Advance Praise

of Revenge

"*The Price of Revenge* is a well-told story full of intrigue, suspense, mystery, shattered dreams, and characters you come to care about. It involves a love affair gone wrong, a murder, and a battle for one man's integrity that leads to consequences you won't be able to walk away from. A very impressive debut."

—Robert Bausch, author of *New York Times* Notable Book *A Hole in the Earth*, and winner of the 2009 Dos Passos Prize in Literature

"*The Price of Revenge* is that great rarity: a compelling legal thriller in which the characters and setting are at least as fascinating as anything in the courtroom. Dennis Vaughn truly knows how to write, and his first-hand knowledge of his subject jumps off every page. This book is one that keeps the reader up all night, unable to put it down before its electrifying climax. I look forward hungrily to Dennis Vaughn's next book."

—Lorenzo Semple Jr., screenwriter of *Three Days of the Condor*, *The Parallax View*, and the television series *Batman*

"Once Dennis Vaughn gets a story underway, the big dominoes start to tumble. In *The Price of Revenge*, one thing leads desperately to another. The world of elegant, distinguished, old-school professionals, he shows us, holds as much trouble as any other. As the secrets surface, true character is revealed—as is the true long-term price."

—Ron Carlson, author of *The Signal* and *Five Skies*, and head of the creative writing program at University of California, Irvine

The Price of Revenge

A Novel

Dennis Vaughn

Synergy Books

The Price of Revenge
Published by Synergy Books
P.O. Box 80107
Austin, Texas 78758

For more information about our books, please write us, e-mail us at
info@synergybooks.net, or visit our web site at www.synergybooks.net.

Publisher's Cataloging-in-Publication available upon request.

LCCN: 2009939672

ISBN-13: 978-0-9842358-1-0
ISBN-10: 0-9842358-1-7

Cover concept by Priyanka Kodikal.

10 9 8 7 6 5 4 3 2 1

To
Linda and Lindie
and
Bill and Billy

I find the great thing in this world is not so much where we stand, as in what direction we are moving...we must sail sometimes with the wind and sometimes against it, but we must sail, and not drift, nor lie at anchor.

—Oliver Wendell Holmes

PART ONE

1

The walk down the stairs that night from the thirty-first floor to the thirtieth seemed more like climbing ten floors than descending one. The stairs felt as though they were pitching. Without even observing them, David Fox passed the oil portraits of the firm's founders hanging prominently at the landing. He had lost all energy, all ability to think. He walked into his office. The automatic light sensor caused the room suddenly to be filled with light. He hit the wall switch, returning the room to darkness, and then closed the door. All he wanted was to put his head down on the desk, but he couldn't risk being found in that position. Even beyond regular business hours, you couldn't be caught with your head on your desk.

Two or three years earlier, a senior partner had walked into an associate's office unannounced and saw his head resting on crossed arms on the desk. "Harmon is down. Harmon is down," the partner yelled out into the hall. It sounded like a dire call on a battle field, not a reference one would expect in the mahogany-paneled, wool-carpeted environment of a large, big-city law firm. Yet, maybe there wasn't that much difference. After all, law firms designated "war rooms" for significant cases and talked in terms of lining up "troops" to throw into battle against tough adversaries.

Jim Ramsey, the firm's chairman, had just threatened him. David was to falsify his internal investigation report in the Ballet matter in order to protect the firm or he would not be made partner. For added measure, Ramsey had said, play ball or the videotape would be released to the partners. Until the meeting upstairs a few minutes earlier, David had been on a sure track to partnership in the firm. Even Stephen Hill, founder of Hill & Devon, had said as much to him, along with smiles and pats on the back. Everything in David's life told him he couldn't falsify the report. He was ethically obligated to report the facts as he had found them, even if the firm's well-being could be endangered. Even if he would not be made partner after working his ass off for eight long years.

As important as partnership was, it was learning of the videotape that hit hardest. How could he possibly have known he was being recorded on that elevator? He often had remembered that night in the elevator with a feeling of warmth. No longer would that be true. Someone might as well have taken a two by four and swung it full force into his belly. He hadn't even been able to respond when Ramsey said that he'd been given the video from building security. Ramsey had supplied the words: What could he have been thinking, using the firm's elevator for a sexual escapade? The partners would have to be informed of a matter showing such colossal bad judgment. They would have to take it into consideration in the partnership decision. Ramsey would even go so far as to tell Stephen Hill; David had no doubt of that. He wouldn't care what the impact might be on the old man. None of that would come to pass, though, if David changed the report.

It didn't seem possible that this could be happening at one of the biggest, oldest, and most highly regarded law firms in the city. A firm well known for excellence in the practice of law, for lawyers of the highest integrity, for good works in the community.

The phone rang. David turned on the desk lamp. Ellen. He looked at his watch. He was late for dinner. He couldn't deal with talking to her now. He had to be clearheaded. He started to shuffle papers into piles and organize his desk for the next day, but he couldn't even do that. Late afternoon telephone messages and e-mails would have to go unanswered, hardly his norm on leaving the office. *How*, he thought, *will I ever be able to tell Ellen? She'll be devastated.* Yet, she had to know what this bastard— the head of her own grandfather's law firm for Christ's sake—was trying to do to him. The son of a bitch. The dirty son of bitch.

He placed a file on the credenza next to a framed photograph of his father. A friend had been in his office a few weeks earlier and asked what the hell he was doing with a picture of himself behind the desk. When David explained that the photograph was of his father, the friend looked more closely and nodded: yes, the man in the photo was older, but David was his absolute clone. David thought about what his father would do in the face of Ramsey's threats. There was no question. The letter his father had written him on his thirteenth birthday told him. One word: integrity. David had made his mistakes before. He wouldn't again.

He put his coat on and stepped out into the hall, slamming the door shut behind him.

△|△

David turned the key in the lock, opened the door, and called out.

Ellen's voice came from the kitchen. "You're late. I was worried. I called the office." She put her arms around his neck as he dropped his briefcase. They kissed and held each other for a few seconds.

David didn't acknowledge the unanswered call. "Sorry. There were a few late-breaking developments."

"Like?"

He put his jacket down on the back of a chair. "Let me wind down. Then we'll talk." He was still absorbed, as he had been during the fifteen-minute drive to her condominium, by how, when, and what to tell her.

Winding down for David meant a couple of beers followed by a bottle of wine shared with Ellen at dinner. There was no time tonight for the beer. Dinner had been ready a long time. He opened a bottle of pinot, and they sat down. Usually, they would burst with conversation over dinner about what the day had brought them. Not so tonight. They ate largely in silence. David looked around the room, not at Ellen.

The scene was comfortable, even if he was not. He was there often, in recent months almost nightly. Her condo set a standard his could never equal, with the antiques, paintings, silver, crystal, and china inherited from her parents. The paintings were not by major names as far as he knew, but they weren't sappy with clowns holding balloons or ubiquitous with waves crashing on rocks. Her belongings exuded class, as did she by her very manner and bearing. He loved to look at her, those large bright eyes dancing as she expressed her thoughts, often enlivened with a quip or two. She had flair. His life never would be boring with her around.

For his part, David hadn't gotten around to fixing up his personal surroundings. His condominium was what might best be described as serviceable. About as far as he'd progressed was to rid himself of some of the junky furniture that had followed him from law school to the apartments he had occupied in the early days with the firm.

"Are you unwound enough to talk now?"

"Sure," he lied. He couldn't hold it off forever.

"What's wrong, David?"

"It's tough."

Ellen's brow peaked, a sure sign she was worried or serious. "Nothing's too tough for us."

"Remember that night, weeks ago, when we were at the office late? When we were in the elevator?"

"No, don't remember a thing about it." Ellen's face changed. Her eyes were stars again. She winked.

"Come on, Ellen." He frowned. "You must."

"Okay. I don't want to threaten your male ego. How could I forget?"

"It's a serious situation." He filled their glasses with more wine. "They have us on videotape."

"What? Who's 'they'?" Her voice rose. The twinkle disappeared.

"That I've got to dummy up the internal investigation report I'm doing for the Ballet or he'll scuttle my partnership." David paused. "And tell the partners about the video."

Ellen was motionless as it began to sink in and then started to shake her head. "I can't believe this. Granddad would—"

"Go crazy if he knew about it? You're right."

"He'll stop Ramsey. He doesn't like him all that much anyway."

"We can't let him be involved. He'll learn about the tape."

Ellen looked steadily at him. With some vague combination of anger and fright, she said slowly, "That cannot happen."

"Only I'm identifiable. You're not."

"Oh great." She raised her arms. "That's a big consolation."

They were both silent. In a low voice, she asked, "What's so terrible about changing the report?"

"They want me not to report some of the things I found in the investigation that are important. It would be dishonest."

"Well, there must be a way to write it to satisfy him, to make your point but still not knock anybody over the head with it."

"Maybe. I don't know. I'm going to have to see." He went to her. Over the fireplace hung an oil painting of the Maroon Bells, located high in the Rocky Mountains near Aspen, a dramatic but peaceful scene of snow on majestic red mountains viewed through fall aspen leaves. He looked up at it, remembering when she'd bought it at a flea market they'd stopped by on a weekend in the mountains at Jazz Aspen. It would never have occurred to him to buy it, but she'd snapped it up without hesitation. He put his arms around her shoulders and back. She trembled. Her cheeks were damp. "Please try," she said as her fists fell lightly on his chest.

His voice caught. How could he tell her there was no way he could change the report? Now wasn't the time. He'd see what could be done. Let her have a chance to absorb it. "It'll be all right, El. We'll work it out. Come sit down."

He guided her to the couch. He held her. They didn't talk. He tried to be calm and to extend his calmness to her, but he was tested by his recurrent thoughts of Ramsey. What an asshole he was. David couldn't believe what was happening.

2

It had started a year earlier with the ring of David's cell phone as he drove to work. Cars were snaking along the off ramp at Lincoln, moving haltingly, their taillights blinking on and off as they inched toward their destinations in the high-rise buildings ahead. David was growing increasingly frustrated by the commute that had become such an immutable part of his life.

At least the cell phone offered the opportunity for diversion. The phone was in a hands-free cradle, and over the speaker came a voice, loud, slightly Germanic, "David, good, Adolph here." Adolph Plotkin was the longtime president of the Denver City Ballet Company, a performing ballet group founded more than seventy-five years earlier.

"Adolph, what has you on the line this early in the morning?" David braced himself for bad news. Plotkin, for all his positive qualities, was a difficult client.

"It's a new problem. It involves Dorothy Chadwell's gift to the endowment fund. It was huge, fifteen million dollars for orchestra pensions. We received a fax this morning written by some ambulance chasers who claim to represent Dorothy's children. The bastards are trying to get the fifteen million back for themselves!"

"Nothing like the prospect of a pot full of money to separate kids from their parents' wishes, is there?" David replied dryly. Perhaps the biggest downside to being an attorney, he'd often thought, was the constant exposure to the ugliest side of human nature.

"I know she wanted that money to go to the musicians for their pensions. God knows I worked hard enough, and over a lot of years, selling her on the idea. David, I need to meet with you right away."

Of course, David thought. *It's always an emergency.* "Adolph, this sounds like a case where you need a good trial lawyer. As a labor lawyer, it's not exactly up my alley." A Ford Taurus wagon had David trapped, its driver seemingly unaware of the opportunities to move ahead that opened and closed before him with irritating regularity. A Lexus SC 430 nosed the Taurus out. Another frustrated driver behind David laid on his horn. Was Monday morning really this bad, or did it just seem so by comparison to the highs of the weekend past? Sometimes David thought that he'd like a hot sexy car too, but for now, he needed a home for his bike and ski racks, so his SUV would have to do.

"I want you on it. We'll have hell to pay with the Musicians Union if we lose that fifteen million dollars."

David thought for a moment. He was overbooked for the week, a state that had increasingly become the norm. How would he work in yet another crisis? Plotkin was always demanding. He didn't care when or where he called you. Everything operated in high gear. There was that time in the hotel room in Washington when he had taken a call on Plotkin's crisis of the hour while engaged in activities that didn't permit full concentration. He had managed to handle the call while stifling his lover's moans. Worse, Plotkin was notoriously cheap, but he was also damned smart and perceptive. Deep down, David was complimented that his advice would be sought on a different kind of issue than usual. "I've got a tight schedule today—"

"I've had the letter faxed to you. I'll meet you this afternoon at one o'clock at Taylor's."

And that was it, the call ending abruptly with a dial tone as David managed at last to maneuver around the Taurus, which sported its proud bumper sticker, "My Child is an Honor Student at Emerson

Middle School." Typical. What else would you expect of someone who drove that way? He pulled in the entrance to the garage and parked the car in his assigned spot. He stopped off at Starbucks for his usual double latte, boarded the elevator, latte in hand, and punched the button for the thirtieth floor. Rose, Hill & Devon's longtime receptionist, waved a warm greeting. He proceeded down the hall and past his secretary's cubicle through the open door to his office.

"David," Amy said, looking up from her desk as he passed, "there's a fax from Mr. Plotkin, marked urgent, like usual. Do you suppose anything has ever not been an emergency with him?" Nearing forty, Amy was in danger of becoming one of those lifer legal secretaries. If she had a personal life away from work, David didn't know about it.

He smiled. "For him, urgent is normal. There's no other speed." He glanced at the letter. It was written by Smithton & Terry, a local firm with a well-deserved reputation for promoting litigation. It was commonly said among the defense bar that Smithton & Terry never saw a case they didn't like.

David sat down and sipped his coffee as he read the fax. The picture was clear enough. Dorothy Chadwell's will had given fifteen million dollars to the Ballet Endowment Fund for the "exclusive purpose" of providing retirement benefits to orchestra musicians. The claim was that the money had been diverted and misspent due to fraud and negligence by the trustees of the fund. Since the donation had not been used exclusively for musicians' pensions, the fifteen million dollars reverted to the residuary legatees, Emily and Terence Chadwell, Dorothy's "devoted" children. Smithton & Terry noted large investment losses in the fund and demanded an accounting. Unless those claims were recognized promptly, all legal remedies would be pursued.

David had to give them credit for creativity, but it sounded like absolute bullshit on the surface. Just because a bequest earned less than the market average didn't invalidate it. His phone rang with Amy telling him that a client had arrived for his ten a.m. meeting. He sighed. The week had begun.

3

David approached the Denver Center for the Performing Arts from Curtis Street through a gallery formed of laminated glass that arched and floated high above street level. The Ellie Caulkins Opera House, the principal theater in the complex, was a beautiful modern facility built inside the facade of an almost one hundred-year-old building, thereby earning the reference "ship in a bottle." The lobby was adorned with the artwork that was obligatory for a public building, a huge representational painting of an opera rehearsal, a realistic bronze sculpture with painted enamel of two ballet dancers, and a Dale Chihuly chandelier. The painting and sculpture had escaped controversy, likely because they were realistic, but not so with the Chihuly. It was an ornate yellow glass composition that seemed too small for the space it occupied. A fuss had accompanied the unveiling of the chandelier, with many in the older, conservative set claiming personal affront that funds that had been picked from the pockets of Denver's society elite had been spent for a so-called piece of art. Time had, however, served to mellow their reaction.

Stephen Hill, the founder of David's firm, given his prominent role in the community, had more or less automatically been a part of the conservative group of fundraisers, but he hadn't been one of those who expressed offense. Indeed, he told David at dinner with Ellen one evening that, while he'd kept his own counsel on the subject, he rather enjoyed the fight that had ensued over the piece that hung so prominently from the lobby ceiling.

The opera house's public areas, elegant though not ostentatious, contrasted markedly with the area backstage where David roamed while working with the theatrical unions on behalf of the Ballet. The public saw Japanese cherrywood, blood red upholstered seats, and thick carpeting. Backstage, the people who made the place work saw none of that: just fluorescent lighting that illuminated concrete-walled corridors.

David walked through the lobby to the stairway down to the Kevin Taylor restaurant, a richly appointed space despite its location in the basement of the theater. David announced the Plotkin reservation and was escorted to the usual table. It was Plotkin's table literally; he was a fixture, having eaten there for lunch on every matinee day, and not infrequently for dinner, since it was built. It was not so much the food, which was good enough, that kept him coming back. It was the extraordinarily deferential treatment he received there as the president of the Denver City Ballet Company.

Wasn't it typical, David thought as he sat waiting, *for the great man to impose an urgent luncheon meeting and then show up twenty minutes late?* It had happened so many times, yet David could never bring himself to assume the pattern as fact and arrive late himself. If truth were known, a few quiet minutes to collect his thoughts before a meeting were not at all unwelcome. And, of course, the meter was running.

David had inherited Plotkin when he had been practicing law for only three years. He'd been thrown into a picketing situation at the center and had done such a good job that Plotkin wanted more of him. Plotkin's wasn't the only case where he'd made a good impression on a client who recognized his talent. The classic high achiever, he'd been on scholarship at NYU and had been named Order of the Coif and President of the International Law Review at Northwestern. His personal appearance, when combined with his academic record, had made him much sought after in the law firm interviewing game. Six feet, 170 pounds, with dark hair and light olive skin, he was good-looking, though he didn't view himself that way; the mirror told him that his nose was too broad and flat to qualify. Everyone said that he could have gone anywhere in the country he wanted. Certainly, he could have joined a larger, more prestigious firm elsewhere, but thankfully for Hill & Devon, he hadn't wanted Wall Street and the megacity life and practice.

"David, my apologies. I've had a frantic morning." Plotkin, breathless, approached the booth and hauled himself along the leather seat. He always seemed to move in a whirlwind of commotion. "Have you been here long?"

"No, besides I needed the time to gather my scattered thoughts, Adolph." David grinned.

"Ha, your thoughts strike me as seldom scattered. Did you get the Chadwell letter we sent?" He gestured to a waiter. Plotkin was in his late sixties, of average height, plump, with thin graying hair. He had spent his life in arts and music management, the last fifteen years with the Denver Ballet, and was, by any standard, a workaholic.

"Yes. Tell me what you know about it." Plotkin ordered a glass of merlot and asked David what he'd like. "Just coffee. Busy day."

"Well, I don't know, but I can speculate about a lot. Basically, it comes down to the fact that Terry and Emily Chadwell are spoiled brats. They received enormous sums of money from their mother during her lifetime. Terry has never worked, unless you call trading your own stocks work."

"I wish I'd had the opportunity." David extended his glass of water forward toward Plotkin.

"Actually, Terry is a pitiful character. Gambling has been a problem, I'm told, along with alcohol…the usual, you know. As for Emily, she's really a pretty decent sort, I think. The problem there is that husband of hers. He married her for money and position and can't accept the fact that she was, as he views it, left out of the will. I know its terms because of the gift to the endowment fund. The kids got the residue, which was, after taxes and charitable gifts, about a million dollars each."

"Not exactly shabby."

"Tell me, can there really be anything to the theory in their letter?"

"That if the funds have been misapplied, the fifteen mil reverts to the children?"

"Yes," Plotkin said impatiently. The waiter served their drinks and took their orders. Plotkin had a sip of wine, dabbing his obviously dyed mustache with a napkin.

"It's a pretty creative theory. If it can be shown that the money has been siphoned off, yes, they can probably get it. But what evidence could they have of that?"

"There is none. The value of the endowment fund has decreased, but that's just been the result of some investments we all wish hadn't been made. Money going elsewhere? No, definitely not."

"What were the bad investments?"

"They're all okay except one, the Owlton fund I think is its name, an offshore hedge fund."

"Did you consider changing it?"

"Sure, I brought it up with Fred. The musicians have raised hell about it with me."

David understood his reference to be to Fred White, the CFO of the Ballet and trustee of the endowment fund, whom the letter threatened would be named as a defendant in any lawsuit right along with Plotkin. "What did he say?"

"He said not to worry. It would even out. We had to look at all of the managers collectively. Rely on Gunn."

"Who is he?"

"Phil Gunn. He's the investment advisor to the endowment fund. Been around a long time. Came in on Fred's recommendation, I believe. Knew him from some other nonprofit. He makes the recommendations where we put the money."

"Speaking of Fred, I thought the air was pretty heavy between him and Austin at the meeting the other day," David said, referring to Austin Wilcox, the head stagehand for the carpentry department at the opera house. "There was a tenseness that went well beyond what you usually see in union negotiations."

"Oh, the two of them get that way from time to time, whether it's at a union meeting or not. It's nothing. You do know they have a relationship?"

David had heard that White and Wilcox were partners, something not all that unusual in the theater. David had never known quite what to make of White. He worked with him on the financial aspects of the Ballet's union negotiations. White was pleasant enough and well regarded, but there was something David couldn't quite put his finger on. People told him that lawyers were a different breed. In his opinion, that went double for accountants, including those with the title of CFO.

There was a pause, interrupted by David. "I talked this over preliminarily with Charles Calhoun, our senior litigation partner. We feel there's nothing to be lost, and maybe something to be gained, by meeting with them."

Plotkin placed his glass of wine on the table so forcefully that some of it spilled onto the white cloth. "Never! I won't dignify it by meeting with them. Let them sue."

"Sounds good now, Adolph, but you won't feel that way when you're served with a summons and complaint, and your board starts snooping around about what we did to head this off."

"The trouble with this world is compromise. Some things should never be compromised," declared Plotkin, his right forearm extended and his hand circling above his head.

"How is meeting with them a compromise? It's to our benefit because we get some idea of the gory details behind the claim. Otherwise, we're in the dark."

"There can be nothing. This is just a selfish effort to take pensions away from the musicians to support the lifestyles of these people. I mean, how can they get away with this?"

David sidestepped the question, knowing that any answer would be fruitless. "We have to decide whether their claims warrant conducting an internal investigation."

Plotkin's eyebrows arched with the question. "What, may I ask, is an internal investigation?"

"Well, we'd investigate the facts thoroughly and make a report to you and the board. If there's fraud, or whatever else they're claiming, this would ferret it out, and then whatever action is appropriate could be taken. We'd make a recommendation."

Plotkin seized on the word "thoroughly," saying, "Oh, could this be, by any chance, another lawyer's full employment opportunity?"

David smiled, again ignoring one of Plotkin's prickly rants. David had a ready smile, not infrequently spreading across his face when talking even about things that were not funny. Much less often did he laugh. "It could buy a lot," he said. "The facts we find might help to convince the Chadwells' lawyers that they have no case, but don't count on it. They like a dog fight. Where the internal investigation would be of significance is with the government agencies that they are threatening to go to. The very fact that you tried to clean up any problem voluntarily would be given weight. And if there are problems, they must be addressed."

Plotkin, his eyes staring straight at David, twirled his wine glass in small circles. "When do you suggest we do this?"

"Right away. The government can be down your back pretty fast if there's a problem."

They were served and ate quietly for a few minutes. The food was not up to par today, but David didn't comment. Their waiter hovered around the table, addressing Mr. Plotkin by name with every comment. Plotkin finished his wine and then grumbled, "I don't like it, David, but I guess you're the doctor. Go ahead. I want you to be in charge, not Charles Calhoun."

"Oh, I'll be in the trenches. But he has a reputation for being one of the finest lawyers in the city. His experience and stature will be very helpful. Besides, he's a wonderful guy. You'll like him." David nodded his head up and down as if to confirm his own statements.

4

David was sitting in a negotiating meeting, listening to Austin Wilcox drone on about a complex wage calculation the union was proposing for the Ballet labor contract. David looked at the BlackBerry he held in his lap, scrolling through messages and then tapping in one as if he were replying. It was not a reply, however. It was to Ellen Hill. "I'm in the most boring meeting I've ever attended. How about dinner at the Rialto at half past six and a surprise after?" His idea for the surprise was the dress rehearsal of the ballet, *Cinderella*, which was being held at the opera house. There would be just enough time between the meeting and the rehearsal to catch a quick dinner at the Rialto on the Sixteenth Street Mall. Within a couple minutes, her reply came: "You're on."

The meeting continued ponderously, ending later than expected and making David late for his date. He left the meeting and made his way backstage alone to the elevator that would take him to the front entrance. Plotkin had departed earlier in the afternoon. Like a passenger in an automobile, David never paid much attention when the two of them made their way to meetings together through the labyrinth backstage. He'd have to think every step of the way to get himself back; getting lost was not quite the image he was trying to convey.

The corridor walls were lined with faded posters and banners for opera, ballet, and symphony performances, some of which David recognized; others had been held in one theater or another in the complex years ago. He walked past the theater manager's office to stage right, where there was a bustle of activity: banging, men calling out instructions, other sounds of work he couldn't place. Stagehands were everywhere, on the stage, up in the grid, adjusting lighting and performing the myriad of activities that led to the finished product. All the work that, on opening night, the audience would take for granted, albeit with raves about its creativity.

He walked to the back of the stage and crossed between the diagonal yellow lines painted on the hardwood floor. The walkway was marked in yellow to lead people away from the activity on stage and out of danger. At stage left, he exited the immediate stage area and walked through double doors into a square room from which corridors ran in three directions, with an elevator on the fourth wall. Was this the place where he took the elevator or did he go on further through the corridor to the next elevator? He decided to try this one. As he pressed the button, he thought, certainly not for the first time, that *Phantom of the Opera* seemed not at all unrealistic in its setting when one learned what the bowels of a complex such as this were really like. Entering the elevator, he pressed the button for the first floor, and upon arrival, he was at the entrance. Success.

Ellen and David had been seeing one another for about three months. It had been slow at first. He was reticent because she was the boss's daughter so to speak. Stephen Hill's name was on the door of the firm he'd founded and nurtured from its beginnings five decades before. Now in his mid-eighties, fifteen years beyond normal retirement age, he had completed the progression from dynamic founder to revered figurehead. He no longer practiced law. He did show up at the office nearly every day, but most of what he did there concerned his interests in the stock market and some small local oil exploration operations he'd been fortunate to get into in the days when wells could be drilled on the cheap. He belonged to the city's establishment clubs and had, from time to time, been a leader of many of Denver's most important charitable organizations.

Ellen was devoted to her grandfather and fiercely loyal to the firm he'd built. In one sense, David's hesitation was understandable as he had always done things on his own—independently, what he wanted, the way he wanted—and he had done it successfully. Now he was facing his biggest challenge. He was up for partnership after eight years as a hard-charging associate. The last thing he wanted was for it to be perceived that he had gained some advantage by virtue of a relationship with Ellen.

Yet, why should he hesitate? After all, he had met Ellen through her grandfather. He'd been invited for dinner at Mr. Hill's home along with two other firm associates, one male and one female, and Ellen had been there. He'd heard it was commonplace for Mr. Hill to have new associates with the firm come to his home for dinner, but he wondered whether it was usual for Ellen to be present too. She'd been introduced by Mr. Hill as his granddaughter and, he added with a nervous laugh, his hostess for the night. David knew that Mr. Hill was a widower, which might explain the hostess reference, but it was not until later that he was to learn that the relationship was deeper than that of grandfather and granddaughter. David thought Ellen was pretty, if not beautiful. She was tall and slender, with long auburn hair and brown eyes. She radiated a sort of warmth and flair that attracted him.

After this first social occasion, Mr. Hill had invited David to the University Club for lunch. He'd spoken proudly of his role in raising Ellen. Her parents had been killed in a bizarre hot air balloon accident outside Aspen. They'd gone up early one morning when a freak wind gust had come up and pushed the balloon into electrical wires. The cables attaching the basket to the balloon had been severed, and the basket had fallen to the ground. Ellen had been only eleven. She'd gone to live with her grandparents, preferring them to her aunts and uncles. She had been withdrawn and depressed as she coped with the loss. As time passed though, her sadness had lifted, and she'd come to life, on occasion to a somewhat troubling degree in her last couple of years of high school.

Lunch at the club had been followed by an invitation from Mr. Hill to go mushroom hunting along with Ellen. They'd driven on a Saturday to the mountains a couple hours west of Denver and walked into an area that was Ellen and her grandfather's favorite spot. They'd found several kinds of mushrooms, some of which they'd picked and some they'd left untouched. David didn't know an edible mushroom from a poisonous one, but they seemed to. It'd been on this outing that Mr. Hill became Stephen at his own insistence. He'd complimented David on how well he was doing at the firm. "If you keep it up, you'll be a leader of the firm someday—someday when I'm no longer around." It felt to David that he'd been talking as much to Ellen as he was to him.

David didn't have to speculate long about what Stephen's thoughts might be concerning Ellen. One day, Stephen had dropped by his office, ostensibly to chat about a high-profile case in the firm. David had taken the opportunity to say again how much he'd enjoyed the mushroom hunt, which couldn't have been further from the truth. He'd found it boring: not at all physically challenging as were his mountain biking, hiking, and running. Stephen had answered, in his most courtly way, "It would be just fine with me, David, if you should want to take Ellen out." And so David had. Over the months, the relationship had become intimate, but not exclusive, at least insofar as David was concerned. The depth of the commitment was not a subject he and Ellen discussed.

A subject they did discuss at length was Ellen's devotion to her grandfather. She talked as well about her grandmother, who had died five years earlier, but it was her grandfather who was her icon. Along with the devotion, however, came a slight feeling of intimidation.

"Granddad and Grammy were sort of rigid. Growing up with them was very different than I think it would have been with Mom and Dad. They were fun, more flexible."

"Well," said David, "you'd expect that wouldn't you with the age difference?"

"All my friends had more freedom. There were so many restrictions on where I went, with whom, what time I got home. Granddad saw things as black and white, never gray. I'm sure I was a giant pain in the ass to them."

"Aren't most teenagers? I was."

"He gave me everything I ever needed. Never held back unless he didn't approve of what it was being spent on, and then the ATM would close. I assume all this was paid out of the settlement the estate got from the accident, but I've never been told or seen any kind of accounting. I have no idea what's left."

"Have you ever asked for it?"

"No."

"Why not?"

"Oh, I worry a little that he might misunderstand the request and think I'm challenging his integrity. I don't have any doubt that's it's all properly accounted for. I'll find out sooner than I want to anyway, I'm afraid."

David didn't offer his opinion. He wasn't sure he understood Ellen's reticence. His own style was to try to be direct but diplomatic in his dealings, both personally and professionally. Her grandfather seemed like an approachable enough person. He would have posed the question to him, he thought, but that didn't mean it was right for her.

Ellen arrived first at the Rialto and sat in a corner of the bar. David had reached her on her cell phone to tell her he'd be late. He came in and, smiling down, gave her a warm hello and a light kiss sideways on her lips. Almost any time he touched Ellen, no matter how perfunctory, it seemed to produce a palpable reaction in her, a sort of shudder, which in turn ignited a feeling of warmth in him. She was just past thirty and had never been married. She was the marketing director for an old-line regional accounting firm.

"How did it go today, Ellen?"

"I was afraid I'd be late or not get here at all. Instead, I end up beating you and doing exactly what Grammy always said ladies don't do...sitting alone in a bar."

"Dangerous sport, that." David laughed. "Why did you almost get derailed?"

"A proposal for a huge piece of new business was dropped on me, at the very last minute of course. The usual partner had it sitting on his desk for two weeks and gave it to us twenty-four hours before the deadline."

"Worse than lawyers."

"You're not kidding." She paused, eyes bright and flashing, and then continued, "However, always the perfect marketing director, I accepted it with a smile, thinking, you bastard, why do you let it sit there and give us no notice? Forget the concept of being considerate of other people's workloads, don't you think we could have done a better job for you—yeah, you—if we had more time?"

"I'm sure I know the answer," David said. "They're too busy."

"No, they just don't think about it until the last minute. But sometimes I feel the real reason is that they want to test you, see how you stand up to having your dinner plans ruined or your weekend away canceled, a firm loyalty test so to speak."

"You're fired up," David said, a broad smile crossing his face.

Ellen looked at him, not responding for several seconds. "You know, David, there's something I've always wanted to ask you. Here I am telling you about all my miseries, and you're smiling. Why do you smile all the time?"

He nodded his head, an awkward smile spreading his lips. "You too, huh? You're not the first one to comment on it. People seem to see it different ways. You?"

"I feel like maybe you smile for punctuation, like an exclamation point, or to underscore something, or to show satisfaction. I don't know."

"Or after a question. I've even been accused of smiling after a threat, not that I go making threats, or to make what I say less threatening. You name it, I do it."

"Actually, I love it. You have a great mouth, and your eyes crinkle up. Sometimes your ears even lift. It's just that it throws me off guard a little. I'm not always sure how to take it."

"I'll let you in on a secret. Most of the time, it's unconscious. It's a habit. My mother tried to break it. She was tough. Dad was the soft one. She'd tell me that it wasn't appropriate to smile when you were talking about something serious. 'Wipe that grin off your face,' she'd say, or, more often, 'that silly grin.'"

"So?"

"She wasn't any more successful with me than she was trying to break the dogs of their bad habits."

They laughed.

David returned to the subject of accountants. "I think the problem is that you just hate accountants."

"Maybe. But not as much as the lawyers I used to work for." Ellen paused and, with an exaggerated look, said, "But I don't hate you."

"The evidence would tend to indicate that," he replied, mimicking her look. "But maybe you'd feel differently if you slept with them too?"

"Watch it, or I won't be sleeping with anybody." They both grinned. "What about your day?" she asked.

"I was at the Denver Center again. Now I've got a new case involving a possible embezzlement from the musicians' pension fund and four zillion documents to plow through. Just what I love."

"Sounds exciting."

"Let's talk about the surprise I promised. Since we're late, we'll finish this drink and then get something to go and a bottle of chardonnay. We can sit in the back of the theater and watch the *Cinderella* rehearsal." There were few perks that went with his representation of the Ballet, but extracurricular access to the theater was one.

"Fine with me, but can we go in with food and wine?"

"Why not? It's dark in the back rows. No one will even know we're there."

Ellen gave him a knowing look. "Perfect."

David took her hand and motioned to the waiter.

David's pass key opened a side door to the theater lobby. The lobby was dark, in stark contrast to the hustle and noise of the crowds on performance nights. He liked it this way, a reminder of the reality that stood behind what happened on stage, the part that the audience never even thought about. It gave him a sense of being special.

"David, tell me about *Cinderella*."

"Well, Cinderella was a young girl who had a mean stepmother and a glass slipper and went to a—"

"I know, I know. The ballet, funny man."

"Oh, the ballet. I don't know much really."

"Well, I've read the reviews," she said. "The story is set in London during the blitz in World War II. The wicked stepmother is a chain smoking, sex-starved witch. So are her two daughters. The prince is a pilot who becomes a hero."

"Cinderella is sex starved too, I hope?" He grinned.

"No, Cinderella is plain old Cinderella."

"That's no fun."

David held one of the double doors at the rear of the theater open as Ellen slid through silently. The rehearsal had started, but with only stage lights and the theater dark, they couldn't see much once inside the door. His hand guided her forward two rows from the back and right toward the middle. They sat there quietly, opening the box with crab cakes and pouring from the bottle of chardonnay that he'd uncorked before entering the theater. He poured with finger poised at the top of the glass to prevent an overflow and handed it to her. They silently toasted one another, as had become their habit on the first, or repeat, of any special occasion. Ellen's enthusiasm for new adventures was an exciting thing to him.

Cinderella was underway, the scene set during a blackout amidst falling buzz bombs. The score was by Prokofiev. The orchestra was, of course, nowhere to be seen, buried in the pit. The conductor's head was visible bobbing below center stage. The dancers' costumes were military uniforms and plain dresses and suits, in dramatic contrast to the typical ballet's tutus, tight pants, and pointed slippers.

David slipped his hand under the fall of Ellen's hair to the back of her warm neck. She turned to him and extended her lips. With bombs pounding onstage, smoke pouring from the damaged buildings, and yellow lights in the broken windows shuttering, they lingered in a deep kiss. The performance, incredibly creative and different though it was, was no match for the overwhelming distraction of his hands on her neck and under the jacket collar on her shoulder, and hers lightly passing over his thigh. It was obvious to them both that they couldn't stop there.

"David, here? They might turn the lights up."

"No way. Just sit on my lap."

"You're sure?"

"Don't worry. It'll be all right."

She stood slowly while he moved his hands down the sides of her legs. She straddled him, slowly lifting and lowering—sometimes barely moving, sometimes deeply—and then thrusting, and they were lost in time and place, not even conscious of the thunderous noise of bombs blasting London in the night.

5

David made his way down the staircase to the Boulder Room on the twenty-ninth floor of the firm's offices where takeout food was delivered each night for the lawyers and staff who would be working late. He'd decided to review the endowment fund's financial statements and records in the quiet hours of the night when there would be no telephone interruptions and fewer people dropping by his office to talk.

He grabbed three pieces of cheese and pepperoni pizza and a Diet Coke and returned up the stairs to his office. Stairs, not elevators, were his habit, at least when time permitted, a reflection of his compulsive focus on fitness and, perhaps this night, a bit of guilt over his dinner choice. As he climbed the steps, he wondered why, with everyone supposedly so busy, there seemed to be to no one around burning the midnight oil. He might not be a partner yet, but he was already thinking like one.

The Ballet documents were discouragingly voluminous. It was exactly the kind of project that turned him off, the only thing that was really boring in his practice, but there was the occasional rush when a truly significant document turned up in his hands. He had the option of assigning the first review to a paralegal, but in this case, he hadn't been sure even what to tell a paralegal to look for among the documents. He had to spend some time with them on his own in order to give meaningful instructions to anyone else. Tons of hours and lots of client dollars could get eaten up in an unfocused document review, and he'd promised Plotkin that he would manage the matter to avoid that kind of thing. No client watched billable hours like Plotkin.

David began to review the monthly statements from the investment managers and hedge funds. As he munched his pizza, he saw that the investment managers' reports were detailed, recording each stock in the account, the number of shares, cost, current value, and dividend yield. Comparable detail was available for bond investments. No secrets there, but he wasn't that focused on the stock and bond accounts since their performances hadn't been problematic.

By contrast, the hedge fund reports were cryptic to say the least. There were monthly, quarterly, and annual reports, but they contained little information, simply a statement of net asset value before incentive fees to the hedge fund, asset value after incentive fees, and the percentage performance, up or down, for the month. There was no information as to what particular investments had been made. Perhaps with good reason, he thought facetiously, as one of these funds, Owlton, was the only investment that had lost money in this up market. Compared to the Dow, which was up 30 percent, the Owlton funds had fallen by 20 percent, reducing the value of the Chadwell gift from its original fifteen million dollars to twelve and one-half million dollars. He would have to interview someone with Owlton to fill in the blanks.

David also reviewed certain endowment fund documents, including the minutes of meetings of the trustees of the fund. He found no helpful information there and, in particular, no document that would resolve the conflict as to who had recommended Gunn to the Ballet. Plotkin had said that it was White, but when David had talked to White, he'd said the recommendation came from George Tate, a former Ballet board member, now deceased.

A soft knock at his open office door startled him. He raised his head to see Saundra, a paralegal in the litigation department, standing at the door. "Hi, David. How are you?"

"Good, Saundra, other than being here. What has you still on duty this late?"

"A document production. You?"

"Same."

"Why don't you have me doing it, David?" she said with an exaggerated pouty look, eyes cast downward. She was, in David's opinion, the best-looking woman in the firm.

"Because I'm not even sure what to look for at this point. I have to know that to tell you what to do, don't I?"

"I do have a little experience in reviewing documents, you know. Let me try and help. We'll need room to spread out. I'll get a conference room." She left the office briefly and then returned, this time without knocking. "The Springs Room is empty. Let's use it. I'll get the files on your desk, and you can bring the boxes."

David followed her down the hall toward the conference room, this one named after nearby Colorado Springs. As a form of subtle marketing, each conference room was named after a city in which the firm had an office: Denver, Boulder, Colorado Springs, Washington, DC, and New York. Each was a different size and configuration to accommodate a variety of meetings. Some had better views than others, the best ones looking west to the Rockies and the less desirable looking east toward never-ending nothingness.

David knew what would happen because it had before, but he found himself unable to resist. Saundra was tall, five feet eleven, with long, slender legs accounting for most of the expanse. His eyes were fixated on the legs as she walked in front of him, her bottom swaying from right to left, or, he thought, was it left to right? His memory was precise in its recollection of just how those legs had wrapped around him and gripped him tightly.

Saundra held the door as David entered with the boxes. They put the documents down on the conference room table. "Let's go through these and get some idea of what we have and how we can organize them," offered Saundra. Instead, he walked to the door and turned off the light. "Hey, how can we do anything in the dark?" she said and then followed with a deep, knowing laugh.

"You know how, Saundra. The same way we already have in every other conference room in the office," David replied. He proceeded to feel his way around the table to her, with only the slightest light from the offices in the adjoining building to guide him.

"Are you just collecting notches on your gun, David? What is it that intrigues you so much about conference room tables?"

"Saundra, if you were half as good at handling documents as you are at handling me, you'd go down in history as the world's greatest paralegal."

David lifted himself onto the table and helped her up. They shed their clothes. He gazed down at her head and long hair outlined in the dim light. Soon even the vaguest thoughts of business were lost to two naked, rigid bodies, aflame, groping, pushing against each other on the slick, cold surface. Ecstasy gripped them as they caressed and kissed and explored each other's bodies.

Suddenly, the door thrust open, and a waving light appeared focused at the floor. David froze, whispering, "My God," and then pushed Saundra's head away from the light and toward the windows. As he did, the light flashed to the table, held them in its glare for a second or two, and then turned and left the room, the door closing behind. David relaxed his grip. She whispered, "What the hell was that?"

"Christ, I don't know. Must be the night watchman making rounds. He never comes in my office that way, though."

"Perhaps," she whispered, "because when you're in your office, your lights are on...maybe even your clothes too!" Saundra moved to his side, slightly moaning as her body touched the cold surface. "Did he see us?"

"He saw us all right, but I think only our bodies. I looked away from him when the light hit the table, and I turned your head. He's gone." David grabbed her around the shoulders.

"He could come back."

"I don't think he will. He's already gotten his thrill. Come on."

"No, I'm getting out of here. David, I really don't understand you and this conference room gig." She felt around the table for her clothes.

David pondered the question. Had he ever focused on it? Certainly, it wasn't a question he'd ever been asked to answer. "I don't know exactly.

Maybe it's the idea of hiding, getting caught, that adds to the thrill, makes the explosion nuclear."

"It didn't quite work this time, did it?"

"Hardly."

"It seems"—she paused—"almost defiant on your part. I mean, I have nothing to lose. I can get a job anywhere and be on the same track. But you have an investment here that you're about to collect on. The thrill can't be great enough to warrant risking partnership, can it?" She turned on the lights and slammed the door behind her.

David dressed and carted the files and boxes back to his office. He had a lot of work yet to do to finish the document review.

6

David leaned forward to look down at the alternating hues of blue that marked the luminescent water below. The beaches were white, long expanses interrupted only by squat native vegetation, palm trees, and an occasional fisherman's hut. The island was Curaçao, part of the Netherlands Antilles.

David had found the flights unusually relaxing. Normally, flight time was spent reviewing documents for a meeting, maximizing every possible billable hour. This case was different. There really hadn't been documents to review other than the cryptic reports from Owlton he'd already examined. He had stared blankly at those, with many more questions than answers. What precisely was the hedge fund invested in? Why didn't they provide more specific information?

But what really made this trip different was that Ellen was along. It was their first time traveling together. He looked beyond her out the window. "Beautiful, isn't it?" he asked.

She glowed, touching her hand to his resting on her knee. "I've been thinking about this ever since you asked me. I know I really shouldn't be here, with the vacation I have coming up with Granddad. Being away from the office twice in such a short time isn't going to make me very popular. But here I am." She laughed her deep, throaty laugh, ending, as it often did, with a snort. Grammy had told her it wasn't a ladylike way to laugh, but most of the time, she couldn't help it.

She and David had chatted about all the things they wanted to do while on the island: tennis, swimming, biking, diving. How much could they pack into three days? Every time she'd mention a new activity, he'd add with a leer, "And?" She'd smile but never take the bait.

David and Charles Calhoun had met to discuss the status of the investigation. An understanding of the Owlton relationship was central to what they were doing. Without more information, they really couldn't go forward. They'd debated whether a personal visit was necessary, finally coming to the conclusion that a face-to-face meeting was required in order to cajole information out of Owlton.

David had been surprised that he was permitted to make the trip. He knew that Calhoun had a home in the Caribbean. He'd seen a photo of it with a sunset over the water filtered through palm trees. The photo rested in a leather frame sitting on a table under Calhoun's diplomas and certificates of court admissions. David had assumed that Calhoun would reserve the trip for himself. However, he passed on the trip, most likely, David speculated, because he didn't want to get dirty in the investigation that early in the game. Calhoun had a reputation for relying heavily on associates to do the grunt work and then stepping in when the facts were all there for him to review. Whatever the reason, it was fine with David since it permitted him to visit a part of the world he had never seen, and to do that with Ellen.

The plane landed and taxied to the terminal building, where they emerged from their air-conditioned capsule into Curaçao's steamy afternoon heat. In the waiting room, they were met by a uniformed driver bearing a placard on which the name Fox was written. With only carry-on luggage, they were able to leave the airport immediately, and in a few minutes, they pulled up to the Avila Beach Hotel in Willemstad, the capital of the Netherlands Antilles. It was a smaller hotel recommended to David by a friend as being a romantic spot on a smooth, white sand beach. The driver said that he'd be back at nine thirty in the morning for David's meeting at the Owlton offices.

The next morning, David stood at the Owlton reception room window, looking out at the water. He wondered if every morning here was as gorgeous.

"Mr. Nels is ready to see you now, Mr. Fox," a male secretary told him. Eyeing the surroundings as he was led down the hall to a corner office at the end of the floor, David's reaction was that the offices, while not extravagant, displayed an appropriate degree of prosperity.

The door to the office was open, and Maarten Nels, senior vice president of Owlton, motioned David in, rising from behind his desk with hand extended. They introduced themselves, and David sat down.

Nels said, "How can I help you?"

"As I wrote you, I represent the Denver City Ballet Company, which is also a client of yours through its endowment fund. There's been a claim filed against the Ballet relating to the fund, and we're conducting an investigation on it. I'll be interviewing all of the investment managers through whom fund investments are made."

Nels's age was not clear to David. About the same as his, he guessed—mid-thirties—but the thick-lens glasses Nels wore probably caused him to appear older than he was. He didn't look fit, as though he could lose quite a few pounds and be better off for it. "You say you will be interviewing. Does that mean we're the first?"

"Yes."

"And why is that? Several thousand miles is a long way to come to have a discussion, or is it the lure of the Caribbean?"

David was already being put on the defensive. "I've never been to this part of the world and have always wanted to try your sun and water, but the purpose of the trip is business."

"I understand you have a traveling companion. It would be too bad not to enjoy our island after coming this far."

David was uncomfortable that Nels knew of Ellen's presence. But, of course, why wouldn't he? The driver would have informed him. "I'll get right to the point. I've reviewed the monthly reports you provide to the Ballet and have a number of questions as you might imagine."

"I'll give you what I can. But much of our information is confidential or, more appropriately, proprietary, so there are limits."

David reached into his briefcase for one of the Owlton monthly reports and handed it across the desk, asking if Nels recognized the document. "Yes, this is the type of report we provide to the investment advisor each month."

"My review indicates that the fund has lost money in the recent past. Can you tell me why that's the case?"

"There are multiple reasons, but the principal one is due to losses in currency hedging transactions," offered Nels, perhaps a bit indignantly, his eyes trained directly on David's.

"What currencies, and when did the transactions occur?"

Nels frowned. "That's where we get into the proprietary aspect of this. If we were to divulge what currencies we hedge, when, how, etc., you could, after all, compete with us, adopt our formula. You do understand?"

David smiled, his lips slightly quivering. "With all due respect, I'm not sure that with these losses your formula would be much sought after."

Nels looked surprised. "Fair observation, I suppose, but that's over the limited period you're interested in. Looking at a longer time span, the picture is different. In any event, win or lose, that's not information we give out to anyone, including our clients."

Questions passed about general matters, such as the size of the Owlton fund, how fees were formulated, and the like, which Nels answered openly. As they talked, David glanced around the office. There wasn't a single piece of paper on any surface, except for a neatly arranged file on the desk. On the few occasions when David had been in an office as antiseptic as this, he had felt an underlying distrust of the occupant. How could anyone be so well organized? Was it as simple as vacant office, vacant mind? He thought of his own office with papers and files stacked on every available surface.

"Tell me about Owlton's relationship with Phil Gunn, my client's investment advisor."

"I can do that. Mr. Gunn is well known to us. He has been investing for clients with us for several years. All are tax-exempt investors because of the nature of the fund."

David looked up from the yellow pad resting on his knee on which he was scribbling notes. "What is your relationship with him exactly?"

"He handles the paperwork for his clients, and usually, though not always, the clients wire funds direct to us. When withdrawals are made, he orders those as well, and the funds are wired to the client's accounts. We provide monthly, quarterly, and annual reports to Mr. Gunn, which, I assume from your files, he sends along to you. That's about it. All very straight forward."

"Does Gunn receive any fee from Owlton?"

"No. His fees are paid by the client. I presume, in your case, by the Ballet. We don't know what arrangement he has with his clients in this regard, nor do we wish to."

David hesitated, "How are Owlton's fees calculated?"

"There's an annual fee of 1.5 percent and 20 percent on the back end."

"Maarten," David said, staring straight at him, "not speaking as a lawyer, but from the point of view of an investor, why would I continue to invest in the Owlton fund when it's losing money, lots of it, and I can't even find out what exactly is being done with the money?" He attempted a smile.

"We develop long-term relationships with our clients." Nels looked around his office as if to say, Doesn't this paperless workspace reflect our clients confidence in us? They don't need documentation. He continued, "They look to our longer-term record. Take Mr. Gunn's clients who are invested in the fund. To the best of my knowledge, not one has left us. While I can't speak for him, I would think some of your questions should be directed to him. In any event, if you don't have confidence in Gunn, perhaps your client should consider leaving the fund."

David stood and walked to the window. He was getting nowhere and decided to change the subject. What he really wanted was to get a glimpse of Nels's computer screen. Given the uncluttered state of the office, he bet he wouldn't find a queue of e-mails on it. But the window didn't get him close enough to see the screen. He asked Nels for a recommendation of the best beach that he and his friend might bike to from their hotel that afternoon. There were a couple of choices, one closer to town and another further out and more secluded. It was a question of how far they wanted to bike and on what kind of roads. The road to the secluded beach was much rougher for a bike, he said, but the beach there was the most desirable.

David returned to his chair. "I can't help but feel I've come a long ways and I'll be going back largely empty handed." He turned his palms up.

"You and your client may not like the losses suffered. Frankly, I'm not happy about them, but it does happen. It's a risk every investor takes and one that we make clear to the advisors. Over the full cycle, our clients are rarely unhappy with a fund's performance." Nels folded his arms over his ample midsection. "You might simply have telephoned. This is the twenty-first century you know."

"You realize that if there's litigation, you may be required to provide the information I've asked for and much more."

Nels nodded as if he'd heard that before. "Our policy is firm. The information is not available. If there's a lawsuit, we'll deal with it at the time." He ended the meeting with customary stiffness, "If there's nothing further, I'll have our driver return you to your hotel, and you can take your bike ride."

Nels called his secretary into the office and asked him to arrange for the driver. He looked at David and rose to shake his hand. "Have a wonderful time while you are here on Curaçao."

Back at the hotel, David and Ellen were fitted with mountain bikes and helmets. The bikes weren't equivalent to the Moots he rode at home. They were some brand he hadn't heard of before, probably a Dutch make, he thought, but they would do on a rough road. The attendant gave instructions as to the bike's gear and brake systems and adjusted the pedals downward on Ellen's bike to compensate for her height. She circled around the driveway entrance to the hotel until she was satisfied she had it right. David thought about how terrific she looked in shorts, a T-shirt, and tennis shoes, even if her hair and forehead were eclipsed by the flimsy-looking helmet she'd been issued. He had one too. While they weren't the carbon fiber ones he was used to, they would work. Bags with picnic lunches packed by the hotel and towels were placed in the bike baskets. David was embarrassed. No way would he be seen at home with a basket on his bike.

They rode out of the driveway. They'd been told to take the highway about five miles where they would turn off on a dirt road to the water. It could be identified by a rose-colored, half-constructed building on the corner. As they made their way there, cars and trucks of all sizes passed in both directions. While there seemed to be adequate room to proceed on the edge of the highway, David was happy to reach the turnoff for the dirt road leading to the cove Nels had recommended. The road was rutted with small- to medium-sized holes and an occasional water hazard, but was no worse than many David had ridden before. As compared to the highway, there was much less traffic. There were no cars essentially, and the trucks were fewer and smaller; though when a truck passed, it didn't feel as though there were an excess of available space.

Eventually, they found a narrow trail off the dirt road to a small, isolated cove, where, they'd been assured, their bikes and few possessions would be safe. They threw down towels and let their bodies absorb the hot afternoon sun. They unpacked the lunches and cracked open chilled Cokes as David related the events of the morning at Owlton. He told Ellen about his vague feelings of mistrust of Nels. He did, however, have to give Nels credit for the recommendation of the beach on which they were then sprawled.

Looking around the private surroundings, David suggested they drop their swimsuits and head for the water. Ellen hesitated and blushed, but after looking around said, "Oh well," with her throaty laugh. She removed her bikini top and bottom and watched as he stripped. He grabbed her, and they ran for the water, their feet burning on the hot sand. The water was warm and clear, clear enough that they could see their toes glisten below them. But David wasn't much interested in toes. He stopped much higher, rubbing Ellen's breasts in the water and bending to kiss her nipples. The result was predictable. She reached for him and dipped down to give him kisses for as long as she could stay underwater. They dove at each other, laughed, played, pressed their bodies together. The feeling of freedom was exhilarating. David never wanted it to end. It was as though they were unconscious of the possibility that anyone else could be present.

Ultimately, they walked from the water, spent, his arm around her waist. They dressed, mounted their bikes, and started back on the trail to the dirt road. A couple of trucks passed them, moving to the left-hand side of the road, kicking up dust and spraying water. David led the way with Ellen falling fifty yards or so behind. His shorts and T-shirt were mottled with muddy water. He heard a couple of trucks from behind and looked to see that Ellen was keeping up. One truck passed him. As he was crossing a cement culvert over a wide ditch, the second truck pulled even with him. There was a thud on his left shoulder, and suddenly, he was circling over the handlebars into the ditch. He yelled as he spun through the air and heard Ellen cry his name. Within seconds, she was at his side, wallowing with him in the mud, her hands on his face. "What happened?" she cried. And then, without waiting for an answer, she stood and screamed at the truck rumbling off down the road, "Stop! You knocked him off his bike. He's hurt. Come back!"

David lay in the water under the culvert, bent on his right side. He didn't speak. The bicycle was at least five feet beyond him, its front tire battered and handlebars askew. His T-shirt was ripped from the bottom, exposing a stomach scraped by rocks and dirt. The water in which he'd come to rest was so brown that his blood, emanating from multiple areas, was diluted and partially hidden. His left arm was turned in an abnormal direction, looking as though it had been dislocated. Ellen made sure his helmet was elevated on a rock so that his head would be above the shallow water line. She checked the strap to be sure it wasn't too tight. She climbed up to the culvert and began yelling for help.

David awakened in a hospital room, groggy, attached to all sorts of intravenous tubes, with Ellen holding his hand. He saw her smiling through the blur. "What happened?" He looked around. "Are you all right?"

"I am, but you're not. You're in the hospital. St. Elisabeth's in Willemstad."

"I don't remember that clearly."

"You were hit by a truck on that dirt road coming back from the beach. It knocked you off the bike into a ditch."

"What's wrong with me?" David wanted to reach his hands out over his body, but he couldn't. He ached from every bone.

"The X-rays show multiple breaks around your left shoulder, as well as a fractured knee cap. To say nothing of the scrapes. You're pretty banged up, David."

"I'm sorry." There was a long pause. He was in a cloud. "I've ruined the trip." A men's tennis doubles match was playing out on television, the sound muted. He couldn't tell who was playing or where. For once, he had no desire to be a contestant.

"That's the last thing to be worried about. I just want to get you out of here to where you can get the best medical attention."

"Who brought me here? The driver?"

"Ha! He drove off. I stopped someone else who arranged for the ambulance. The police are looking for the driver."

David mumbled, "Nice of him."

"The police asked what hit you. I didn't see it, only heard you yell as you somersaulted over the handlebars."

"I don't know."

"Was it the side mirror, do you think? They stick out so far, and the truck had to pass pretty close to you."

"I'm not sure. It didn't feel hard. It was softer, like a punch or something."

"I called the man you met with, Mr. Nels, and he recommended this hospital. I also took your American Express Platinum card and called its medical services department. They're deciding whether they'll fly you back to the States for treatment. It looks like they might." She was serious, as she always was when talking about business matters.

"What kind of treatment? Where?"

"Your shoulder will have to have surgery. It's fairly complicated, with plates, screws, wires. We're trying to convince them that it shouldn't be done here."

"So, I'll be setting off metal detectors at airports from here on." He smiled weakly.

"Maybe. Your knee is in a cast and probably won't require surgery. And the abrasions will just take time."

"I've got to get back to Denver. I can't," he struggled, "be sitting around on my ass in a hospital here for Christ's sake."

"I'm trying." The phone next to David's bed rang, and Ellen rose to answer it. "Granddad. Hi. How are you?" Ellen cupped her hand over the receiver and whispered to David, "It's Granddad. He's trying to help get us out of here."

"Yes, he's doing better." She said little else other than an occasional "yes" or "I don't know." Her grandfather had seemed pleased that she and David were going away together, and now it was clear that he was genuinely concerned. He had never been accepting in that way to the other men in her life in the past.

She leaned toward David, whispering, "He wants to talk to you. Are you up to it?"

David nodded his head equivocally, as much side to side as up and down, and extended his right hand toward the phone.

"David, I'm damned sorry about what happened. Don't worry about anything. Just take care of yourself. The firm will do everything necessary to get you back here and into the right hands."

"Thanks. I do...I do appreciate it." David's right arm swayed. Ellen took the phone.

"I think that's enough for now. He's sort of darting in and out. It's the morphine."

A few minutes later, David opened his eyes. Ellen's face was in front of his, looking down. "I love you, David."

He smiled and nodded his head. With that, he slipped under again.

7

David was transferred to Presbyterian/St. Luke's in Denver, where he underwent surgery on his left shoulder. On the day following the operation, he was fairly alert when awake but had a hard time concentrating, tending to drop off after only a few minutes of focused conversation. Ellen sat in a chair by the window, working from her BlackBerry. She had been with David full time since the accident five days before and was trying to keep up with her marketing responsibilities at the same time. Proposals for new accounting business necessitated almost immediate turnaround, a requirement that was hard to meet when she was out of the office. She had made arrangements with American Express for an air ambulance out of Curaçao to Miami. The ambulance came with a paramedic, and there had been room for Ellen as well. Amex picked up the entire tab, except for the relatively small added cost of flying David home from Miami for surgery, an expense which Hill & Devon assumed.

Charles Calhoun rapped quietly on the closed door and was met by Ellen, who was acting in the protective position of gatekeeper. Locking her hands on his shoulders and kissing his cheek, she said with evident relief, "Charles, I'm glad you're here."

He patted her on the back. He'd always expressed a paternalistic attitude toward the attractive, spirited young woman, whom he'd known for some twenty years. "How is he, Ellen?"

David answered, "I'm fine." He chuckled. "Don't let all these tubes and the wiggly lines on the monitor fool you for one minute." He was pale, and his face looked thin, but if one could ignore the tubes and the monitor, he looked healthy. In fact, the lines on the monitor were fairly rhythmic.

"I like your nurse, David. Pretty lucky patient."

Ellen waved him away. "All he can talk about is work, the things he should be doing." She threw her head back with some combination of exaggerated disapproval but knowing acceptance.

"Before we get to that, what exactly did happen?"

Ellen answered, "His left shoulder has multiple breaks and required extensive surgery. His left knee cap was fractured and is in a cast. All the abrasions are covered with bandages. Other than that, hardly a thing." She forced a laugh to underscore her resentment.

David held the TV remote in his right hand and turned off CNBC, where he had been trying to follow the financial news. "I've been worried about the Ballet investigation. We could get a letter from the Department of Labor any day."

"Don't worry about it. When I got the call about the accident and found that you'd be out of the picture for at least a couple of weeks, I started interviewing witnesses." Calhoun added, "You're tracks in the files are clear, and I picked right up."

"You don't know yet what happened at Owlton."

"Well, I am curious about that, of course, but I don't want to press you now. Let's wait a couple of days."

"It won't take me long to report. What happened was exactly this…" David dropped the remote and formed a circle with the thumb and index finger of his right hand. "Zip, nada. They say they can't give us proprietary information because we might steal it and compete with them. I'd laugh, but it hurts too much." Pushing around in the folds of the sheets and blankets resting on top of his stomach, he managed to regain possession of the remote. "I don't trust them either."

"Why's that?"

"Their guy, Maarten Nels, isn't credible."

"To say nothing of having David pushed off his bike into a ditch," added Ellen as she moved her fingers through her hair, letting it drop to the sides and back of her head. She had a habit of doing that when she was excited.

"Is that what happened?"

"I can't prove it, but I'm suspicious that what hit my shoulder was not the car or the side mirror but an open hand."

Ellen returned to her chair. She looked tired, under strain. "The police are investigating it."

David would have shrugged, but he couldn't. One shoulder wouldn't work without the cooperation of the other in this movement. "But they've got home court advantage. Nothing will ever be established."

"I'll keep on with what I'm doing," Calhoun said. "And after you're feeling better, I'll send you the witness statements I've taken, so you can see where I've been." He didn't add that the Chadwells' lawsuit had been filed three days before. That news could wait to be delivered when the statements were sent.

"God, I'm sorry about this," David said, looking at Calhoun.

"What's wrong? Don't you think I can do this digging stuff anymore? I may not be as rusty as you think."

"The only hard part about this assignment is the client."

"I can handle him. David, don't worry. The firm will stand behind you 150 percent. Stephen wants you to know that, but he'll be coming around to see you himself."

Calhoun kissed Ellen on the cheek and, pointing a finger toward her face, said, "You try and get some rest too. You need it." By the time they finished talking, David's eyes were closed again.

Later the same day, Stephen Hill dropped by the hospital. He gave Ellen a hug and shook David's hand. He was courtly and formal, always appointed in traditional business attire. He would have nothing to do with the new business casual look adopted by his firm over his muted protests.

"I feel terrible that this happened to you in the line of duty."

"If the truth were known, Stephen, the 'line of duty' for that day was over. I was on my way back to the hotel after an afternoon lounging on the beach with your granddaughter." David looked at Ellen to catch her reaction to this seemingly innocent, but charged, description of their activity that afternoon. Her only response was to lower her head and lift her eyes upward as she looked at David.

"Speaking of my young lady," Stephen said, looking down at her, "has she been a good nurse?" He was a strong-looking man, almost six feet tall, though now slightly stooped, with white hair.

"The absolute best. I don't know what I would have done without her."

"No," Ellen interjected, "it was Granddad who got you back here to a first-rate hospital and surgeon."

"Hardly. That was the least the firm could do. The important thing is for you to get well. Don't worry about your cases," Stephen said with an elegant swoop of his hand. Mannerisms like this one, combined with his general appearance, gave him an authoritarian aura. "The one I understand that is occupying most of your time, the Chadwell case, is being taken care of by Charles. He'll be sending you the file once you're home. You can get up to speed and right back in the thick of it as soon as you're ready."

"I should be getting out of this place soon."

Ellen changed the subject. "What's been going on at the firm, Granddad?"

"Nothing special. I know you're a whiz at all this, Ellen, but I'm still doing my best to hold back the marketing tide that seems to be overtaking our profession these days."

"No need to apologize to me."

"Well, Jim Ramsey's doing a good job running the firm, but he's buying into some ideas I sure don't believe in."

"Like?" David asked.

"Branding. That's one."

"What's your objection, Granddad?" Ellen asked, knowing full well the answer.

"We're professionals, and professionals don't worry about branding. We're not slick. We don't need to advertise to have an 'image.' We've built this firm pretty successfully by just digging in, working hard, and getting good results. That's all that counts."

"In my world," Ellen said, "all the big accounting firms are doing it."

David struggled to prop himself up in the bed. "I've been meaning to mention the rumor I heard before we left about the new offices. That the firm will be the lead tenant in the building and we've negotiated naming rights. Our name's going to be at the top of the building, at the sixtieth floor."

"Over my dead body. I won't have the name Hill & Devon blinking in multicolored lights above this city."

"The banks are doing it, too," Ellen interjected.

"I don't care. They're different. They are huge, worldwide companies with thousands of employees."

"So, suppose," Ellen teased, "the lights weren't colored and didn't blink. Would it be okay then?"

Stephen laughed with her and turned to David. "You don't have to worry about anything. You're the best of the best among all the partnership candidates this year. Just get yourself well, and we'll make another mushrooming foray."

Oh, God, not mushrooming, David thought. He hated the activity, but Ellen and Stephen loved it, so he played along. It was something the three of them could do together that was important to Ellen. He reconstructed in his mind their last trip to the mountains. Stephen and Ellen had walked along slowly together, chattering about the characteristics of mushrooms, those that are poisonous, like amanitas, and those that are sweetest, like chanterelles. They had ranted about the people who picked the poisonous ones and then dropped them by the side of the trail, commenting on how dumb they were to pick them in the first place. Actually, it had seemed to David that, rather than being dumb, these people were pretty smart to recognize what they had ended up with and leave them right there. A lot of time had been spent too with

43

Ellen and Stephen identifying the wildflowers they passed along the trail: fireweed, paintbrush, king's crown, queen's crown, you name it. From time to time, they had consulted small, well-thumbed books that pictured and described their discoveries.

To David, the process was painfully boring. For the life of him, he couldn't remember one wildflower from another, particularly the blue ones that all started with an *l*, like lupine and larkspur. And about the most he could remember in the mushroom department was that the prettier they were, the more likely they were to be dangerous. When he was in the backcountry, he wanted to be on the move toward a destination, hiking or running, not roaming around in circles under trees, staring at the ground in search of edible mushrooms. He and Ellen shared a number of sports interests: they both played passable tennis, they both liked hiking, and they both skied, though she was a lot tougher than he in powder and moguls. One area in which they parted company was running; it helped him clear his mind but meant nothing to her.

On the last mushroom-hunting trip they'd made together, after a respectful period nosing around with them, David had announced that he needed to work off some tension and was going to run up the trail; he would meet them on the way back on the trail or, if not, then at the trailhead in two hours. They'd been fine with that. They just seemed to like having him along on the excursion even if he didn't participate fully. He had pounded up the trail, dodging over, around, and on the rocks, sucking it all in: the noise of the streams, the rustling of the wind in the trees, the blue skies and white clouds. This was what he loved.

Now, he would be forced to participate in their activities because the doctors had warned him that he wouldn't be up to much more for several weeks. Three months was the prognosis before he could resume his usual more strenuous activities. For a time, mushroom hunting it would have to be.

8

David had been exhilarated by the thought of finally returning to the office after several weeks out of the action, first in the hospital and then at home recuperating. He'd been bored without the daily interaction he found at the firm. True, Ellen had been attentive, but her daily visits and nights and weekends spent with him filled important, but obviously different, needs than those served at the firm. She was away only once, and then not until the latter part of his recuperation, when she went on a long-planned but short vacation with her grandfather to Barbados. She had said she was worried about being away from David and was also uncomfortable about leaving her responsibilities at the office again so soon after having gone to Curaçao. Her role as marketing director was critical in the development of new client presentations, and her absence wouldn't go unnoticed. But there was no way she would disappoint her grandfather.

David's shoulder had improved, though slowly. Sleeping was the most difficult. He still required Percodan at night before he went to bed to get any sleep at all. When he was up and busy, the pain was less noticeable.

During most of the recuperation period, his telephone, e-mail, BlackBerry, and fax kept him tethered to the office and to clients. Mail had been delivered to his condominium in a daily pouch. He tracked his time as though he were at the office, but he fell well behind his daily budget of billable hours. The authorities in Curaçao had seemingly dropped the investigation into the cause of the accident. They hadn't been able to identify either the truck or the driver; there was nothing more they could do, they said.

He and Ellen had talked often about his bad luck in being injured in the very year that he was up for partnership consideration. Rather, he talked of it, while Ellen scoffed at the idea that it would hold him back. After all, the accident had occurred while on a business trip. It wasn't as though he'd screwed up his shoulder and leg heli-skiing, she argued. Logically, she was right, of course. Still, he couldn't remove the concern totally from his mind. More than any other single factor, billable hours were often what decided who became a partner and who didn't.

His first day back was a daunting one that included a meeting with the Stagehands Union. It wasn't easy for him to get around, given that his left leg was encased in a hinge brace and only one shoulder, the right, was available to use with a crutch. He sent files ahead by messenger and caught a taxi. At the artists' entrance to backstage, he ran into Austin Wilcox, the head stagehand in the carpentry department at the opera house and a member of the union's negotiating committee, who welcomed him back. "You know, we haven't had a negotiating session while you've been away. We wanted to give you a chance to get back if we could."

David laughed. "Ah, so you can get me in a weakened condition."

"Got it. But seriously, now we're going to have to move it forward pretty fast."

"I know. It'll be one of my main priorities."

"You have the pension fund investigation going on too, I know. I talked to your partner in your absence. Will you be picking that back up?"

"Yes, that's another one of my priorities. You met with Charles Calhoun?"

"Yes. I'm interested to know what your reaction is to the information I gave him. I've never heard from him again."

David pressed his memory but drew a blank as to any memo in the investigative file concerning a meeting with Wilcox. He had reviewed all the work product of Calhoun's investigation. There was no smoking gun. It appeared the Ballet was going to be in the clear, so he wondered what Wilcox was talking about. "Well," David fudged, "when I've reviewed everything, we'll see what the next steps will be," adding, "I'll get back to you if there's something we should pursue further."

Wilcox looked at him quizzically. "If? Here you have the fox, if you'll excuse the expression, literally in the hen house, and you don't think it's important?"

David smiled. "I get the pun, but I'm not sure I'm following you."

"I'm talking about Fred White and Phil Gunn, that's what," Wilcox scoffed. "You don't even know about it, do you?"

"We're looking into all of the claims that have turned up," David answered honestly if not evasively. He had noticed an odd peculiarity in Wilcox's manner of approaching a serious subject. He would stand sideways, hands in his front pants pockets, turning his head over his shoulder to look at the listener, rather than facing the person head on. It seemed defensive, like talking to someone with your arms crossed over your chest. He was doing it again.

"Then," Wilcox said, "you'd better hear it straight from me." He looked at his watch. "We have time before the meeting starts."

They walked into a small vacant office down the hallway, and Wilcox closed the door. "I met with Calhoun at the art museum. I asked for the meeting when it wasn't clear when you'd be back. I told him there was something wrong with the fund, to put it mildly. I spelled out what I called a hypothetical theory. I think he understood it wasn't really hypothetical, but I'll be more direct with you. Phil Gunn has relationships with the hedge funds he steers his clients to. They give him kickbacks for producing the business, an easy thing for them to hide because they don't provide any information about their investments. Fred White, a trustee of the fund and an old buddy of Gunn's who brought him in as the investment advisor in the first place, is cut in on the deal in exchange for getting Gunn the business. Neat little arrangement and hard to trace. Even harder to find when the reward is," he paused, "in artwork, not in cash deposited into some bank."

David was stunned but struggled not to show it.

Wilcox continued, "When Calhoun asked how I knew this, I told him to think about how Fred, the CFO of a nonprofit ballet company, could have a wall-to-wall, floor-to-ceiling painting by Richard Diebenkorn hanging in his living room. It was clear from his reaction that Calhoun knows how valuable a Diebenkorn painting is."

"White could have independent means."

"That's what Calhoun said, but he doesn't. Trust me."

David held out his hand out, palm up, moving his fingers toward his chest. "You'll have to tell me how you know all this if you want me to rely on it."

"No. You go out and investigate it."

David was astonished. It was always tough as a lawyer learning that there was a major hole in your case. He fought not to show his surprise. There must be some explanation for the fact that he had found no interview memorandum for Calhoun's meeting with Wilcox. It must have been misfiled. David said simply, "Thanks for the information. I'll look into it."

"I hope it means more to you than it apparently did to him," Wilcox said in a snippy tone. With that, they opened the door and walked back down the hall to the negotiating meeting.

The doctor's orders, if followed literally, called for David to go directly home that evening from the Denver Center following the stagehands meeting. Instead, he grabbed a cab to his office and called Ellen, telling her that he'd be delayed a bit before he could get away for dinner. Her response was tense for she had become increasingly frustrated in her assumed role of doctor's enforcer. About the only time she had influence was when he was focused on making love, an inclination that seemed to be returning as the days passed and he grew stronger. The problem was that the execution, with his mending shoulder and knee, was a bit challenging. Ellen said, "Okay, one hour. I'll be there at seven," and hung up.

He rifled through the Chadwell file in his credenza and found the section containing witness interview memoranda sent to him from Calhoun. There he found tabs for interviews with White and Gunn and numerous others but, as he had remembered, nothing for Wilcox. David wandered down to the area outside Calhoun's office to look through the official file in the case, which was maintained there. Again, he went through every file tab for every witness interview but found nothing for Austin Wilcox.

David approached Kathleen, Calhoun's secretary, who was still at her nearby desk at that late hour, even though her boss was out of town. He said, "I understand that there was an interview with an Austin Wilcox in the Chadwell case, but I can't find it anywhere, not in the materials sent to me by pouch or even in the files here."

"There should be. I seem to recall typing one." She ran through the tan files that contained witness interview memoranda and then raised her hand to her head. "Oh, no, that's the one we deleted. There isn't one for that person."

"Deleted? Why?"

"I don't know. One day Charles said delete it, that we didn't need that one, so I did."

"I have to take a look at it. There's been a development that might make it have significance that wasn't apparent before."

"Okay, I'll look in the system and see if I can retrieve it. I'll let you know first thing in the morning."

David returned to his office and sat down at his desk. The phone rang; it was Ellen calling from in front of the building. He put on his coat and walked slowly to the elevator, crutch braced under his good shoulder. At the ground level, he pushed through the circular door and saw her car at the curb. She got out and came around the side to open the door. He loved the gesture even though it was a bit much. He could handle getting the door open.

"Thanks, El."

Back in the car, she said, "You need a policeman."

He laughed. "You think?"

"I know."

"I love you."

She looked at him, leaned over for a kiss, and drove off. It was dark outside. The sunset had given way to a black sky. The only color was red, a string of red lights ahead for them to maneuver.

They were both silent, she frustrated and he absorbed. Why, he wondered, having conducted an interview and having dictated a memorandum about it, would Charles have deleted the memo? Even if it shed no helpful light on the subject, it wasn't normal procedure to delete a memorandum. After all, many witness interviews produce nothing particularly significant, just a lot of circular excursions and dead ends. There was some good reason he knew.

9

David arrived at his desk at eight thirty before the office opened. The blinking red light on his phone signaled that messages were awaiting him. He touched the message button to find that there were seven. The third one was from Kathleen at eight o'clock the night before, saying that she hadn't been able to retrieve the Wilcox interview memo from the system and wanted him to know first thing. Feeling that there must be some way to find the memo, David decided to call Saundra, whom he hadn't seen since the incident in the conference room. In addition to her several other talents, she was adept with the firm's computer systems. Luckily, she answered. She was there at all hours it seemed. David couldn't help but wonder whether she might have the same relationship with others as she had with him. Or used to. There would be no more of that. His new tight relationship with Ellen made that impossible.

"Saundra, it's David."

"Yes, I know."

Given the coolness of her response, he decided it best simply to pose the issue.

"It has to be in the system. She doesn't know how to get it."

"Do you?"

"Of course," she replied. "Every night, all work product is backed up. Anything in the system can be retrieved from the backup tape. In other words, it may have been deleted from Kathleen's work station, but she wouldn't have deleted it from the backup tape. It's simply a matter of locating it. Do you know the document number?"

"No."

Saundra sighed, "What about the date, subject matter?"

"I don't know exactly. It would have been last month, and it's in the Chadwell case. The file number," he paused as he looked at the file, "is 472397. The memo concerns a witness interview with an Austin Wilcox conducted by Charles Calhoun. He's away currently, but I'm working on the case with him. Can you tell me how to go about getting it?"

"Let me take a crack at it. It would take me longer to walk you through the process than to do it myself, and it's not exactly a skill you need to master. It's seldom that we ever have to do this."

"How soon can I get it?"

"So now you want me to drop everything and turn right to your very important project, is that it?"

"It is very important, Saundra, and I'd really appreciate it."

"And I suppose that you'd like personal delivery to a conference room? Which one this time, David?" But before he could even reply, she added, "Oh forget it. I'll send what I find by messenger." She hung up.

An hour later, a messenger entered David's office and placed an interoffice envelope in the inbox on his desk. If one were to judge from his inbox, David had a lot to do. Papers and files on which this envelope was dropped were stacked at least seven inches high. The inbox matched the rest of his office. Every square inch, desk, credenza, tables, bookcases, was stacked with files and papers. They were even beginning to creep along the carpet at the perimeter of the office. It was all tidy; organized clutter might be the appropriate description. David could put his finger on any file at any time.

He put the letter he was reading aside and opened the envelope. There was a one page memo from Calhoun entitled "re: Interview with Austin Wilcox."

I met with Austin Wilcox at the art museum on November 15, 2006, the meeting having been arranged at his request and at the location of his choosing. He asked for a confidential meeting, and my assumption is that he did not wish to meet at our offices.

Wilcox's statements were a mixture of assertion and innuendo. The innuendo is to the effect that we ought to be looking into the relationship between Phil Gunn and the hedge funds that he has put the endowment fund in; that he could be getting kickbacks; and also that we ought to be looking into the relationship between Gunn and Fred White. The implication is that the kickbacks have something to do with artwork, with the further hint that White owns a very valuable work by Richard Diebenkorn from his Ocean Park series, which he lent to the new museum building for its inaugural show. The specific assertions were that Gunn was brought into the scene at the Ballet by White some years ago and that White didn't have independent means that would explain ownership of a valuable Diebenkorn. How Wilcox would have information of this type was not explained. Obviously, these relationships should be explored, and I assured him we would do so. He was not responsive to my efforts to fill in the blanks.

David sat back in his chair and stared out at the morning sky. Huge, billowy clouds passed along in front of the crystal blue backdrop. The bottoms of the clouds were brown, sliced flat as though by a dirty knife. He looked for the memoranda in the file reciting Calhoun's interviews with Gunn and White. He skimmed them quickly and then doubled back to read each one carefully. White was cooperative but had nothing that shed light on the problem. Gunn had been almost impossible for Calhoun even to see. When he did, he was abrupt and unhelpful. It was interesting that nowhere in the memoranda was there the slightest reference to the kind of questions that should have been asked to elicit answers to Wilcox's accusations. Why would that be? There must have been something that subsequently occurred that made Wilcox's accusations look like they would just lead up a blind alley. But still, why delete an investigative report from the file? It was a puzzle, and there was no way to get to the bottom of it short of asking Calhoun directly.

10

The first time Calhoun's schedule permitted a meeting following his return to town was on a Saturday, and predictably for a Saturday, it was at his home. Apparently, he hadn't thought about how David was going to get all the files there that might be needed. Recognizing that the most he could handle was one litigation briefcase full of documents, David had culled through the files to find those that most likely would be needed. At least now he could drive.

David pulled up in front of Calhoun's home, a large brick structure set well back from the street on a sweeping lawn. Several chimneys rose above the roof line. The neighborhood was one of Denver's best, the country club area. As he parked the car, he found it hard to picture his ever being in the position to summon associates to his home, to, in effect, "pull rank," particularly to a house like this. He loaded the large briefcase on a handcart and walked it to the front door.

They sat in the sunroom overlooking the pool and garden. Calhoun offered David a soda, observing that he hadn't intended that he should drag all that with him, considering the condition of his shoulder. "I thought we ought to meet to discuss the report you'll be drafting now that we've pretty much buttoned up the investigation."

Calhoun was dressed in tan chinos and a polo shirt with sweater. He was short and solid, his light hair contrasting with a tan face. The overall impression was of a strong, healthy middle-aged man. David was dressed similarly. It was an acceptable uniform for the office too, except that at the office the required shirt was collared with long sleeves. Actually, David more often saw Calhoun at the office in a suit, due undoubtedly to the frequent court appearances that were a part of his life as a trial lawyer.

"You feel the investigation is complete?" David asked.

"As much as it can be. When I had to step in, I went through everything you'd done and then launched into it myself. The bottom line is that I think Adolph is right."

"Meaning?"

"That there's nothing to the claim. It's a market gone bad as far as Owlton is concerned. Sure, we could wish that they hadn't put the money there, but you do that kind of thing in order to diversify. Some investments are going to go up and some down. They happened to catch a big one in a real drop."

"What about the principals? Do you think they're all clear?" David asked cautiously.

"Yeah. Plotkin didn't pay the kind of attention that ideally he should have, but you know Adolph. He's big on creativity, not on detail. As for White, he's probably not the smartest CFO around, but if he were, he wouldn't be working for this client would he? Gunn's a promoter, that's for sure, but there's no law against that. If there were, a lot of people would be behind bars."

"Yeah, including a few lawyers we know," David said. He looked through double doors into the living room on one side and into a den on the other. It looked as if every wall surface was covered with paintings and drawings, mostly abstract and colorful, and in many spots on the floors, steel or marble or bronze sculptures stood like sentinels. "It looks like you're into the art world."

"It is a big interest of mine."

Most of what he saw didn't intrigue David that much, but his eyes caught a piece across the living room. It was a sculpture of a nude woman, a thin, well-proportioned, luscious young woman. Pointing, he asked, "What about the nude? Who did that?"

"That's Robert Graham. It's bronze, done in the lost wax process. Most all of his sculptures are of nude women or girls."

David decided to go for it. He'd put it off as long as he could. "What about Austin Wilcox's claims?" he asked as offhandedly as possible.

"Who?"

"Austin Wilcox, the head stagehand you interviewed, though I couldn't find the interview report in the file."

"Then what makes you think he was interviewed?"

"He told me he was. He asked what was happening and why he hadn't heard anything."

"A thin guy with a black mustache?"

"Yeah, that's him."

"Yes, I remember him. I didn't think his story was believable."

"Why is that? I've read the memo, and there's nothing on the face of it that makes it seem doubtful."

"Read the memo? What do you mean?"

David knew that Calhoun was on weak ground when it came to computer technology, not that he was any expert. "When I couldn't find a file memorandum, I checked with Kathleen, and she said there had been one but she'd deleted it. I had it retrieved from the backup system." Calhoun's color turned almost white. "I can't understand why it would have been deleted."

"Because the accusations were potentially explosive. I could find absolutely nothing to support Wilcox's claims. To the contrary, he had a motive for fingering White, the familiar role of a spurned lover. I assume you know that the two of them had a relationship for years which has recently blown up?"

"Pun intended, Charles?" David said with a wink and a grin, hoping to lighten the load a bit.

Calhoun didn't react. "In fact, his motives were so suspect I considered it unfair to grant them even the credence a file memorandum would lend. We can't be certain we'll be the only ones to see the files. They may have to be produced to the government or our adversaries, as you know."

"I can see that," David answered, "but don't we have to be in a position to show that we've weighed all the facts?"

"We have. That doesn't mean that every last assertion has to show up in the report." Calhoun paused as if the matter were closed but then continued. "What I'd like you to do now is to produce a draft of the report confirming the conclusion we've discussed and taking what you feel should be included from the investigatory file."

David sighed. He didn't know what more to say. They were at a stalemate.

Calhoun rose, and David stuffed files back into his briefcase. As they walked out of the sunroom through the living room to the entry hall, Calhoun talked about some of the artwork, apparently responding to David's interest in the Graham sculpture. There were a lot of names of artists whom David had never heard before. His eyes flitted over the walls. It might as well have been a museum. He commented on what a beautiful home it was. Calhoun laughed and said his wife didn't agree with all the contemporary art being mixed with antiques, noting that the former was his department and the latter hers. David felt an aura of prosperity that he hadn't realized the senior partners of Hill & Devon enjoyed. Stephen Hill's house had not been nearly as grand. In fact, it had looked almost in a state of disrepair with shabby upholstery, threadbare spots on the carpets, and framed mirrors that hadn't seen a cleaning in a long time—undoubtedly a reflection of the fact that there was no woman of the house.

David felt too ignorant to even attempt questions about what he was looking at, but did ask, "How did you get started collecting?"

"It's a long story. Some day when we have the time, I'll tell you. But I'd advise you not to start. It can become addictive."

David stepped to the door. "I understand that Fred White is interested in art too, contemporary art. You two may have a lot in common."

"I know. In fact, we've already exchanged site visits. He came here to see our stuff, and I did the same at his home. He's got a real collection."

"How can he do that on his salary?" David asked.

"I don't think he does. He mentioned paintings that had come from his mother."

"Oh," David said, "to be in the inheritance business. I'm afraid I missed that one."

"That makes two of us."

11

Ellen sat across the table. She looked especially desirable, David thought, all the more so as she'd been gone for a couple of days on a business trip. They were having dinner at Ellen's place. He'd gone by a Japanese restaurant and picked up sushi and sashimi and a bottle of sake. The one real advantage in dating the boss's granddaughter was that, if anything, she was more loyal to the law firm than he was, and she never tired of hearing about what was going on there. She was the only woman he'd ever been with to whom he could talk shop without watching eyes glaze over, but tonight she'd given the impression of being a bit impatient discussing the office. She played with chopsticks and looked around the room as if she were redecorating it. He changed the subject to his visit with Calhoun the preceding Saturday, mentioning how beautiful his home was.

Her mood changed; she became engaged. "I think it's one of the prettiest houses in the entire city." She hesitated. "Did I show you the photos of their house in Barbados?"

"No, I don't think so."

Ellen was familiar with his Barbados home because Calhoun had invited Stephen Hill to spend a few days there, and Stephen, in turn, had asked Ellen to join him. Knowing that he wouldn't go without company and that there weren't many eligible companions of his vintage, she'd agreed.

"I'll get them." She rose from the table and started down the hall toward her bedroom. David's eyes followed. He loved her walk; there was a deliberate quality to her step. He called out, "So does the beach cottage show I have something to aspire to on becoming a partner— that is, I should say, *if* I become a partner."

She walked back into the room with an envelope. "Of course you will. At least according to Granddad, there's never been a clearer or better choice." She sat back down at the table. "It's not exactly a cottage." She thumbed through the photos, explaining the rooms and the views. He was impressed by the luxury of the home and beauty of the grounds, but not really surprised after what he'd seen of their establishment in town.

"Yes, cottage it isn't," said David.

"You couldn't have a better setting. You walk out of the house and stroll fifty feet to the water, where little lapping waves hit the beach. I love the sound of the waves to put you to sleep at night. Maybe someday we can go there together."

"That sounds like the best part, El, and speaking more precisely of that subject..." He moved toward her.

"Naughty boy. I just got back—"

"That's the point, and against your will, I'm here for dinner, right?"

"You got it." She laughed heartily, ending with a trademark snort.

David settled back into his chair. "I know Charles is interested in art. It's quite obvious from his home."

"Well, he's saved some of the best for the Caribbean. This, for example, is a Richard Diebenkorn. It's very valuable. And," she passed more photographs, "here's a Jim Dine, and an Eric Fischl and—it goes on and on."

"Sounds like you learned more in that art class at Boulder than I'd thought." David smiled. He looked carefully at the photographs. He couldn't figure out what anyone saw in the Dine painting of a bathrobe, but he liked the Diebenkorn painting. He held the photograph out. "Tell me about what's his name—"

"Diebenkorn. It's from his Ocean Park series."

"Yeah, what's that mean?"

"That's a name he gave a series of large paintings he did while living in Southern California years ago. Ocean Park is a place there. They're numbered. They have generally soft colors and sort of an architectural feeling."

"What number is this one?" asked David.

"What difference does it make? All I know is that it takes a lot of money to buy one of these babies."

"I imagine." David felt himself suddenly filled with rushing thoughts. This was the same artist whose painting Wilcox had mentioned to Calhoun. David focused on what Wilcox had told him and the contents of the deleted memo. The thrust of it had been that White had profited in the form of artwork that he had no possible ability to buy. And here was the same artist, what sounded like the same series as far as he could recall. A coincidence undoubtedly, as the series was numbered, and there might very well be a lot of them. But still, it seemed strange.

It was all too speculative to share with Ellen. Charles Calhoun was her hero. Besides, there was other business to conduct. He turned to draw her into his arms. He had been thinking of this for days. "There's something of beauty I'd like to see right now. But first we've got to get you out of all of those cumbersome clothes."

12

The new addition to the Denver Art Museum stood as a tribute to a fundraising effort spanning several years and fueled by social and political intrigue among the city's power elite. The new wing, designed by Daniel Libeskind and built at a cost of one hundred million dollars, was both exciting and controversial. The structure was like an explosion of triangular titanium, rising four stories and emanating from the formidable fortress designed for the museum decades earlier. The addition jutted forward like the prow of a ship. There seemed to have been no effort to marry the two structures, other than by connecting them with a light green gangway. If the gangway was the umbilical cord, the child appeared to dwarf the mother. The contrast to the gold-domed capitol building nearby was jarring. Some thought that such a dramatic statement served to distract from the works of art it was designed to house.

The interior of the Libeskind wing was almost as unconventional as its exterior. The galleries were divided into smaller asymmetrical areas. There were few right angles. Some walls were not at ninety degrees to the floor; they were canted inward or outward, leaving paintings to hover in space. The feeling was exciting, dramatic, but also disorienting. All in all, the environment seemed that it would be successful for large-scale contemporary work but not hospitable for the museum's vaunted collection of art from the American West.

David entered the new wing and was directed to the office of a curator where he introduced himself and inquired about the Diebenkorn painting that his investigation had indicated was in a recent museum show. He wanted to know more about this famous artist. The curator, who appeared nearing retirement, commented expansively on the piece, noting that an anonymous donor had made it available on loan for the show. With David's question as to what number in the Ocean Park series this work was—offered with about as much authority as he could muster—she left her desk, opened a file drawer across the room, and returned, answering, "I wanted to be sure. It's 141." She handed him the catalog of the show and urged him to keep it.

David left the office and walked upstairs. He passed paintings done by painters now deceased, Mark Rothko and Robert Motherwell among many others. He recognized some of their names from Ellen. He sat on a bench in the center of one of the galleries and reached into his coat pocket for Ellen's photo of Calhoun's Barbados living room. He then opened the catalog to the photograph of the anonymously lent number 141. David had taken this one of the photographs Ellen had shown him at dinner several nights before since he knew that he'd need more than just a general mental recollection of its composition. He compared the two photographs, space for space, color for color. With a sinking heart, he realized there was no doubt. They were the same painting.

David returned to the curator's office and knocked on the door. He thought he'd take a try. "You said the Diebenkorn was lent anonymously. I was wondering whether the donor is local or whether it came from out of state or out of the country for that matter?" He tried to give her an engaging smile.

This time the curator didn't have to consult the file. "It's from an individual who's quite generous in lending his works to us. He's an executive with an important cultural organization here in Denver."

David wanted to supply the name, Fred White, but he couldn't bring himself to do it. Or was it that he didn't need to? He became immune to the architectural and artistic drama he had just experienced, feeling almost sickened by the thoughts rolling through his mind. Calhoun now had the Diebenkorn painting that White had acquired in some way or another from Gunn. And Calhoun had deleted the memorandum of his interview with Wilcox that had provided the tracks to follow. Calhoun's explanation of why he deleted the memorandum had seemed only superficially plausible when they met. Now, there was no doubt that the explanation was false.

To reject the explanation was impossible. Charles Calhoun had an impeccable reputation on every score, professionally and personally, and he was far from dumb. He couldn't be involved.

⚖️

David set the afternoon aside to devote to drafting the internal investigation report, but he spent more time staring out the window, lost in thought, than he did getting words down on paper. Despite every attempt he made to express the conclusion that Calhoun expected, whitewashing the Ballet and the trustees' involvement in the case, he couldn't make it work. Reluctantly, he was forced to the conclusion that he had to confront Calhoun. It couldn't wait any longer.

David picked up the telephone. "Charles, this is David. Can we set up a time to talk about the Chadwell report?"

"Of course, come along. This is as good a time as any…that is, if you're ready."

While David hadn't anticipated an immediate meeting, he said he'd be right there. Down the corridor and up the stairs, he practiced, for perhaps the tenth time, how he would phrase his concerns. There had to be something he was missing, he was certain. He was aware of the reputation he had in the firm for displaying a fair degree of diplomacy in tricky situations; he hoped it was true and that he could come up with a bit of it for this meeting.

Calhoun waved him into the office, inquiring as everyone did incessantly about his injuries. It seemed no conversation could start or end without a discussion of the subject. In many cases, the concern expressed was real, but in still more, it was rote. He wouldn't want to have to characterize Calhoun's inquiry, but the subject had grown boring. He was tired of it.

"Charles, I have concerns about the report that I have to talk out with you." David's downcast smile spread, revealing his long, straight upper teeth. "Frankly, the conversation won't be an easy one."

"Yes."

"I wasn't able to disregard the accusations of Austin Wilcox, and so I went back to him. He's in a position to know a lot, living with Fred White for years and, well, obviously sharing confidences as two people would under those circumstances. He says he can prove that the painting by Richard Diebenkorn, the Ocean Park series, number 141, came to White from Gunn. It was not inherited from his mother as he told you. He knows there's no way White would have had the wherewithal to buy it."

"What does that add up to?"

"It means that we can't write a report without getting to the bottom of Wilcox's accusations that Gunn is on the take from the hedge fund and that White somehow shares in that."

Calhoun could not have reacted more innocently. "I still don't see any real evidence of that. Isn't it the kind of thing that comes up in your sexual harassment cases, a lover gets jilted and turns against the person, in this case Wilcox against White? Besides, I've heard that Wilcox is a busybody, sticking his nose into a lot of things around the Denver Center that aren't his business."

"Of course, I've considered the source and the possible motivation, but I still want to explore the accusation as far as I can. I wouldn't delete a memorandum from the file as if the claim had never been made." *So much for diplomacy*, he thought as the words rolled out of his mouth. David looked down and then up. There was no longer a smile. "And what about the Diebenkorn?"

"What about it?"

David paused. "I understand it's not with White anymore."

"Oh," said Calhoun.

"That's right. It's at your home in Barbados." David was so nervous that his voice broke.

Calhoun hesitated for what seemed to be an interminable time, but in fact was only a split second. David was prepared for him to deny it. Instead, Calhoun said, "And?"

"You tell me, Charles, because I don't get it."

"On what are you basing your information?"

"Ellen was telling me about what a beautiful art collection you have there, the highlight being a Diebenkorn and—"

"You know, David, I'm surprised you'd be so careless before making such an accusation. Richard Diebenkorn was quite a prolific painter and printmaker. I'm very lucky to have one of his pieces. A number of them are quite similar to the untrained eye."

"I understand the one you have is number 141."

"The Ocean Park series especially all look alike…very architectural, large, muted colors," said Calhoun, ignoring the statement.

David shook his head. "It's identical to the one in the museum's catalog that White lent for the show. I have a photograph of your living room. I've compared the painting in it and the one in the show. It's the same painting."

Calhoun rose awkwardly from his desk and walked to the window, his back to the room. He turned. "You…you have a photo of my living room? I can't believe that." His face was red. "I tried to do something nice for Stephen, and your Ellen. I wouldn't have thought that someone, a guest, would be going there and taking photographs of the contents of my home."

"There was nothing covert about it. Ellen loved your house and took photos because she admired it."

"What Diebenkorn I have and how I acquired it has no relationship to this case…totally irrelevant." Calhoun waved his arm as if to dismiss the whole subject.

"I'm sure that's right, knowing you, Charles, but there is an appearance problem, don't you think? I mean why would I even have looked into it if not? You recognize this can't be easy for me."

Calhoun looked up at the ceiling and started to comment when David continued, "White lied when he said the Diebenkorn came from his mother. I've had the painting's provenance investigated. She never owned it. Approximately two years ago, it was purchased at auction at Christies in New York by no less than one Phillip N. Gunn."

Calhoun turned from the window and looked at David. A long silence between them passed. "David," he said calmly, "I'd suggest you think long and hard about where you're treading. Whatever mutual interest in art Fred White and I may share, whatever transaction may or may not have occurred between us, has nothing to do with this case. I have a reputation I've nurtured for my entire career, and I won't see it undermined by you or anyone else. And I think it goes without saying that, if you persist, it could have an impact on..."

He didn't need to complete the sentence. Yes, David understood that his opportunities for partnership were fast fleeting out the door. He rose from his chair and stood behind it. "I'll have to sort this out. I'm in the process of drafting the report, and what I've discussed with you obviously poses a real problem. I'll get back to you when I have something to look at."

"When will that be?" Calhoun asked coldly. "There have been so many delays, not that anyone is to blame, but we can't wind this up until the report is finished. I'm leaving Wednesday for Barbados for another week of R & R and would like to have your draft to review while I'm there."

"I'll make it happen."

13

David continued work on the report. He spent a lot of time organizing and outlining its contents before sitting down to draft the statement of facts and conclusions. He wanted to think that he adopted this approach because it was the most efficient way to proceed, but suspected that it was, in reality, a tactic designed to delay having to put pen to paper—a phrase quite outmoded in this computerized world.

There was no way to rationalize the omission of Wilcox's accusations from the report. The fact that he had a long standing relationship with White that ended messily was hardly a basis to ignore his claims. The accusations didn't have to be taken as true, but they certainly deserved further investigation and consideration. Some of the most salient facts in an inquiry came from sources with an ax to grind.

The reality was that somehow, someway, Calhoun had acquired the Diebenkorn, presumably from White, during the course of the investigation. Maybe innocently, and knowing Calhoun, David certainly wanted to think so, but clearly it gave the appearance of impropriety, which Calhoun should have fully appreciated—and avoided.

The easy way out was to follow Calhoun's lead. Hadn't that been exactly what David had done in the biology course his freshman year when he'd prepared for the final exam with a copy of the test somebody had managed to swipe? Had he really stood up for his buddies who'd been charged with possessing and using coke at a party his senior year when he happened to be outside getting sick and so was not arrested with the others? He didn't like to look back at some details of his life. He wasn't proud of them. Thank God he'd pretty much been able to put that kind of thing, including his experimentation with drugs, behind him as he matured and moved on to law school.

Could he live with himself now if he didn't disclose all the facts? If he did reveal them, would he lose the partnership for which he'd been working the last eight long years? Would anyone believe him anyway with Calhoun's impeccable reputation? A relatively young lawyer with a good but fledgling reputation pitted against a member of the establishment bar, a senior partner of one of the largest and oldest law firms in Denver? David and Goliath, but would it end up the same way?

As he always did, he measured the question against the words of his father's letter. He could see the words, written in that familiar hand, slanting evenly to the right: "Success in life is not measured by wealth, power, or prestige, but by character, honesty, and integrity." He could remember the day it was handed to him, his thirteenth birthday. His father, sometimes given to emotion, had tears in his eyes. Hardest, though, was David's torment over the fact that the letter, which had meant so much to him, had not survived his own irrational rage, a rage born of frustration and despair when his father had died less than one year later at only age forty-seven. Despite the irrationality of the act, maybe because of it, the words had survived as a mantra by which David had attempted to guide his life.

Though his father had been gone for twenty years, many lessons David had learned from him remained clear in his mind. He remembered particularly one evening when they had taken a walk up the street together and his father had posed an ethical question. The specific issue he couldn't recall, but it had been clear that his father had been asking for his advice on a question confronting him at work. Nor could David remember what advice he had offered. But he could still feel the swell of pride that his father had sought his judgment—at such a young age—on a sensitive matter.

Not that his father had been perfect. He'd straight-armed David's attempts to get himself confirmed in the local Episcopalian Church, proclaiming whenever David wanted to go to Sunday school, "You're closer to God in the garden than in any church." His father's avocation had been gardening, which had occupied his Sundays, and he'd wanted David's help, at least that's what David told himself. But deep down, he knew that his father had wisely understood it was the desire to be with friends, not the advancement of his religious training, that was the real reason for David's interest in church.

David noticed the sky darkening and looked at the clock on his desk, a required device for someone who had to account for his every working hour in one-tenth or one-quarter hour increments. It placed an abnormal focus on the value of time, so much so that even on weekends, when he was playing, David thought of the time he was not billing.

It was seven p.m., and he had promised Ellen that he would be at her condo for dinner. He saved the portion of the report that he'd completed, arranged the files to get back into it the next day, and left the office. The time had come when he would have to tell Ellen about Calhoun. His future was at stake. His being.

After they had finished dinner and opened a second bottle of merlot, David said that he had something to discuss. He was nervous and hoped it didn't show. "Under no circumstances can you discuss this with anyone." They were seated on the couch in her living room, the fire dancing against logs that looked real enough, but weren't.

With this ominous admonition, she became immediately serious. "I think you know that I'm pretty good at that. I mean I couldn't have grown up around Granddad and not understood the importance of keeping confidences."

"You'll find this one hard, Ellen. It concerns the Chadwell investigation. I've turned up something that's disturbing, and I'm trying to decide how to deal with it."

Ellen sat up, her bright eyes aglow thanks in part to a good bottle of red wine. "Let's hear it."

"In a way, you're involved because of your trip to Barbados." The corners of his lips braced back to form an uneasy smile.

"What?"

"Let me go back." David proceeded to explain Wilcox's accusations about White and Gunn, Calhoun's omission from the file of any reference to the Wilcox interview, and his stated rationale for deleting the statement.

"Okay," Ellen's brow wrinkled, "what's the question? He made a judgment that doesn't sound irrational, even if it's one that you or I wouldn't have made ourselves."

"Now, let me muddy the waters a bit," which he did by taking her through the steps of his investigation, from which it was clear that the Diebenkorn White had loaned to the museum show was the same painting she had photographed in Calhoun's home.

She was startled. "Are you suggesting that Charles didn't report what Wilcox had said because he was paid off with the Diebenkorn painting?"

"Precisely."

"That's absurd, David. There is no lawyer in this city more respected than Charles Calhoun. Granddad thinks the world of him. He loves art and has a wonderful collection. Who's to say that he didn't buy it, or trade it, or whatever."

David poured yet another glass of wine for each of them. "I considered all that, which is why I gave Charles the opportunity to explain how he came into possession of the painting. And when I did that, instead of offering an explanation, he threatened my partnership in the firm."

"What? Come on," she said impatiently. "I mean, surely, you must have misunderstood what he said."

"No. There was no misunderstanding. You need to know this too…he was angry that you had taken photographs inside his house. I assured him it was all innocent but—"

"Jesus, David. He's going to think I was spying." Ellen looked dejectedly toward a wall where an Ellsworth Kelly lithograph was hanging. David followed her eyes. He had never quite understood why she'd hung this simplistic, bright-colored form on her wall. It seemed like something a sign painter would do.

He decided to try to lighten the conversation, pointing to the Kelly and saying, "I wish things were as simple in life as his work seems to be."

She didn't bite. "Do you realize what the implications would be here? The firm, and my grandfather's reputation, would be destroyed."

"Well, I don't think it's that extreme, but I recognize there's a problem. That's why I'm torn."

"You can't do it, David." Ellen hit her knee with her palm. She paused and then added, "I really resent your having shown that photograph to Charles. It makes me look terrible. I think you owed it to me to have my permission to do that. How did you get the photo? I didn't give it to you."

"I borrowed it." He smiled with awkward embarrassment and stood. "I'm sorry. I should have said something instead of just taking it. It was only a suspicion, and I didn't want to involve you. What do you think your grandfather would do in my position?"

"I can't answer that. The point is *I'm* asking you to let this go."

"Ellen, I can't just whitewash it. Don't you understand?"

She dropped her head to her arms crossed over her knees. Her breathing was palpable. He sat down and put his arm around her back. She accepted him at first, but then removed his arm, stood, and walked from the room. No, she did not understand.

Within the hour, Ellen had come back into the living room. The tears were gone. She looked fresh. She said she was sorry, adding that she knew that it was hard for him and he would do what was right. He asked her to sit down and give him a kiss. This was always his ploy, actually no longer a ploy because they both knew full well that they would join together. The pattern: fight, make up, make love.

He started to remove her clothes deliberately, kissing her shoulders and breasts and legs. He then removed his, not deliberately but urgently.

She looked intently at him. Suddenly, her mood changed. It was amazing how she was able to withdraw from a tense or angry situation. No longer seemingly mad or even serious, her eyes sparkled. This was the way he loved her. She was bright and exuded spirit, the latter being a characteristic with which he knew he hadn't been abundantly endowed. "David, are you CIA?"

"What do you mean?" he said, extending his arms around her waist and pressing his body to hers.

"Because you seem to be constantly in a state of heightened alert. It's true, look at that," she pointed and laughed.

His eyes followed her motion down, and he fell back on the couch. "Well, it is true, I have to confess. I'm a secret agent, and I'm required to have this smart bomb with me at all times. It's one that penetrates caves at depth with deadly accuracy and explodes."

Her eyebrows pointed upward. "I see."

"Let me give you a little demonstration." And their bodies moved and smothered one another. Their arms and hands and kisses and caresses and whispers and heat and urgency intermingled, until finally the friendly fire was spent.

14

David completed the report and handed it to Calhoun as he was leaving the office to catch a plane to Barbados. He seemed to be spending a lot of time there lately. "I'll review it, and we'll sit down and have a discussion when I return next week," Calhoun said, not meeting David's eye.

"Charles, you aren't going to like it. I've felt compelled to say that I don't feel the investigation is complete. And I've gone into certain things that I think you'd rather I not. But you're the person signing the report. Obviously, the final decision is up to you."

Calhoun said, "You've got that right," and went out the door.

David tried to put the matter out of his mind. He'd had no further discussion with Ellen about it. She had seemed a bit distant, not as lighthearted as usual. He didn't know how to tell her that he had completed the report in the only honest way he felt he could.

The following Monday morning, David was called by the firm chairman's secretary for an urgent meeting. Meeting with Jim Ramsey was, by definition, an anxiety-producing event, all the more so in this case given its proximity to the announcement of partnership decisions. David had little time to ponder its implications as he quickly made his way up the stairs and down the hall to Ramsey's corner office.

As David entered, Ramsey hung up the telephone and turned to face him across the desk, looking grave, almost shaky. He said, "Close the door," and motioned David to a chair across from his desk. He remained seated, drinking water from a glass filled with ice; he didn't offer any. People talked about how Ramsey used to come out from behind his desk and sit in a guest chair for a meeting. It was seen as a sort of leveling action. Now, with a certain imperiousness that had developed over his years as chairman of the firm, he remained seated in the throne and conducted meetings across his desk. "You've been working with Charles on an internal investigation in connection with some litigation." He rifled through papers sitting on his desk. "The Chadwell case, I understand."

"That's right."

"You're doing a report."

Again, another declaratory statement that sounded like a question. "Yes."

"What's the status? Is it complete?"

"Well, that depends. I don't feel it is. Charles may think the contrary. He has it with him on his trip."

"Are you sure?"

"Absolutely, I gave it to him personally as he was leaving for the plane last week. He was to review it and get back to me on his return tomorrow. We're under a time limit to produce it."

"They've found no trace of it." Ramsey came around the desk and started to pace. He was tall with wavy gray hair and, today, as always, was perfectly groomed in the most expensive suit.

"I'm sorry. Who is 'they'?"

"Confidentially, Charles has disappeared. It's very strange. He went for his usual swim after dinner in the waters fronting his house. That was two days ago, and he hasn't been seen since."

A grandfather's clock in the corner of the office ticked softly.

David whispered under his breath, "Good God."

Ramsey continued, "There's probably some simple explanation, but so far no one has been able to figure it out. Considering the range of possibilities, anything from an accident to foul play to...who knows

75

what. Everything has been carefully searched. They've found no papers relating to clients, or the firm for that matter, which, of course, is not in character. Everyone knows that he goes off loaded with work when he makes these trips. I asked his secretary, and she told me about the Chadwell case."

"I don't know what to say." David added, "Was there a note?"

"No, they've found nothing. The only thing at all unusual is that Charles gave Celeste a kiss as he went out the door for his swim, a nothing, a peck on the forehead, yet not something he usually did. She told police he had been withdrawn, drinking more than normal, but the night before his disappearance was quite jovial."

"That doesn't prove anything, of course," David said, wanting to deny even the possibility of the unspoken worst alternative.

"I hope you're right. But until the situation clarifies itself, I'll have to step in and review the report to see where we are."

David knew that he didn't want the report out in its present state. He had taken comfort in the idea that the conclusions and wording were Calhoun's final call as a partner and the senior lawyer on the case. David thought about how he might have worded the report differently, and certainly how he might have changed the note accompanying it, had he known they might reach someone else's eyes first. But as these thoughts rushed, he also knew that he had no choice. He had to tell Ramsey of the conflict. "You should know that Charles and I had a sharp difference of opinion. I expected that the report would be changed significantly before leaving his hands. I'm a little uncomfortable with someone other than Charles seeing this draft though I accept the necessity." He paused. "It's all been so strange. He had to take over the case for me when I had the accident, and now we're having to take over for him."

Ramsey sat down. "Have a copy delivered, and I'll read it right away. I'll call you when I finish."

David returned to his office and put together a copy of the package he'd handed to Calhoun. He lingered over the transmittal note that had accompanied the report, a note that he had spent much time crafting:

Charles:

As you will see, I cannot agree that the investigation should be considered closed without further investigation of Wilcox's claims. I think they leave unanswered questions, but it's your call. As for the Diebenkorn, I haven't included its present whereabouts in the report, but I am troubled by what some would view as an appearance of impropriety in its travels. I am confident, of course, that there was no impropriety in fact.
David

The note had been his best effort at being firm but at the same time diplomatic. Well beyond merely an appearance of impropriety, he thought, in fact, that it looked terrible. He simply couldn't understand how Calhoun could have put himself in this position. He was too smart. If his passion really required him to possess a Diebenkorn, why not buy another one from the Ocean Park series somewhere else. After all, they were all supposed to look relatively alike, at least to the uneducated eye.

He opened a manila envelope and placed both the report and the note in it, marking the envelope in hand, "Jim Ramsey Personal and Confidential."

⚖

David was up early the next morning after a miserable night's sleep in which he had run and rerun his judgment on the report. He dressed in sweats and left for the river on his usual five-mile running course. It was the activity that best helped him clear his head and diminish his anxiety levels. He had missed it during the weeks of forced inactivity. At this point in his recovery, the run was not really even a jog; it was more of a brisk walk. There wasn't a lot happening on the path next to Cherry Creek that morning, only an occasional runner headed in the opposite direction or, to his chagrin, past him.

When David arrived at his office with the obligatory double café latte in one hand and office clothes to change into in the other, the red voice mail light on his phone was blinking as usual. The first message was Ramsey directing David to come to see him immediately on his arrival at the office. With a stomach suddenly turned to acid, he showered quickly in the gym provided by the firm, dressed, and went directly to the chairman's office and knocked. Ramsey motioned him to close the door.

"I've read your report, but it's the note that bothers me. What does it mean?"

"I meant that only for Charles's eyes but felt that since it had accompanied the report, I had to include it for you to see." David explained the interesting travels of the Diebenkorn and his concern as to how it ended up in Calhoun's hands.

Ramsey was not one known to reveal his thoughts, but his concern was obvious as he listened. The crevices etching his face from nose to mouth looked deeper than ever. "Do you realize what you are saying? You are taking a person who has an unblemished reputation for honesty at the bar and in the community and saying, in effect, that he sold his soul for a lousy painting?" He came out from behind the desk and stood in front of David. "And has it occurred to you that your assertions might even be the cause of his disappearance?"

David couldn't let that stand. "That's unfair," he protested. "I merely raised questions. I made no assertions. As you well know, there is a big difference between an impropriety and an appearance of impropriety. I did nothing more than suggest that some might see the latter."

"This could ruin the man's reputation irrevocably—if he's still with us. And it could forever impugn the firm's good name."

"Perhaps," David offered weakly, "someone independent should look into it and come to his or her own conclusions…someone who can see the forest for the trees. Maybe I can't anymore. I've been involved for so long."

Ramsey stared David down, now clearly angered and more than a bit impatient. "That will just give it even more currency. No, we have to stop it here, with the two of us."

"That may not even be possible." David had thought this out many times in debating what to say in the report. "The Chadwells' lawyers

have threatened that if we don't produce a written report, they'll peti-
tion the court to force us to. In that event, I would probably be called
to testify as to the circumstances surrounding the development of the
report. There could well be questions that I couldn't dodge."

Ramsey returned to his desk. He seemed to soften. There was a
long silence interrupted by the sound of him crackling ice. Here was
this supposedly classy guy chewing on his ice. Even David knew not to
do that; his mother had told him a million times it was bad manners.
Finally, Ramsey said, "Let me think about it. Please understand that
I'm not mad at you. I'm angered at where this puts us, that's all. It's just
that the circumstances, the innuendo, and then this disappearance, look
strange, even sinister, as though he were really guilty of wrongdoing. It's
Charles's reputation, even more importantly the firm's, that we're dealing with here. We've got 350 lawyers to think about. And we do have
Stephen to think of, don't we?"

Ramsey, who knew, as did everyone in the firm, about the seriousness of the relationship between David and Ellen, needed to say
nothing more about the firm's founder. Now éminence grise of the firm,
Stephen Hill had been a fixture in Denver society virtually his entire
life. Born to a wealthy and connected family, his father a banker, he'd
gone east to prep school at an early age and stayed there to complete
his education, first at Dartmouth and then at Harvard Law School.
Upon graduation, there was no doubt he would return, the prodigal
son, to his roots and join the city's most established firm. He broke
out of the mold only once, but then significantly, when some twelve
years later, he founded his own firm with one other partner and two
associates. The firm that was now a colossus. His oldest child, Robert,
had dutifully joined the firm down the line and practiced business law
until he and his wife were killed tragically, leaving Ellen to be raised by
Stephen and her grandmother, Grace. Stephen warmed to high-achiev-
ing younger men in the firm, probably in an unconscious attempt to
fill the loss occasioned by Robert's death. Grace had devoted untold
hours to the plight of the homeless at the Denver Rescue Mission, not
always with the overwhelming approval of the more conservative of her
friends, who thought, "those people ought to go out and get a job."

Yes, Stephen was now too removed from the scene to have any real influence in the firm or to be personally tainted by the conduct of its partners, but David knew that is hardly the way Ellen would see it.

15

Two uncomfortable days passed with David receiving no call from Ramsey or even a sighting in the halls. If this were such a priority with the chairman, which it surely must be, then what in the hell was he waiting for?

Jim Ramsey was a mercurial character. He was formal, some said cold, but while walking through the halls, he never failed to nod or say hello to even the lowliest file clerk. He didn't have close friendships within the firm. He was all business. But he was respected for his brilliance, hard work, and commitment to the firm. He even found time to take leadership roles in the bar and in the community.

On Thursday morning, the call came. David was summoned again to the great man's office. Ramsey's was sitting, a row of freshly sharpened yellow pencils on the desk before him. His manner was abrupt. "I've had an opportunity to review not only your draft report but the entire file. Sadly, Charles is not here to speak for himself—nor will he ever be from all reports. But I agree with his conclusion that nothing of substance turned up supporting the Chadwell claim. In other words, the investigation need not be continued. The report should be finalized."

Ramsey's strict tone made it clear he had made a final decision. All David could muster was, "What are you saying, 'nor will he ever be'?"

"We received the preliminary investigative report of the Barbados authorities last night. Their conclusion is that Charles committed suicide."

David's fear had become a reality. "God, it's impossible to believe."

"He'd been lifting a lot of weight. I think we have to assume that he read the draft report you presented to him and then destroyed it. Your insinuations imposed huge pressures on him. Words can be extremely destructive, as I'm sure you are learning."

The accusation was outlandish. David was so stunned that he was frozen; there were no words.

Ramsey, organizing and reorganizing the yellow pencils, continued, "And there is another matter we need to discuss. I received a visit from building security shortly before these terrible developments concerning Charles came to my attention. They told me a story that, well frankly, seemed unbelievable to me."

David sense of uneasiness grew. "Yes?"

"They said that late one night, a Friday night several weeks back, there had been an incident in an elevator that involved a couple of our lawyers," his head tipped to one side, "as they put it, 'our little love birds.' According to the chief guard, a man and a woman got on the elevator together, stopped it on the twenty-eighth floor, where she, shall we say, provided him with oral services. After a few minutes, they put the elevator back in operation and left."

David tried to be casual, even though he was raging inside. "You know those security guards. They sit around all night with nothing to do, fantasizing about what they'd like to be doing."

"I wish it could be dismissed that lightly."

"What would you like me to do? Look into it with my associate relations committee hat on?" David shrugged, "Potentially not a bad assignment, I guess."

"Well, you were in the office late that Friday according to security's computer records. They say it was you, David."

"I've been here on Friday nights lots of times and every other night of the week too. There are always people around. It could have been anybody." He paused. "How would they know who it was anyway?"

"There's a recessed camera in the elevator. It's on tape." Ramsey seemed to utter the words, the right side of his mouth and lips turned slightly upward, with satisfaction.

"I see." David cleared his throat. He actually felt as though he were on an elevator, out of control and falling.

"Yes, you're quite identifiable, I'm told. By your face. You're leaning against the wall opposite the camera. Your pants are down. The woman's face cannot be seen, they say. Her hair hangs forward and obscures her features—as well as other details of this intimate little scene."

David felt cold, close to panic. He wondered if this was a ruse and they really knew it was Ellen who had been with him in the elevator that night. After what seemed an eternity of silence, Ramsey said, "How amazingly stupid. What could you have been thinking?"

Obviously, it was stupid. But at the same time, he remembered vividly the excitement of the experience that night, the first in an elevator, fingers in her hair, the slow thrusts, the softness, the strength, the warmth, the heat, the stillness, the noise. He remembered having tried to restrain the intensity of his response. What a waste, worrying needlessly over the audio, while being oblivious to the video. He didn't know whether to laugh or cry.

"David?"

"How can I disagree? It was stupid. But without the camera, it was a private matter." At some level, he had understood that his penchant for dangerous times and places would lead to trouble. It was inevitable. He just wished it hadn't involved Ellen and that it hadn't surfaced now. He had to do something to get himself under control. What he really wanted to blurt out was, Who are you to talk, Ramsey? Here was the chairman of the firm who had just married the chief financial officer of one of the firm's biggest clients. Did he really think that people weren't going to suspect that maybe, just maybe, the marriage had been preceded by a violation or two of the firm's unwritten, but strongly held, rule against fraternization with clients? But obviously, that line of discussion wasn't going to get him anywhere.

"You know, we associates spend lots of hours around this place in close proximity with each other, and I suppose, sometimes we get a little carried away. But there's really no excuse, I know. A little privacy and no klieg lights might have been more appropriate, to say the least." David paused and then added, "I want that tape." He opened his mouth, smiling for emphasis.

"Building security assures me it's secure."

"Fuck building security. They'll be sitting in their little cubicle getting off as they watch it endlessly, night after night."

Ramsey smirked. "Who's the woman, David?"

"This is bad enough without getting her involved."

"They said long darkish hair." Ramsey paused. "You suggested another associate. Is it? Or could it be Ellen Hill? I hope not. You know, Mr. Hill would have your head if it turned out to be her."

David could hardly keep himself from yelling, "You fucker." Instead, looking directly into Ramsey's eyes, he restrained himself. "I want to ask you to do whatever is necessary to get that tape for me. You can imagine how I would feel having it out there."

Ramsey made a light shrug. "Maybe we can work an exchange, David."

"Meaning?"

"Oh perhaps, I give you the tape, and you give me the report. How about that?"

He had wondered how far Ramsey would go. He was in disbelief. Then, he felt defeated as he could see no way to turn. He looked at the grandfather's clock ticking softly in the background. He had to play for time. Should he ask the question directly? He stood and walked over to the clock. The finely carved silver face bore the name "J. Cruden" and beneath it "1797." It was a handsome piece. So quiet but majestic as it chimed out the hours day after day, year after year, decade after decade. How many tense scenes had it presided over in its two hundred plus years? Could any have been as ugly as this? He turned back and faced Ramsey. "What effect will this have on my partnership consideration?"

"None, of course, *if* no one knows about the incident. I've not discussed it with the executive committee. I'm the only one in the firm who knows at this point."

"Then, what will influence your decision whether or not to raise it?"

"Look, David, I'm human too. At one level, I can understand, even sympathize. None of us is perfect. At another level, I have to think that it shows colossal bad judgment on your part. Do I owe it to my partners to share it with them as they evaluate you? It's a tough question. If I do, you're sunk. If I don't, well, you remain on track. You can make it a much easier decision if you choose to."

What a beautifully, precisely calculated response, thought David. Ramsey did not have his reputation for smoothness for nothing. He was a presence. On the surface, he was perfect for the role of leading one of the most distinguished law firms in the city. But today, for the first time, David was seeing him below the surface for what he really was.

"Before you leave, tell me...How was it?"

David looked back at him, shook his head, and walked through the doorway.

16

David had always thought the characterization of "woodshedding" a witness a curious one. But after his long session with Ed Baker, the firm's partner who'd been assigned to represent him at the hearing on the Chadwells' motion to force the investigatory report to be handed over, he damn well knew he'd been there. They'd started at eight in the morning and ended at six in the evening without a break, unless taking time to chew the ham and cheese on rye and slam down the soda delivered to their conference room could be called that. David was exhausted and angry. Probably no more than Baker was as well. But he didn't much care anymore what Baker thought.

The bastard tried his level best to direct David away from the honest conclusions to be drawn in the investigation. In Baker's hands, everything was so obfuscated that the true facts would hardly be recognizable. He didn't like Baker. He might be a good litigator, but David thought his reputation overrated. Regardless, he was an important partner in the litigation department and getting on his bad side would hardly facilitate the process to partnership.

David drove to Ellen's. As he opened the door to her condo, she stood and asked, "How was it?"

"Unbelievable. I'm bloodied and battered."

THE PRICE OF REVENGE

"So where's the blood? The broken bones?" She kissed him.

"I need a martini. You?"

"White wine. I had an easy day, apparently in contrast to yours."

David went to the bar and made a gin martini straight up, a drink that not a lot of his contemporaries seemed to like. He sat next to Ellen on the couch and handed her the glass of wine. "You go first," he said.

"I took Granddad to lunch." She shook her head. "He talks about the firm, how proud he is. I'm afraid he's really not in touch with what's going on there in today's world, particularly in the marketing arena. And we talked a lot about Charles. It was an accidental drowning according to Granddad. Suicide isn't part of his vocabulary."

David looked into his glass. A martini straight up was a sexy drink, he thought, or was he confusing the drink with the aftermath?

Ellen sighed, shoulders dropping. Alpha Blondy's rhythmic tones spilled out from the stereo. Ellen loved reggae. Its monotonous sounds seemed always to be present in the background at her place.

David continued, "My day was miserable. If your grandfather knew what the firm was up to, he'd go ballistic. Except, of course, he wouldn't use that term. He'd be far more genteel. Baker was hard as nails on me, had me in the woodshed."

"Woodshed." Ellen hesitated. "I've heard the word of course, but I'm not sure what it stands for?"

"In the old days, there were woodsheds adjacent to courthouse buildings. Lawyers used the woodsheds to prepare their witnesses to testify. The reference definitely isn't complimentary because it conveys the idea that the lawyer is telling the witness what to say in his testimony, rather than really pulling out the true facts. Well, today that art was being practiced vigorously by one of the best litigators we've got."

"So, what does it boil down to?"

"We were preparing for the hearing on Monday before Judge Felix. I'll be required to testify on the investigation process. Baker is trying to convince me not to mention my disagreement with Charles's view that there was nothing further to investigate. That means I'd have to dummy up about the Wilcox memo that Charles ordered destroyed. Even more important to Baker is that nothing be said about the Diebenkorn happening to end up at Charles's beach house."

"What did he say about that?"

"Oh he tried to make me feel guilty, digging on the reputation of the firm, the reputation of Charles Calhoun, your grandfather and his feelings. Baker is an asshole, a crude asshole."

"Was anyone else there?"

"Don't miss this. Ramsey, who is never in the office on Saturdays, just happened to drop by the conference room to see how things were going." David didn't want to get into the video thing again; she'd gotten so upset when he told her at dinner the night Ramsey threatened him over it. But how could he avoid it. He blurted out, "And they brought up the video."

He went to the bar for a refill. "Ellen, I can't tell you how sorry I am for getting you into this. I should have been able to figure out that the elevator was likely to have a camera for emergency use, but it didn't occur to me. It's not as though I was thinking clearly under the circumstances." He smiled resignedly, raising his shoulders.

David could almost see the wheels turning in Ellen's head. She was smart and could get to the heart of things quickly. She could well have been a lawyer but had dropped out of Columbia Law School after the first year when she decided that her grandfather's genes for the practice of law had not found their way to her. She thought it was boring. She sat, not saying a thing, looking down at her lap.

Then she said curtly, "It didn't have to happen you know. Why do you always have to push to have risky sex? What is it with you?"

There really was no answer other than to observe that it wasn't as if he'd forced her. He decided to remain silent.

She continued, "You seem to have a risk addiction, a weird little streak that makes you want to take the chance of being caught."

He could see her on Google researching the term "risk addiction." What could he say?

"If it got to Granddad, I'd kill myself."

"Not before I'd kill Ramsey."

She stared at him and then went into the kitchen. He heard the rattling of dishes. It struck him that there was an unusual amount of noise emanating from the room. He offered to help, but she asked to be left alone. After about fifteen minutes, she returned to the living room.

"David, I'm going to try my best to be logical about this, not emotional. Does it feel at all like you're doing a little bit of a Don Quixote act here? You don't even know that there's anything to Wilcox's claims, do you? Charles could have been absolutely right in rejecting them as accusations coming from a disgruntled lover. You also don't know that there was anything untoward about Charles having the Diebenkorn for that matter."

"You're right. I don't know that there's anything to Wilcox's claims, but I do know that they were serious enough to warrant further investigation. Sure, I don't know that there was anything unlawful about Charles ending up with the Diebenkorn, but it sure as hell raises a problem on the appearance-of-impropriety test. Even if he paid full price for the goddamned thing," his voice was rising, "he shouldn't have been buying it at that time from that person. And why did Charles commit suicide? Just a coincidence?"

Ellen started to cry, resting her head on her arms at the fireplace mantel. She turned to face him. "If this comes out, David, it could kill Granddad. He's getting so old. He sits there, his hands covered with brown spots, stubble showing against frayed collars. He doesn't care anymore."

David didn't answer, deciding to let her go on.

"It would do huge damage to the firm, which is his life now. He loved Charles, and look what it would do to his reputation. He respects you so much."

Finally, David said, "That's a heavy burden to put on me."

"Oh you must feel proud of yourself, sitting up there on a white horse, prepared to tell whatever it is you've convinced yourself is the truth. But from here, it doesn't look all that noble. You'll be running the risk of destroying something very wonderful, something very close to me. If you do, I really don't think I could believe you love me."

David stood and extended his arms and hands toward her. "I don't think you appreciate the ethical dilemma I'm facing, Ellen. You're asking me to go into court Monday and be prepared to lie. How can I do that? No self-respecting lawyer could."

"I'm tired, David. You should go. Obviously, it's your call on Monday. All I can ask is that you think it out carefully between now and then."

At the door, David leaned to hug her. She responded. They held each other strongly, swaying slowly from side to side. Neither spoke. There was nothing more to be said.

17

The click of David's shoes sounded against the expanse of polished marble as he walked the nearly deserted hallways toward Judge Felix's courtroom in Denver's Federal Courthouse. David was early, and the corridors were not yet teeming with the usual noisy court life— lawyers, litigants, witnesses, and the customary court followers who thrive simply by observing controversy in action. He was tense, as was his way whenever he made a court appearance. It was always the same no matter how many times he opened the thick wooden doors into those quiet, stately rooms.

But today was not his usual appearance, and he was beyond nervous. He had never appeared as a witness before. As he contemplated the experience, he found himself considerably more sympathetic toward the witnesses he had put through this as a matter of course. Yet he tried to rationalize that they hadn't really had as much riding on their testimony as he had on what he was going to be saying today under oath. It was a conflict between his sense of loyalty to his principles and profession and his loyalty to his firm and Ellen. How he would walk the line depended largely on what questions he was asked. The world of ethics was often murky, various shades of gray and too rarely black and white. It was possible to compromise so innocently and then end up giving into temptation. But he believed himself to be a man of integrity. He had never knowingly crossed the line in his professional life.

When he reached the courtroom, he found himself standing before Ed Baker. No greeting was exchanged. Baker, his cheeks flush from years of alcohol dependence, the lines of his mouth turned down, rested his eyes on David's and said simply, "And what have you decided?"

"Remember the old saying, Ed, 'When all else fails, tell the truth'? That's what I've decided."

David turned toward the entrance of the courtroom. He glanced through the slatted windows in the ten-feet-high wooden doors and pulled their straight steel handles. His right hand behind his back served to ease the door closed; he still favored his left arm. There was a whoosh as the door settled against the jamb.

The scene was normal. A short lineup of lawyers gathered in front of the court clerk's desk, their business cards in hand to extend when they got to the head of the line to announce their appearances to the clerk. To the side, close to the bench and the witness stand, the court reporter was busily arranging the equipment with which she would record every word spoken on the record that morning. Two law clerks entered the courtroom through a side door and took their places.

The courtroom had a high, arched ceiling. The walls were paneled and decorated with paintings of judges who had earlier occupied the courtrooms in that building. Black marble adorned the wall behind the bench, marking it as the throne. Intruding on this serene setting was the latest in television monitors and other electronic equipment required in today's technological world in the presentation of complex cases.

Today, David wasn't proceeding forward to the clerk to announce himself since he was not appearing as counsel. He took a seat in the front row of the wooden benches that were reserved for the lawyers, litigants, and witnesses awaiting the calendar call to reach their cases. The seats were hard but comfortable, contoured in a way so as to catch the lower back and butt, at least the back and butt of a six footer. The design seemed intended to lighten the severity of the surface without providing enough comfort to lull the sitter into a disrespectful doze.

The clerk stood, calling the courtroom to order, directing that all rise, and announcing the judge. Judge Felix entered amid a flurry of black robes, took the bench, and directed everyone to be seated. This was the protocol followed in most courtrooms. In others, only a few, those in the courtroom were directed to remain seated as the judge entered. David felt that this one little procedure reflected a lot about the person walking into the room. Maybe it wasn't as extreme as regular guy versus little tin god, but it tended toward those ends of the spectrum. Not unexpectedly, there were few generalizations that could be drawn from this ancient process. But one that David took based on his experience was that judges who were abusive to counsel—and some seemed to thrive on it—were invariably of the tin god category.

Pondering this not so weighty aspect of judicial procedure did little to ease his anxiety in anticipation of taking the witness stand. He felt flushed, and his hands were sweating. He unconsciously crossed and uncrossed his legs. Having seen the court's calendar for the morning, he knew that he would have something of a wait before Chadwell ads. Denver City Ballet Company, number eight on the calendar, was called. He had the option of sitting there and observing the distinctly depressing process of the criminal calendar being called for arraignments and sentencing, or going outside in the hall to wait, where he would just have Baker on his back again. With that choice, he stayed, watching as criminal defendants, most there because of drug charges, some handcuffed and in the company of officers, came and went. Sometimes, the appearance of this assortment of people didn't telegraph their problem. More often their jail garb left no mystery about where they had spent the night before. They were given priority on the calendar, a fact that always struck David as reflecting a distorted societal standard.

What an inefficient system it was. High-priced lawyers, witnesses, parties, all sitting around waiting for their cases to be heard. Often matters were not concluded but postponed until another day, requiring that everyone gear up for action yet another time, and another, and another.

Finally, the Chadwell case was called, and Baker walked to the lectern, followed by the Chadwells' lawyers, Maynard Smithton and Sam Terry. It was plaintiffs' motion, and Smithton went first. He took his place behind the lectern in front of the bench to explain why his clients were seeking production of the report.

Judge Felix peered over small reading glasses and spoke briskly, "I've read the papers, Mr. Smithton. You need not repeat what's already before me."

"Very well, Your Honor. Unless you have questions, we will submit on the papers." Smithton stepped to the side and then sat with his co-counsel.

Baker now moved to the lectern and began, his voice a bit too high-pitched for a litigator from an establishment firm, where litigators' voices always seemed to compete for the lowest possible octave. "Your Honor, I wish to emphasize that plaintiff's motion, even if it were appropriate at some future time, is premature here as there is no completed report in writing, nor—"

Judge Felix interrupted, "You've made those points in your opposition papers. I don't want to have anything repeated."

Baker complied. "Very well, Your Honor." He sat down at counsel table.

Judge Felix shuffled papers around and then spoke, "I think plaintiffs are entitled to determine the status of the investigation, the status of a report, if any, and the surrounding facts and circumstances. Otherwise, I have no way of determining whether or not, and under what circumstances, there is anything that must be produced, do I?" It was a rhetorical question that no one was foolish enough to answer.

"I am mindful of the attorney-client privilege issues that may be presented," the judge continued, "and I expect you, Mr. Smithton, to be sensitive to that as you proceed. No questioning about the substance of the investigation or report, only questions at this point about the status of the investigation and the report. Mr. Smithton, are you ready to proceed?"

"Yes. Plaintiffs will call Mr. David Fox as their first witness. Mr. Fox is called, of course, as an adverse witness."

David rose from the gallery bench and proceeded toward the witness stand. He had never crossed that threshold before without a briefcase in his hand. Without it today, he felt naked. David turned, faced the clerk, and automatically raised his right hand to be sworn as a witness. There was something almost surreal about the experience. He'd seen it happen to witnesses hundreds of times, never thinking that he would someday be in the same position. The words, "To tell the truth, the whole truth, and nothing but the truth, so help you God," which were always so mechanically delivered it seemed, had special emphasis to him today. Each one of them echoed. He replied, "I do," and took his place in the witness stand.

Judge Felix acknowledged him with a nod, "Mr. Fox."

"Good morning, Your Honor," he responded, summoning all the self-assurance he could muster. David could exude confidence, though often he didn't feel it within himself. He was tall, had erect posture, and a commanding presence. No one would suspect this man's stomach was churning as only he knew it to be at this moment.

Maynard Smithton's initial questions were simple enough, designed to establish who David Fox was, where he was employed, how long, his status as a senior associate, his areas of specialization, and the like. David's attention wandered a bit as he looked out across the courtroom. There in the gallery was Jim Ramsey, whose attendance was hardly a surprise.

Smithton asked a series of questions about the so-called investigation to set the stage for the critical questions to come. His emphasis on "so-called" was obviously intended to deprecate the very mechanism designed to get at the truth when serious allegations of wrongdoing are made.

Ultimately, Smithton got to the question: "As for Mr. Calhoun, in response to our subpoena, we were informed that he was unavailable for this hearing. Can you explain the situation?"

David looked down and arranged his suit coat. He was wearing a dark blue suit, a "sincere" suit as they were called at the firm because dark blue was the invariable uniform for court appearances. "Mr. Calhoun is missing. He was visiting his home in the Caribbean, went for a swim one night, and has not been seen again."

"Have there been legal proceedings there with respect to his disappearance, an attempt to determine the cause?"

Ed Baker rose. "Objection. The circumstances of Mr. Calhoun's disappearance have no relevance in this proceeding. Even if they did, Mr.

Fox would not have knowledge with respect to a legal proceeding in a foreign jurisdiction."

"Overruled. You may answer the question, Mr. Fox."

"It's my understanding that there have been, but I have no personal knowledge of the matter."

"Did Mr. Calhoun commit suicide?" Smithton asked pointedly.

Baker was on his feet, "Objection, Your Honor, objection. The question is irrelevant—and, I must say, impertinent."

"Sustained as to relevance. Mr. Smithton, while impertinence is not a recognizable evidentiary objection as we all know, I find myself in agreement with Mr. Baker." The judge grimaced as though in pain. Whether he was or not wasn't clear; perhaps it was just a habit. What it revealed, though, was a strange configuration of his mouth, more accurately his teeth. They were all, on both the top and bottom, of the same dimension in length, stunted as if they had been filed down to be entirely even.

"Very well, Your Honor." Smithton proceeded to the next question without so much as a ruffle at being admonished by the court. "Mr. Fox, is there or is there not a written report of the internal investigation?"

"Objection," Baker interjected, "the question is ambiguous as to what the meaning of 'a written report' is?"

"Overruled."

David hesitated. He and Baker had debated the answer to this question at length over the weekend, and it was on this question, as well as several others, that their views diverged. His answer or Baker's? "Mr. Smithton, there is a written report, but it is in draft only. It is not a final report."

"Has it been sent to your client, the ballet company, Mr. Fox?"

"It has not."

"Why not?" Smithton was known for his curt, acerbic questioning of adverse witnesses. The delivery was rapid fire, as though he were being timed by a stopwatch.

Enough, David thought, *just enough, not too much, not too little, a factual answer without opening any doors unnecessarily.* "I drafted a report for review by Mr. Calhoun, and the draft had not been finalized at the time of his disappearance."

"In your opinion, Mr. Fox, is the investigation complete so that the report could be finalized?"

This was the trigger question David had feared the most. Looking out into the courtroom at Ramsey, who looked back sternly, he hesitated and then answered, "In my opinion, there was more investigation to be done." He saw Ramsey lower his head and look down.

"And was it done?"

"No."

"Why?"

"Mr. Calhoun and I weren't in accord on that. He thought that enough had been put into the investigation. I did not. But I recognized that the investigation was his ultimate responsibility and that it was his decision to make."

"More investigation of what type?" Smithton stood and walked forward.

"There was a person who had implied," David thought that as equivocal as he could make it, "that certain others may have taken advantage of their relationship to the endowment fund for their own benefit."

"And that 'implication,' as you put it, hadn't been pursued?"

"Not in full, no."

"How did this come to your attention?"

Smithton's co-counsel, Sam Terry, motioned him to counsel table and whispered in his ear. Smithton looked up, startled, and then down at his pants pocket. David didn't need to hear the words to know what Terry had said. "Stop jiggling your change." David had also been distracted by this irritating habit that morning.

"There was a memorandum concerning an interview with the person making the accusation, and I discussed it with Mr. Calhoun." The series of questions that followed required that David disclose the contents of the memorandum about the Wilcox interview, that it had been deleted by Calhoun, and then restored by David who thought it should be a part of the investigatory file. From the questions Smithton asked, he was certain that Wilcox must have told Smithton of the interview himself.

"What form did these kickbacks—"

"Objection."

"Sustained."

"That is, payments from the hedge fund take?"

"Art."

"What kind of art?"

"Paintings, or a painting. I'm not certain."

"Can you identify the painting?"

"Your Honor," Baker protested, "if I may, this is going far, far afield. What possible difference can it make what painting, if any, was involved? I think the questions are now going beyond your admonition to stay out of the actual facts turned up in the investigation."

"Overruled," the judge stated quickly, demonstrating impatience with Baker.

"The implication was that it was a painting by Richard Diebenkorn."

"Was it identified?"

"Yes," replied David, trying to follow his own directions to clients to answer only the question posed and no more.

"How?"

"Part of the so-called Ocean Park series. The series is numbered. It was number 141."

"And what happened with respect to it?"

David traced the painting to White but stopped there. He was awash in sweat. He didn't know if he'd turned white or red, but his skin tingled, and he felt his breakfast rising to his throat.

Smithton reached to his eyes, his fingers clutched. He dropped his hand. Smithton's eyes had that vacant, exposed look that sometimes accompanies a transition from glasses to contact lenses. David suspected that the motion was a habit, a theatrical movement he had probably used a score of times in the courtroom, a habit he hadn't been able to break with the change to contacts. "Then who does have it?"

Baker stood, almost shouting, "Objection." But again, before he could even articulate the grounds of his objection, it was overruled.

David was boxed. He looked at Baker and then Ramsey. Ramsey appeared rigid but dignified as always. His aura of total self-confidence drove David, who knew only too well what was going on in his own stomach at that time, ape shit. His safest answer: "At this time, I don't know."

"Let me put it another way. When the painting left Mr. White, where did it go?"

David's choices were to either say he didn't know or say what he knew about Calhoun's possession of the painting. He was at the end of the line. Though he'd gone over the question and his answer to it numerous times, he hadn't known before that moment exactly which answer he would voice. "It ended up in the home of Mr. Calhoun in the Caribbean." He thought he saw Ramsey's shoulders sink slightly and his head move from side to side. From that point, there was a flood of questions relating to Calhoun's possession of the Diebenkorn, which brought out almost all of the story, including the pressure Ramsey brought to bear on David to change the draft report.

There was a long pause as Smithton walked from the witness stand back to counsel table, apparently trying to organize his thoughts. He turned and said, "No further questions."

Baker rose from his chair but chose not to ask any questions. He had decided upon a technique that David seldom found the confidence to adopt. He could only assume that it reflected disgust on Baker's part, that David's answers had so damaged their position that there was no way to rehabilitate him as a favorable witness.

Judge Felix said, "Do you have other witnesses, Mr. Smithton?"

"Yes, Your Honor. James Ramsey."

"Very well, we stand adjourned until one thirty this afternoon."

David stepped down from the stand. Bad as it had been, thank God there had been no question that required him to disclose how Ramsey had threatened him over the videotape. That, perhaps more than anything, was what David had feared about the appearance today. Testify in open court about the elevator? Face the possibility of "outing" Ellen to the world? At least he had that element of good news to bring home to her. He walked toward Baker, who did not speak. David continued through the gallery. Ramsey was ahead of him, moving toward the doors and the hallway. He turned his head back, casting a fierce look at David.

David walked into the hall. He felt as though he might get sick. He was flush. He needed to stop and think, not walk. He turned right rather than follow the hallway to the left out of the building. He approached a window overlooking the street and rested his forehead against the warm metal window frame.

Often following a court appearance, David revisited the scene in his mind, thinking that he should have asked this question, not that; should have objected to this question or that; should have phrased something differently. Endless second guessing. The need to think and respond on your feet was what made litigation exciting. Nothing was pat. You had to be able to feel your way in the courtroom.

On this occasion, however, his feelings went well beyond reliving the event as was his way. "You fool, you fucking fool," he whispered. He looked down at the street. There were Ramsey and Baker walking to lunch together. He could see Ramsey's right arm spiraling above his head, undoubtedly condemning him. Clearly, his chance for partnership was irrevocably gone. Ramsey wouldn't have to pin it on his performance on the stand today, though all in the partnership would silently know. It would be obscured in some sort of competitive "need" analysis, that the need for him as a partner was not as great as the need for someone else under consideration that year. Ramsey wouldn't have to fire him. He knew David too well, knew that David would quit because his pride and ego would never permit him to stay on as an associate or any status other than partner.

The decision, in one sense, came as a relief. If David were out of the picture, there would be no need for Ramsey to play the video card with the partners to scuttle his partnership. That had just been a threat to secure his compliance. Even Ramsey, despicable as he might be, respected Stephen Hill too much to see him hurt in that way.

He bent over for his briefcase. Remembering there was none, he turned to walk down the stairs and, soles clicking against the marble corridor, out of the courthouse.

He didn't think he could come back this afternoon and sit there listening to Ramsey lie. It was over.

18

The reception room at Sperry, Reid & Hutchins was busy with the opening of the office. People walked through the double doors, nodding or saying hello to the receptionist. Most were dressed in business casual attire. David, dressed in a dark gray suit, white shirt, and solid red tie, was there for his nine a.m. interview with Gates McGarey, the managing partner of the law firm. He held the morning's *Wall Street Journal*, though his eyes were fixed elsewhere. He was absorbing the room's starkly modern design. What a comparison to the wood-paneled room up the street, adorned with its plein air paintings and Oriental rugs, that he'd passed through daily for so many years. Lawyers invest lots of money in reception rooms to create a mood for their clients. But they don't live in those reception rooms. They only walk through them.

This one, he thought, was dramatic. A bank of floor-to-ceiling windows faced the distant Rockies. Cappuccino leather and blond oak rested on a dark brindle carpet. The feeling was not one of total luxury. Probably it had been the intent to look prosperous but not extravagant. Certainly, the open marble stairway that rose from the middle of the room to the floor above set a prosperous tone. In contrast was the faux marble wall behind the reception desk. Was the wall treatment decided upon to save a few dollars? Or was it studied, to let clients, whose first contact with the office was facing this wall, *think* that the firm had tried to watch the dollars? Either way, there was something to be said for it as it fit their pitch, adopted from Avis, "We're number two, and we try harder."

David thought back over the interviewing process he had gone through since he left Hill & Devon two months earlier. There certainly had been no rush to pick up his contract, a fact that had somewhat surprised him. When he graduated from Northwestern, he could have gone to any of the white-shoe law firms on Wall Street, but he hadn't wanted that kind of firm. What a misnomer. White shoes were the last things those New York corporate lawyers wore, at least to the office. Their shoes were black or dark brown. Now, there was a problem posed by his eight years of experience at Hill & Devon. Any firm would have to slot him in its lineup of legal talent at a level that recognized his years of practice. But this was increasingly difficult as law firms focused more and more on bottom-line dollars. He had almost given up the idea that he could walk into another firm as a partner, most likely not here at the Sperry firm.

There had been numerous meetings with Sperry partners, and the invitation to return to see McGarey gave him encouragement. But did he really want the job? To some, it would be seen as a step down, going to a second-tier firm in the city as an associate when he had been assured of a partnership at a first-tier firm. Hill & Devon was older by a couple of decades, larger in headcount, and had as clients more of Denver's old-line banks and energy companies. Yet, Sperry was not all that far behind, and he liked the people he'd met here. Several of them, entering the reception room, recognized him and stopped to shake his hand.

David had felt like number two his whole life, and he didn't want a step down now that would confirm that. His relationship growing up with his older brother had been competitive. Better-looking, smarter, more popular, a natural athlete, Brian was always out in front in David's mind. While their parents had tried to build David's sense of self-assurance, insisting that he had all those qualities in equal measure, he was never convinced. Brian forever tore away at his confidence, telling him that he was adopted but threatening dire consequences if he ever mentioned it to their parents. David didn't really believe it was true—he was a clone of his father—but still it rattled around in the recesses of his mind.

One effort that David's parents made to instill some self-assurance in him ended with particularly disastrous consequences. They bought him a horse with the idea that having responsibility for something would be a confidence builder. The horse was a Western saddle pony, appropriately named Pronto for his speed. David loved riding him on the trails near their home. Along with the fun of riding came the chores of feeding and grooming that fell to him. One day, Brian came running through the pasture toward the house yelling, "Something's wrong with Pronto. He's frozen." David stumbled as he raced through the pasture to the barn. There was Pronto, standing on all fours, unable to move. David pulled, pushed, and pleaded, "Come on, Pronto. You can do it." But nothing worked. A veterinarian was called and quickly pieced together what had happened. The day before, David hadn't been able to find the padlock to the feed room, so in order, he thought, to secure the door, he'd wedged a piece of wood where the lock would normally go. Pronto had managed to nose the stick out. He'd gotten into the container of oats, eaten without limit, and then drunk from the water trough. The result: he had foundered and become paralyzed. The verdict was that he had to be put down. David was devastated. It was horrible. His beautiful pony, dog food? On the day Pronto was to be shot, David went to school, only a block from his house, and as eleven in the morning approached, he cupped his hands over his ears and hummed. He didn't think he could live through hearing the gun go off. He had never forgotten the experience. It was his fault because he'd cut corners. The lesson was a good one on the importance of being careful, but rather than building self-confidence, the tragedy had shattered what little he had. Brian, to his credit, didn't rub in the stupidity of the mistake.

David progressed through school successfully, managing to do well academically and in extracurricular activities. He had to work hard to keep up with Brian's accomplishments.

Following college, Brian became a CPA with a midsized accounting firm in the city. Partnership at Hill & Devon for David had promised an opportunity to change the ranking with his brother. Now that was gone. Still, he thought that through hard work and some luck, he could, even here at Sperry, ultimately reverse the relative positions of his brother and himself.

Not far from his mind was Ellen. He had left her condominium that morning after they had rolled together in bed, the sun cascading through the windows to warm their bodies. Their morning romp had followed a night talking over too much wine about the "what ifs" should Sperry extend him an offer. While they hadn't yet formally moved in together, their relationship had become deep and loving, and all of their free time was spent with one another. His decision as to what he would do with his career was his, but it would be reached only after long discussions with her. They had worked their way through the tears, recrimination, and guilt that followed learning of the videotape. The idea of going to her grandfather in an attempt to have him intervene with Ramsey hadn't been feasible. There was little choice but for David to leave Hill & Devon.

Ellen wasn't comfortable with the idea of him joining a firm that competed with her grandfather's, but she couldn't stand the thought of him moving to San Francisco or Seattle for the right job, much less of her following him there. She wanted to stay right here in Denver where she had family, a history, and a challenging job she enjoyed. The Sperry firm was a viable candidate.

His thoughts were interrupted by the receptionist, who offered to take him down the hall to Mr. McGarey's office.

As David entered the room, McGarey rose from his desk and greeted him with a wide grin and a strong grip. David had thought from his first meeting that McGarey was a bit rough around the edges, certainly not polished. He was stocky and had a ruddy complexion with a few strands of hair to match. Gusto was the word that best described him. He was noisy, ebullient, and seemingly so open. What a contrast, David thought, to the refined and polished Jim Ramsey. On the face of it, Ramsey was far more impressive. Underneath, he was ruthless. McGarey gave the impression of someone who meant what he said and who could be trusted.

McGarey slouched down in a chair across from his desk and motioned David to the chair opposite. The chairs, it appeared, had been around awhile. The brown leather upholstery was worn and cracking. They fit the generally disheveled appearance of his office. McGarey, a trial lawyer, pulled at his loosened tie and made his opening statement. "David, I'll be candid. We like you a lot. We have a topflight recommendation from Dirk Underhill. It says a lot that it comes from the chair of the department where you spent so many years. We need to build our employment law practice, and we think you're a person who can do that."

"I appreciate that, Gates."

"But I'll be frank. There's innuendo from your former firm that we need to discuss. I can't disclose the source. Unfortunately, investigating even mere innuendo goes with the job I've taken on around here. You know, that management role for which my partners shower me with bags of gold." McGarey laughed, his head nodding up and down as if to confirm the humor of his statement.

David smiled. Managing a law firm he knew was like being in the eye of a storm, pounded on all sides by huge egos with special interests to advance. It required a strong guy, and from what little he could see, McGarey might just meet that qualification. He held his breath. "What's the accusation?"

"Not exactly an accusation, David. Innuendo as I said. Hard to pin down, even where it's coming from exactly. The innuendo falls into two areas. One is the Denver City Ballet case you handled. There's been some criticism. The other relates to a matter of personal conduct on your part, maybe sexual harassment, maybe not."

Before the meeting, David had resolved that, if necessary, he would have to trust McGarey with the information about the Ballet report and the way Ramsey had tried to stifle him. He couldn't go forward interviewing with one hand tied behind his back. But the personal conduct area wasn't as easy.

A drop of sweat fell from David's chest to his stomach. "I realize you said the sources are unclear, but that becomes pretty important. If it were Dirk Underhill—"

McGarey held up his hand in a motion to stop. "No. He's high on you, has no criticisms."

"Then, have you asked him about the so-called innuendo?"

"Yeah. He sort of clams up. The impression I get is that he thinks you got a raw deal on both counts, but he doesn't quite come out and say how. Maybe he can't."

"If," continued David, "it comes from Jim Ramsey, that's another matter. We got crosswise on something. I doubt that he'd have anything good to say about me."

McGarey looked at his extended fingers pushing off one another. "You should know that Jim Ramsey and I have had a couple of real run-ins over the years. We're two aggressive guys heading firms in direct competition with each other. If that were all, I'd think no more about it. But he can't be trusted. Let's face it. He's a prick."

David let out a muffled laugh, as though to put an exclamation point on McGarey's characterization. He was to second base already. "Then you already know what I would have to tell you. He may deserve his reputation as a smart corporate lawyer, but I wouldn't trust him to get from your chair to mine."

"Tell me more," said McGarey as he got up to close his office door.

"Long version or short?"

"Shit, I don't know, as short as you can and still give me enough to go on. Spare me the gory details." McGarey's eyebrows arched. "Except as they relate to sex of course."

What did that mean? Did McGarey know? David decided to start on the Ballet report. That story made the Hill firm, really Jim Ramsey, look so bad that McGarey might not be all that interested in the details of the other issue.

David proceeded to relate the whole story about Calhoun, the deleted interview memorandum, and the Diebenkorn painting ending up in his vacation home.

"David, I'm blown away by the idea that Charles Calhoun could be bought, if that's what you're saying. His reputation at the bar was unassailable."

"It was hard for me to believe too. It was even harder to sit there and tell him that the report should include those facts. He took the draft with him to the Caribbean. He went swimming one night, and well, you know the rest."

David went on to explain how Ramsey had then entered the scene and threatened him with denial of partnership. "I really don't think what happened is representative of Hill & Devon as a firm." David continued, "Stephen Hill would be appalled. It's a case of one rotten apple getting power in a firm and abusing it."

McGarey sat silently for thirty seconds and then frowned. "But why would Charles have done such a thing?"

"I can only speculate that his passion for art and this painting overcame his other instincts. I don't know anything about art, but I'm told the painting is very valuable, in the millions. It's a Richard Diebenkorn. Are you familiar with him?"

McGarey chuckled, his stomach jiggling. "Are you kidding? I'm not much into that world."

"Calhoun was a collector of contemporary art. He was successful but not wealthy enough to buy that painting. My suspicion would be that to get this great painting, he threw out all his standards."

McGarey's normally bright face looked drawn and serious. "And you were denied partnership for writing an honest report?"

"That's right. But there was something else that was used against me, or at least was threatened to be used against me. It's embarrassing to relate, but it's probably what they are trying to explode into a sexual harassment case."

"I think I can handle it. I'm not shy, in case you hadn't noticed," McGarey chortled.

"There's a videotape," said David. He coughed and looked down at his lap. "I haven't seen it, but I'm told it shows me in, ah, a sexual act. Ramsey had the tape, still does I'm sure. He threatened that if I didn't play ball on the Calhoun cover-up, he'd use the tape with the partners to defeat my partnership."

"Jesus Christ. You've got to be kidding."

"No. I tried to get it back, but there was no way." David paused, wondering if McGarey would ask next what sexual act it was. He didn't. What a contrast. McGarey, the rough hewn one, didn't even ask what they were doing. Ramsey, the smooth one, had no trouble asking how it had been.

"David, I wasn't born yesterday." McGarey stood and paced behind his desk. David looked at a table lined with framed photographs. Two of them showed McGarey, in each case with what appeared to be a different woman and different sets of children. David wondered what they represented.

McGarey continued, "I can't begin to tell you about the things that go on around here with our lawyers, whether it's associates with associates, partners with associates, staff and lawyers, clients and lawyers, conventional, same sex. You name it, we have it." He threw his arms upward and guffawed. "I sometimes wonder how our people bill so many hours when they are as lusty as they seem to be. Trouble is," he laughed, "I damn well resent being reminded of my age."

David said, "I want you to know there was no element of sexual harassment involved. That's a total setup on their part. Given my employment law practice, I understand those rules pretty well. Whether what I did was dumb or not is one thing. But nothing I did raised the specter of liability for the firm."

McGarey returned to his chair. "I'm satisfied, and I think our partners will be too. I'll have to figure out how to present it to them."

David was relieved by McGarey's statement, but felt compelled to add, "Basically, I was told to follow Ramsey's lead. When I couldn't, the music ended. And, well, I'm here."

"David, I think you could help us build a first-rate employment practice that will rival the great one you come from. You know, I'd like you to come in as a partner—"

"I would too."

McGarey continued as if not interrupted, "But that won't fly. The best I could do would be to bring you in with the understanding that you would be considered for partnership in a year. It would depend on your performance, of course, but I think you'd stand a good chance. And you know what? I think we might have some fun teaching one Mr. Jim Ramsey a thing or two, don't you?"

The two men looked at each other. With conspiratorial grins, they shook hands.

19

Ellen and David were married three months after he joined the Sperry firm. The wedding was a small but elegant one in the living room of Stephen Hill's home. Ellen wanted it there because this was really the place where she'd grown up. Her touch was evident. A gray Berber replaced the worn carpet in the living room, and the furniture was newly upholstered in contemporary fabrics. Stephen escorted his granddaughter down the aisle with evident pride. Her twinkle was as bright as his smile. She looked beautiful, dressed in a simple beige silk dress that emphasized her natural elegance. Despite David's defection to another firm, Stephen embraced him at the wedding as his new son, warmly toasting his talents and virtues.

In fact, Stephen had been shocked and upset when David first told him he was leaving the firm and had done everything he could to talk him out of the decision. He'd kept telling David, and Ellen, that he was the best partnership candidate the firm had had in years. David hadn't disclosed the real reason for his departure. He'd stuck with the line that he thought it best to establish his career independently. He didn't know how much Stephen learned from other sources about the conflict he'd had with Ramsey. Stephen either didn't know or didn't want to talk about it, but he did seem to grow somewhat more distant. Ellen went along with the vagueness.

Ellen's large extended family attended the ceremony. David's mother, brother, and sister-in-law were the extent of his family. Friends and business associates of Stephen, the bride, and the groom counted for the balance of the guests. Lawyers from both the Hill and Sperry firms were thrown together for drinks, dinner, and dancing. David had not wanted Jim Ramsey to be invited, but since he was the chairman of the firm, Stephen felt he had to be. David deferred to his wish, believing that he probably wouldn't have to talk to him anyway. Things didn't work out quite that way. After the ceremony, David and McGarey were drinking champagne and talking when Stephen approached with Ramsey in tow. Stephen started by saying, "I thought I might help break the ice a bit. Have all you fellows shake hands. I'd like to see us return to when our firms had a better relationship with one another. Not today, but—" A photographer interrupted Stephen and asked him to pose with Ellen in the corner. "I'm sorry. I'll be right back."

There was an awkward silence. This was classic Stephen Hill, ever the diplomat, utilizing a direct approach to get a problem out on the table. David debated whether to say anything but decided against it. This wasn't the time to dredge up the past. McGarey, who could charm anyone under almost any circumstances, offered nothing.

Ramsey, dressed in his usual expensive uniform, looked uncomfortable, as though he'd been dropped behind enemy lines and deserted. His lips trembled faintly. He said, "Perhaps a place to start would be for you to stop stealing our clients and our lawyers."

McGarey looked at David and then smiled and shrugged. "We can't help the fact that they come to us. That's not theft."

It looked as though Ramsey wanted to say something, but no words came out of his mouth. He squinted, turned, and muttering what sounded like "we'll see," walked away.

David shook his head, his eyes following his old adversary. "What an asshole."

McGarey nodded. "I think maybe we're getting to him."

The other somewhat difficult encounter for David on this otherwise happy occasion was with Celeste Calhoun, Charles's widow. She, Ellen, and David chatted together. He didn't know Celeste Calhoun, but he sensed a certain coolness on her part toward him, though not toward Ellen. What had she known about the report? Had she seen it? Had she destroyed it? Had there been a note? Had she destroyed that too? He couldn't help but recreate the scene in Barbados with Charles entering the water after giving her a kiss. *No, don't think about it. Get it out of your mind,* David thought.

After a relaxing honeymoon in Greece, David and Ellen threw themselves back into their professional lives. Ellen's career much of the time was every bit as demanding as his. She worked hard, traveled on business more than she would have liked, and helped achieve new milestones in business production for her accounting firm. While Ellen wasn't happy with the fact that David was no longer with Hill & Devon, she enthusiastically entered into a whirlwind of activities to support him in his new firm, participating in firm recruiting efforts, attending business development dinners, and even joining him at American Bar Association committee meetings in distant cities.

The months passed, and David had increasing success in building the employment law practice at Sperry, Reid & Hutchins. On his first anniversary, he was rewarded with a partnership in the firm, as McGarey had all but promised. David liked his partners, none more than McGarey, whose approach he continually experienced as refreshingly direct. You knew where you stood with him and that counted for a lot in a tense and stressful law firm environment.

To some extent, David's success at his new firm was at the expense of Hill & Devon's practice. A few of his more important clients came with him when he moved. More came later. It also began to be the case that there were some defections of senior associates and younger partners from the Hill firm to Sperry. David and McGarey gave each other high fives, sometimes supplemented with shots of the latest boutique tequila, with each new client or lawyer acquisition. They were on the move.

20

One Saturday afternoon when David got home from the office, he was approached by Ellen. She was agitated. She stood directly in front of him and said, "I had breakfast with Granddad at the country club. He says your firm is stealing their clients, raiding their lawyers. He says you're doing it."

"That's not true, Ellen. We're not stealing clients. I can't help it if some of my clients have wanted to follow me. And as for their lawyers, we're not raiding them either. They ask to come with us. They initiate it." Without waiting for a response, he added, "What are we supposed to say, 'No, you've been at Hill & Devon. We can't talk with you'?"

"You don't need to do that to be successful. He says you and Gates McGarey are deliberately provoking a confrontation. I'm in the middle, you know, David."

David blew a short stream of air through his almost closed lips. "You don't understand, the rules of the profession have changed. It's no longer a gentlemanly, clubby profession. Civility is out the window. Look at the way I was treated by that asshole Ramsey."

Round and round they went over the weeks and months, with the conversation, in various forms, repeating itself time after time. Calm questions provoked defensive answers leading to angry exchanges.

Still, Ellen had a hard time summoning the courage to be explicit with David as to the full range of her thoughts and emotions. Slowly, she withdrew from those of David's efforts that could undermine Hill & Devon. It developed to a point where David could no longer even speak to her about the contributions he was making to his new firm. And she didn't ask. Her grandfather seemed no longer to want to be with her if David were present. The warm connection between the aging icon and the leader of the new generation was all but severed. Ellen and her grandfather continued to see each other, usually just the two of them. Sometimes David and Ellen were with other family members at events planned around birthdays and holidays, but if the family patriarch were to be there, David wasn't welcome. The triangle was a strain on everyone. David said that Ellen should support *him*, that there was nothing for which he could be blamed.

The videotape added to the tensions. Seldom ever mentioned, it lingered like an iceberg deep below the surface. David had more or less dismissed it as an issue, but not Ellen. Early on in their ever more intense exchanges, Ellen threw up her arms, saying "I feel like I'm living with a time bomb. I can't get the tape out of my head. As I see the pressure building between your firms, my nightmare is that Granddad will find out about it, that it will become a public thing."

"It's a dead issue, El. Remember, I quit. The asshole didn't have to use it."

"But he still has it." She looked up and then down. "David, I need to talk with someone about it, about my fears, even if they are irrational. It's better than letting them fester."

David took his time in responding. "If you think it would help, fine." He didn't ask, and she didn't offer who and when this would be.

It was true that David's move to the Sperry firm had been largely successful, with a number of his clients at Hill & Devon following him, but one who didn't was Plotkin. When he learned what Calhoun and Ramsey had been up to, the explosion was louder than a set falling backstage. He fired Hill & Devon on the spot and ranted to all who would listen that it was his own lawyers who turned out to be "shysters." He didn't attribute this appellation to David, but he didn't see him off to the Sperry firm with any continuing work either. Compromised by the mess that had been created, Plotkin was forced to settle the case. An undisclosed amount of money was paid to the Chadwell estate from the funds held by the Ballet for musicians' pensions. The Ballet filed suit for malpractice and fraud against Hill & Devon, Ramsey, and Calhoun's estate, which remained unresolved. Both White and Gunn were fired, but neither was prosecuted, another example of lax vigilance when it comes to white-collar crime. Something about the evidence not being adequate to prove a crime beyond a reasonable doubt.

David discussed it with McGarey. "It's a miserable result. Sure, there was some monkey business in the administration of the fund, but we know the case was nothing but a strike suit."

McGarey grinned. "What's really eating you, David?"

"Now you're going to play shrink, I suppose?"

"I'd say you're just pissed off because, with a settlement, you'll never get a finding that Ramsey lied when he testified that he didn't threaten you. Right?"

"He's a liar. You know that," David said in the agitated tone he seemed to reserve for Ramsey. "He parades around like he's God's gift to the profession. Don't forget that Mrs. Chadwell's only interest was in seeing to it that the musicians received halfway decent retirement benefits. With this, they're going to get less, and her ne'er-do-well children will line their pockets with the difference."

"So, we'll have to find other ways to make Ramsey pay, won't we?" said McGarey, tipping his head to one side and looking at David knowingly.

Like it or not, David knew he'd be there with him.

21

David looked at his calendar on Monday morning and was reminded of his appointment at ten thirty with Ted Goldstein, a partner at Hill & Devon who had been a contemporary of his there. Goldstein, a business lawyer working on mergers and acquisitions, had called David and said that he had something confidential to discuss and would like to meet at his earliest convenience. He didn't offer, nor did David ask, what the subject of the discussion would be.

Goldstein walked into David's office and looked around the room and then out toward the majestic Rockies and Mt. Evans. "Nice view."

"Yeah, I graduated a couple of months ago. I was happy to leave the prairie view toward Kansas." They chuckled.

Goldstein turned to a series of framed works on one wall of the office. They appeared to be color photographs, but they were abstract. "I don't remember these. What are they?"

"Ellen and I bought them when we were on our honeymoon in Greece from a photographer selling his stuff on the street. They were super cheap. I like them because you can't really tell what the subjects are. That one, for example," he pointed, "is a close-up view of the hull of a fishing boat. The one in the middle is a shot of the top of a jagged wall."

"Interesting."

David removed the papers from the guest chair next to his desk to make room for his visitor and placed them on the floor. He motioned Goldstein to sit down. Goldstein glanced behind him in a nervous way that David took as a signal to shut the door.

"David, I appreciate your time. This is highly confidential."

"Of course."

"I've been thinking of leaving the firm and thought maybe you could advise me."

"I have had a little experience there, haven't I?" David laughed, trying to make light of it. He was flattered that Goldstein would seek him out.

"I just wish I'd been a little more perceptive way back and gotten out then," said Goldstein.

"The difference is, Ted, you weren't thrown out. You were made partner."

"Word had it at the time that you were screwed by Ramsey. You never confirmed that, but that's what the rumor mill put out."

"One case where the rumor mill was correct." That was the most David had ever said to anyone at Hill & Devon about the reasons for his leaving, though he had been sorely tempted.

Goldstein began to blink uncontrollably. David had seen this odd tic many times before. It seemed to telegraph that Goldstein was nervously approaching a sensitive subject. David glanced away, fearing that, otherwise, it would appear that he was staring. He had always wondered how his friend could be an effective negotiator when he wore his tension in such an obvious way. But he was effective, a "rainmaker" or an "elephant" in law firm parlance. A fantastic business producer. Business production was increasingly the way law firms measured the worth of their lawyers.

"Well, now he's got another target in his sights."

David lowered his head slightly and said, "And that target is?"

"Me."

"Hmm. For the smoothest-looking and acting guy in the world, he sure is a viper."

"He's on the board at Grathway. You know about Grathway, of course?"

David had been following the story in the press. Senior management of the company was being accused of cooking the books to inflate earnings by more than a billion dollars over a two-year period. There were claims of lavish spending by the three top officers for parties, boats, and other toys that had no corporate purpose yet were charged as company expenses. "Only what I know from the press," answered David.

Goldstein looked around, absorbing what he saw. He pointed toward a black-and-white photograph in a silver frame sitting on the credenza. It was next to the phone on the one surface area in the entire room that was not obscured by a stack of files. Many times when David looked at the photograph, he thought how lucky he was to have Ellen. "How is she?"

"Well, thanks."

"Tell her I said hello. You know, her grandfather still comes into the office every day, like clockwork."

David didn't comment. Goldstein returned to the subject. "There's much more to come out about Grathway. Ramsey's the front man on the account, and he does what you'd expect of an outside director. But when it comes to the lawyering, I'm the guy on the firing line getting the work out the door."

"Still doesn't like to get his hands dirty then? Some things never change," David replied.

"Right, in general that is, but his hands may be really dirty here."

"Oh."

"There are facts, it turns out, concerning Grathway's accounting of earnings that have been kept from me. Had I known them, I would have raised questions." Goldstein hesitated and then looked at David before proceeding, his eyes remaining fixed but blinking rapid fire. "It gets even worse. I think Ramsey himself may have been on the take. But I don't have proof…yet."

David tried unsuccessfully to repress a knowing smile. "How did he do that?"

"I believe he got a special little bonus of ten million dollars—ostensibly for being the marriage broker in Grathway's acquisition of Qualto Drilling. Ramsey, you know, is an asshole buddy of Grathway's CEO. They play golf every decent weekend, and Ramsey has been on the finance and compensation committees of the board for years. He also had a relationship with Qualto's senior management. Supposedly, his maneuvering got the deal done."

"What a prick. He has you out there walking the plank for him, keeping information from you, letting you go forward in the dark as to what's really happening." David tapped the desk with his fingers. "I'm really not surprised. What are you going to do?"

"That's why I'm here." Goldstein stood and walked to the window. "If I get the facts and disclose them, he'll see to it that I'm thrown out of the firm. He wields plenty of power as chair of the executive committee. The committee just rubber stamps what he wants. If I take the risk that he won't or can't throw me out, and I go ahead and spill what I find, the firm will be so harmed I'm afraid that I wouldn't want to stay there anyway. I mean, it's a great firm with great people and great clients, but no firm can withstand having its most high-profile lawyer on the take with a dishonest client. People in this community wouldn't believe it if they learned about it." Goldstein returned to his chair and sat down.

"Actually, that's an understatement," David said. "Ramsey looks golden in this city. Always has pissed me off. But that's not the issue. The issue is what do you do?" David felt agitated; he needed to move. He stood and walked toward the closed door and, with his back to Goldstein, said, "One thing you could do is come here, Ted." He was startled at his own suggestion but, returning to the chair, continued talking as if trying to convince himself that it was a good one. "Others have come here recently as you well know. Some of your best lawyers have become refugees at our firm."

"Yeah, those have been real losses to us. Three more partners and double that in associates in the last two years. That's tough. It drives Ramsey mad."

"Good. But, you know, we didn't go after one of those people. Every one of them came to us, unsolicited, and started the discussion. I don't think Ramsey will be able to hold the firm together, not if this comes out the way you suspect it will. You're in an area where we have real need. You'd only have to sell yourself."

Goldstein beamed, his eyelids flapping. "I'm flattered that you think there might be a match."

"Understand that I don't have the authority to proceed with something like this on my own. I don't hold much sway around here."

"That's not the way I hear it."

David continued, "Be sure you have the facts. He'd be crazy enough to sue you for defamation if he had the chance."

After Goldstein had gone, David propped back in his chair and put his feet up on the desk. Try as he might, he couldn't repress the feeling of warmth running through him. He might finally be able to get even with the bastard. How could he push this forward? How could he get the information to the right people without being identified by Ramsey as the source? He picked up the phone and rang McGarey. "Gates, I have some interesting information for you. Can I come up?"

22

That night, it took all the restraint David could muster not to tell Ellen over dinner what he'd learned about Ramsey. She thought he was so tough on him. What if she knew the kind of a person he really was? Pocketing ten million dollars for doing what he should have been doing as a director. Would she feel differently about going after him if she also knew that he had screwed his fellow partners, including her grandfather, out of their rightful share of the bonus?

As it turned out, it wasn't David who raised the subject. Ellen did over dessert. "When I was at the mission today, I heard some stuff about Jim Ramsey."

"Oh?"

"It sounds terrible. Something about him stealing millions from the firm." Ellen moved her spoon through the dessert she'd made, meringue torte with whipped cream and raspberries, David's favorite. "It's hard to believe."

David wanted to say, "No, it isn't," but restrained himself. "Who said it?"

"We were sitting around having one of those god-awful lunches we serve, and it came up in a discussion across the table."

"What did you say?"

"Are you kidding? Nothing. I'm not sure they were completely candid about what they did know. Most of them, I'm pretty sure, are aware of my connection with the firm."

The Rescue Mission was a shelter for the homeless on Park Avenue West in downtown Denver. The street name seemed a bit incongruous. Ellen had recently become a volunteer there, continuing the tradition started by her grandmother years before. Ellen's marketing background was helpful in the fundraising game. It wasn't a long step from that to being sucked into serving on the food line once a week. Being born and bred in Denver and an alumna of Boulder, she knew many of the volunteers who were there helping out.

Since she had raised the subject and given him an opening, David decided to go ahead and tell her what he had learned about Ramsey. She listened, shook her head, and asked what impact it would have. He said it could be very bad for the firm but that it wouldn't directly impact her grandfather. Ellen became quiet and then said, "I had hoped there was nothing to it." She dabbed her eyes with her napkin. David didn't know how to respond. Increasingly over the months, these emotional reactions occurred. They could be counted on when the subject turned to the two firms. Even beyond that, sometimes she just sat and stared, appearing lost in thought. Some of the light touch, which had attracted him so, seemed to be disappearing.

"Look, Ellen, your grandfather's a great guy—even if he won't speak to me anymore. But you're not being realistic about him. He's the firm patriarch but not its leader. He's above the fray. He can't be impacted by this stuff anymore."

She started to turn pink and responded rapid fire. "That's what you think. It's his firm, his baby, his family. Everything he's got is tied up there. The reputation of Hill & Devon can't be separated from his own."

David knew that there was no way to shake her view and decided he might as well get it all out. That included the information he'd received from McGarey about the possibility of Sperry filing suit against Grathway on behalf of a major client, Reliance Corp. "Ellen, we represent a bondholder who has a claim against Grathway, and it could be that Ramsey and Hill & Devon will have to be named as defendants."

Ellen looked at him for the longest time, incredulous. "I thought law firms didn't sue one another."

"They don't usually. But you can't take a case and then not pursue all the defendants against whom your client may have a claim." He didn't add that McGarey had almost jumped with excitement over the prospect of including Ramsey as an individual defendant. And he certainly didn't add that McGarey had also encouraged David to leak the information to a couple of sources who could help advance the client's cause.

David had predicted it correctly. Ellen exploded, "Then don't take the goddamned case." She walked out of the room, closing the door firmly behind her. Now it was out, and she would cool down.

David decided first to tip Nathan Oliver, a financial reporter at the *Denver Post*, who would have his own resources for investigation. The tip was on deep background to protect David's identity as the source. He could trust Oliver, whom he had known since their early days in the legal practice. Oliver had gotten bored lawyering and had decided after a few years to bring his expertise to his real love, journalism. They had a regular racquetball match on Tuesday mornings at the University Club. After playing one morning, as they sat in the locker room, sweating and drinking quarts of water, David took the opportunity to tell Oliver what he knew about the ten million dollars going into Ramsey's pocket.

"That's a pretty serious accusation."

"It is, Ollie. That's why I'm coming to you. You have ways of getting to the bottom of it."

Swigging from a water bottle, Oliver said with a quizzical tone, "You haven't missed the fact that if this is true, it has serious implications not only for Ramsey, but for Hill & Devon too?"

David didn't respond immediately and then said, "It goes where it goes." He smiled.

David's second contact was with Jessica Turrell, a fellow Northwestern Law School graduate who had been a year behind him.

They'd had in the past a sometimes amorous relationship at school. He'd worked hard at Northwestern to maintain a position toward the top of his class. This was vital in finding a first-rate job. She'd done even better, but without as much work. After graduation, they'd ended up in the same city, but their relationship hadn't deepened. They simply became good friends. If David had any feelings of regret when Jessica married, he had hidden them from her. Now she was working with the Denver office of the IRS, investigating charges of tax evasion.

"Jessica, it's David. Will you get off the speaker phone?"

He heard a click. "Sure. Hi, David."

"Would you be interested in ten million dollars in unreported income?"

"I've got to go back on the speaker phone."

"Why?"

"So I can rub my hands together." She laughed. "Tell me."

David proceeded to fill her in on what he knew. With the right investigatory subpoenas, he thought the agency might be able to establish that the ten million dollars had been paid to Ramsey. And he suspected it wouldn't have been reported to the IRS. But he couldn't guarantee anything, and he couldn't be identified as the source. She said she'd take it up with her supervisor, adding "You'd pass up the finder's fee?"

"Gladly," he answered.

23

The story exploded in the *Denver Post* in a bylined piece by Nathan Oliver. It wasn't relegated to the financial section as were most such reports. It was the headline.

The press had been filled for months with stories of fraud, dishonesty, and corporate malfeasance of one type or another involving several huge companies. This one, based on the same claims, was not unique. What made this story worthy of front page coverage was that the players were right here at home, important people in the city of Denver. The suit was filed by the Sperry firm on behalf of Reliance Corp. It named as defendants Grathway Corp., its senior officers, certain of its directors, and its accountants and lawyers, including Hill & Devon and Jim Ramsey. It didn't hurt that some of the more extreme facts alleged clearly overstepped the norms seen as acceptable in this essentially conservative community. Jets filled with birthday revelers off to the latest chic resort, all paid for by Grathway, were facts not lost on the *Post's* readers.

David found the article on his desk when he arrived at work, with a note from McGarey. He read the piece carefully. He could just imagine what the reaction would be up the street at Hill & Devon—Ramsey scurrying around for damage control, convening a meeting of the partners to deny the allegations of the ten-million-dollar payoff in which they hadn't shared, fielding calls from his East Coast Harvard Law School buddies asking uncomfortable questions, and maybe even throwing papers across his office, but only after closing the door in order not to jeopardize his reputation for equanimity. While the fantasy may have been a little sick, it was delicious.

But it wasn't delicious for long. A few minutes later, Ellen called. She was borderline hysterical. "David, what the hell are you doing? Granddad called. You've sued his firm. You've sued Jim Ramsey."

"Ellen—" But she wouldn't stop.

"Granddad says law firms don't sue law firms. It's an unwritten rule. He says—"

"Ellen, give me a chance—"

"You're," her words were interrupted by tears, "trying to destroy his firm. Destroy everything he's worked for." She hung up the phone.

David went down to the street to take a walk and restore his balance. This is the way it was becoming with Ellen: arguments followed by tears followed by silence. Sex at the conclusion of that kind of exchange couldn't be counted on as a remedy anymore. She would retreat into a state of listlessness and withdrawal. For days, he wouldn't be able really to reach her.

How could she defend Ramsey? The guy was a crook. David's imagination refocused on him, picturing him walking into the University Club for lunch, trying to portray his usual self-confidence, with people leaning forward in their chairs to whisper to one another about the news. Who would have the courage to ask? How many would believe the allegations? Ramsey's response would be to brush it off as nothing, wildly irresponsible claims, you know Gates McGarey. He wouldn't dignify the lowly David Fox by even mentioning him.

David would soon learn that Ramsey's response was to come in a unique, almost diabolical, way.

24

David, as head of the Hill & Devon alumni at Sperry, had been the logical point man for the firm in dealing with the recruitment of Ted Goldstein. Several weeks had passed since their first meeting, and there had been a whirlwind of activity in the meantime. Goldstein had gone through the lateral entry recruiting drill, during which he interviewed almost 90 percent of the partners in Denver.

David was pleased with the progress of the project. Goldstein and two other Hill & Devon partners joining him would be a strategic addition for Sperry, greatly strengthening its merger and acquisitions practice. Most importantly, the group would be immediately profitable to the firm. That was critical because any reduction in the incomes of existing partners was unthinkable in a world with all its emphasis on the almighty earnings per partner.

Secrecy was the watchword as Goldstein couldn't afford to have his firm find out that talks were being held. If Ramsey learned of his disloyalty, he'd have his ass. Worse yet would be the impact on the other two partners whose futures Goldstein controlled. The three were a team, whose individual effectiveness was enhanced by, perhaps even dependent on, the presence of the others. All were interviewed, yet the negotiations on status and income levels were handled in discussions with Goldstein alone.

Finally, all the details were worked out. The vote was unanimous to admit Goldstein and his two cohorts, Janice Outerridge and Thomas Malone, as full equity partners. The plans for the announcement were agreed upon. Goldstein would disclose his move internally at Hill & Devon. Later the same day, Sperry would issue a press release. David was triumphant. This catch couldn't help but enhance his stature in the firm.

As usual, the feeling of triumph was not one he could share with Ellen. But she would have to be told before learning of it in the press or through the rumor mill or, even more likely, as a result of an indignant call from her grandfather. It would be hard enough for her to take without David patting himself on the back. But getting Goldstein was a huge win. The bottom line was that Ramsey would go nuts. David couldn't wait for the howls of anguish to rise from up the street.

The howls, however, came in an unexpected form. It took only two days for a headline in the *Denver Post* to trumpet Ramsey's bizarre response. "Departing Law Partner Accused of Sexual Harassment." The article told an incredible story. An unnamed source at Hill & Devon stated that, even before his announced departure, the firm had reached a decision to terminate Goldstein because of an accusation of sexual harassment made by a female associate. The implication was plain. Rather than acquiring a nugget, Sperry had inherited a lemon.

McGarey came rushing into David's office waving the morning paper. "Have you seen this shit? It's fucking unbelievable."

"I was reading it online."

"Is Ramsey trying to commit hari-kari? It's the dumbest ass thing I've ever heard of."

David tried to remain calm in the face of McGarey's explosion. "The guy has spun out of control. Why would you invite a libel suit by making a public statement like that?"

"No shit."

"You've been around a lot longer than I have, but this is the first time I've ever seen a firm swing back like that when losing a partner."

"Sure. The norm is to say nothing at worst and something polite at best." McGarey's motor was beginning to slow even as he was pacing around David's office with the *Post* in hand. "The profession may not be the gentlemen's club it once was, but this is unbelievable." McGarey removed his glasses. With his head thrust forward over David, he said, "Goldstein will sue his ass off." He paused. "Won't he?"

David thought back to the elevator tape, and the innuendo based on it, that he too had been a sexual harasser. When he heard that the claim was most likely emanating from Ramsey, he had thought lawsuit, but there hadn't been adequate grounds for it. In that situation, there had been no clear accusation, just innuendo, nor had there been an identifiable source. In contrast, here the accusation was explicit and the source, Hill & Devon, clear. David squinted as he spoke in a husky voice, "It's still the law, isn't it, that truth is a complete defense in a libel case?"

"Last time I checked."

"So," David said, "the question Goldstein has to answer is whether Ramsey can prove that he engaged in sexual harassment? The facts in those cases are never clear. They are really glorified dog bite cases. She said this. He did that."

"With one big difference. There are big monetary consequences."

David nodded. He stood behind his desk, shuffling papers on the credenza. "And juries are unpredictable, as you know better than anyone."

McGarey pulled at the suspender straps he often wore. In most cases, they read eastern establishment, but not in his case, where they seemed to be part of a somewhat disheveled appearance. "Where does this leave us with reference to the offer? Can we withdraw it? What are the ramifications if we do? Among the staff? Clients? The bar? What about Outerridge and Malone?" With each new question, his voice rose in volume. "You know, this is a fucking potential disaster. I'm calling an executive committee meeting for three p.m. I want you there."

The executive committee met in conference room A on the twenty-fifth floor. Sitting together toward one end of the long walnut table with David were Judith Strong, a fifty-year-old tax department partner, who, despite her name, was small and seemingly fragile, and Frank Goshen, an older and outwardly quiet partner from the firm's business law department.

McGarey entered the room and walked to the head of the table, his customary position. He never looked entirely put together, and this was no exception. The knot of his tie was pulled slightly down, and his shirt was less than well pressed. One always had the impression that he arrived and left in a tumultuous spin. It was said that, in his earlier days, his shirt tail was persistently to be found hanging out of the back of his pants, a habit that, if true, he had managed to tame over the years. By contrast, Judith Strong was always so neatly attired that people kidded that she must dress at the cleaners.

McGarey looked at best, agitated; at worst, angry. At least he was calmer than he had been earlier that morning. He said that everyone in the firm, from the mail room up, had read the *Post* article. The talk in the halls had been about nothing else. The consensus was that the firm was screwed. Ramsey had destroyed Goldstein's value. The women in the firm wouldn't accept a sexual harasser in their midst. Who cared that a letter agreement had been signed, confirming that he would be joining the firm? Who worried about the concept of innocent until proven guilty? He was soiled linen and an embarrassment to the firm.

Complicating the matter even more was what to do with Outerridge and Malone. They were service partners for Goldstein's clients. He was the business producer. They got the work out the door. They were of zero value to Sperry without him. Yet, those who most opposed him also felt most strongly about the inequity of hanging Outerridge and Malone out to dry. That their leader was accused of sexual harassment was no fault of theirs. It wasn't fair to them to refuse to go forward. They were out at Hill & Devon and could never expect to be taken back. A letter agreement with them too was enforceable, even if they, like Goldstein, had not yet gone through the formality of signing the partnership agreement.

All three of them could sue if the firm now backed out of the deal. What a "frickin' mess" was McGarey's repeated refrain. The only answer they could agree on was to meet with Goldstein to get his position and then decide on a course of action.

And what about Ramsey? He had set himself and his firm up for a libel action if the accusations against Goldstein were not true. What was he thinking? Or was he a brilliant, diabolical strategist who had absolutely fucked his adversaries at Sperry?

David walked back to his office from conference room A, charged with the responsibility of setting up what could only be a difficult meeting with Goldstein. He couldn't help but think of the impact that this debacle could have on him. As long as it was going well, he could take a lot of credit. He wasn't the architect of the deal. He just brought it to the firm. But he was the point guy. Pulling off the acquisition of a seven-million-dollar practice would be a real feather in his cap. Conversely, while not his fault or responsibility, being associated with a project that detonated in the firm's face was not a plus. It would bring negative publicity in the community and the usual Monday morning quarterbacking within the firm. It was turning into a no-win situation for him. Lose at the firm, and lose on the home front with Ellen as well.

PART TWO

25

Ellen thought about the Monday afternoon when she arrived at Elliott Asher's office to be greeted in an unexpected way. He was the psychiatrist she'd been seeing three times a week for a period of time. The process had always been the same before. She would enter his tiny reception room ten minutes before the hour and take a place in one of the three chairs that lined the walls. She wouldn't bother with the pitiful selection of magazines sloppily spread over the corner table. She would spend her time thinking or sometimes making notes of points she wanted to discuss with him. She would hear an inner door close and then the door from his office to the reception room would open. He would shake her hand, motion her into the room to the chair reserved for the patient, and close the door. He then would flop into the Eames chair against another wall of his small office. To the side of his chair was a low couch, almost more like a day bed. The office was plain; the carpet and upholstered chairs were well worn; there were no photos or paintings on the wall to reveal anything about his taste or his life outside that small space. The occupant obviously was not particular about his environment.

That Monday afternoon in the reception room, she thumbed again through an article Dr. Asher had given her the Friday before, one that he had co-written with a colleague and published in a psychiatric journal. It concerned sexual relationships between psychiatrist and patient. Erudite, not erotic, it balanced evidence of the beneficial therapeutic effects of such relationships against the overwhelming evidence of their deleterious impact. But what came through clearly was that it did happen. He had handed her the article at the end of their last meeting after telling her that he'd like to make love to her, but of course, he couldn't because of the professional relationship between them.

At the beginning of their therapy sessions, the discussions had concerned her issues, predominately the conflicts that centered around David, her love for him, yet her extreme discomfort over the fight with Hill & Devon, in which she felt he fully participated. How to balance her love for David and her love for her grandfather had been the primary subject of discussion at every session. Asher pressed her to think about how many years her relationship with David might be expected to last versus the number of years that might be left for her to be with her grandfather. Her unrelenting fear about the videotape becoming public was discussed at every session. Their difference about having children was an important subject too. She wanted them; David wanted to wait. After a while, she found herself becoming more critical of David's thinking and his habits, with which she had lived since before their marriage. Short periods of silence developed in the sessions with Asher when there didn't seem to be that many urgent things to discuss. They moved on to other subjects, philosophy, religion, and finally at their last meeting, the studies that he'd been involved in about sexual relationships between psychiatrists and their patients.

Ellen had read and reread the article over the weekend, hiding it in a stack of towels in the linen closet. She hadn't been able to get the thought of Elliott out of her mind. She'd fantasized about being with him. What it would be like. She'd been afraid, yet she hadn't really believed it would happen. When she entered the room that Monday afternoon, he didn't shake her hand or motion her to the chair. He closed the door, approached her, and took her in his arms. He kissed her deeply. She felt him pressing against her stomach. She stepped back and looked at him and then down at herself. He nodded, just once.

She fumbled with her blouse and then turned to her pants. He made not a move, just looked at her. When she finished, he motioned his head back and to the side as if to come to him. She did and started to unbutton his shirt and then unzip his pants. They fell to the couch, he still in his socks, jamming roughly into her, sweating, breathing hard and loud. The ceiling lights glared down at her. It wasn't the way it was with David. Elliott's body was slim, but the skin was loose and seemed to wiggle. His back was grossly hairy. David's body was firm yet supple. Why was she doing this? She felt as though she were swirling.

Much later, when they were dressing, he said, "You realize, of course, I can't see you as a patient any longer."

She nodded. She wasn't surprised.

A buzzer rang announcing the arrival of the next patient in the reception room. He stepped to the exit and opened the door for her. She wondered if he would kiss her good-bye. He didn't. She left the building and looked at her watch. She had been with him almost two hours. It was the first time in all her visits that the buzzer announcing the arrival of the next patient did not ring fifty minutes after the commencement of the session. And it would be the last.

She continued to see him on a regular basis in his office, but no longer was she billed. The meetings resumed a fifty-minute schedule. It was always the same. She undressed herself and then him. He moved not a muscle before they hit the couch. She began to wonder if this was to protect himself, so that he could claim that he was never the aggressor. Their connection was quick but passionate, followed for a few minutes by talk about whatever, movies they'd recently seen, books they had read. Sex had been substituted for therapy. As time passed, the "whatever" increasingly concerned Elliott's fear about what David would do if he found out: sue him, ruin him, worse. Sometimes Elliott was unable to perform. What was the cause of that? Was it that he feared David so? Was it that he had the same relationship with others, collecting firsthand data for his studies? She couldn't bring herself to ask the question of the friend who had referred her to him: is he fucking you too? It was like the daughter who has an incestuous relationship with her father and is unable to ask her sister whether she does as well.

He never invited her to meet him away from the office, not even for a lunch or a walk, much less for dinner or a weekend away. Once, when she asked him to go mushroom hunting, he agreed but seemed short-tempered and distracted until they found a hidden spot and fell into each other's arms.

The relationship was demeaning. Fifty quick minutes in an office by appointment. She didn't know why she continued. It was so wrong. She didn't really enjoy it. She knew she loved David. The issue was one she began to discuss with her new psychiatrist, Dr. Gwendolyn Gordon. Was it that she felt complimented by Elliott? That he thought she was smart? That he appreciated her? Gordon didn't hesitate to say that Asher's conduct was despicable and violated all of the ethical rules of the profession. She sought Ellen's permission to take steps against him before the local psychiatric society. She said she feared for Ellen's mental health, that leading a dual life, one with the man she loved and one with a man she didn't love but who controlled her, risked an eruption that could have devastating effects on her and her marriage. Ellen heard it. Increasingly, she had difficulty concentrating, finding the right word, even completing simple tasks. She couldn't sleep at night but wavered from sleep to wakefulness during the day. Inaction became her default mode. She had a strange feeling that her brain was floating out there, somehow disassociated from her head. Is this what it was like to lose control? She knew Dr. Gordon was right, but she didn't seem to be able to stop.

26

David was on his morning jog, thinking as he ran about what had happened a couple of weeks before with Ellen. He'd received a call at the office from Dr. Gordon, the psychiatrist Ellen had been seeing after leaving another psychiatrist she'd been with for some time before that. David had met neither of them, nor had Ellen offered much of an explanation for why she had made the switch. Dr. Gordon had called to say that Ellen was with her and was so upset that she couldn't drive home. She'd suggested David pick her up. When he'd asked what the problem was, noting that Ellen had always been able to drive home before, the doctor had declined to answer. She'd said that Ellen would have to explain it to him.

He had gone to get her, leaving her car at the doctor's office to deal with later. He'd asked her what was wrong. She hadn't replied. She'd just sat in the car, looking ahead. When they'd reached home, he'd had to coax her to get out and into the house. She'd immediately walked upstairs to their bedroom and closed the door. There'd been no dinner and no communication. Things had been somewhat better the next day or two, but he still couldn't get any explanation out of her as to what had caused her to be unable to drive. He couldn't call Dr. Gordon for an answer. He hadn't understood it then, nor did he now.

It was a daily ritual for him to run through the old, established country club area where they had recently been able to purchase a fifty-year-old Tudor home. It was a pretty place on Race Street that needed attention. They'd been challenged just to buy it; a new kitchen and master bath had to wait. It was too big, for now, but that would change when they had children.

David loved the neighborhood with its large homes and massive trees hovering over the streets and gardens. It had an aura of prosperity, and he was happy to be a part of it. As he ran, he dodged to avoid being crushed by cars backing out of driveways and going on, in most cases he supposed, to the high-rise office buildings downtown. He tried to maintain a good pace, but he didn't run hard enough or long enough to reach the endorphin highs that some others claimed. He looked down at his watch, a black Casio with a plastic band, a runner's watch that would tell him when to head back home, shower, and be off to work himself. The watch conveyed a different image than their establishment home. He was conscious of the ambiguity and promoted it. Leaving people wondering, a bit off guard, had its advantages.

The problem facing him at work that morning, though it paled in comparison to the mystery surrounding Ellen, was a tricky one. Horton, the chair of the employment law department, wouldn't touch it, as was typical of him in any kind of a delicate situation, so McGarey leaned on David to get the job done. The lawyers involved would understand it better coming from David anyway, McGarey said, than from some old fart, in which category he slotted himself. He was an old fart maybe in demeanor, gruff as he was, but certainly not chronologically at age fifty-five or on an energy scale.

It had been reliably reported that Jerry Tennett, a third year associate, and Trish Osbourne, a summer associate, had been having occasional afternoon trysts at the Brown Palace, Denver's old-line grand dame hotel. McGarey went nuts over the idea that they were taking firm time, during which they were supposed to be billing clients, "to fuck their eyes out" as he put it. Endless discussions at executive committee meetings concerned how to deal with the issue. Management had learned of it through one of the associate's secretaries who, in a fit of anger, suggested that someone might check room 507 at the Brown Palace to see where Jerry was. And oh, by the way, there might be someone else of interest with him there as well. It didn't take much observation after that to find the pattern they followed.

David decided to get the confrontation over with first thing on arrival at the office. While he was not entirely inexperienced in such matters, David was embarrassed to raise the subject. He felt trepidation with Tennett, even more with Osbourne, whom he found quite attractive. He could easily understand Tennett's going after her, but that certainly wasn't something he was planning to say.

David asked Tennett to come to his office. Tennett was tall and reputed to have been a reasonably good basketball player at Princeton. He was also thin. His height and lean frame combined to remind David of a great blue heron, a prehistoric-looking bird he sometimes saw swaggering along the banks of mountain streams he was fishing.

David still vividly remembered the meeting when he was called in to see Ramsey about the elevator incident. He wanted to handle the situation better than Ramsey had his. The overriding feeling he had after that meeting was one of complete and total stupidity. He wanted to spare Tennett that. Besides, the two cases were very different.

"Jerry, I'll get right to the point. I understand that you and a summer associate have been going to the Brown Palace one or two afternoons a week for a couple of hours. I'm sure you recognize this raises a firm discipline problem. I mean, what would happen if a partner called up to get some help at three o'clock on a Friday afternoon, and all of the associates were at the hotel, missing in action?" He smiled while nodding his head up and down for confirmation.

Tennett leaned forward in his chair. His neck and head were extended with his hands resting on his knees. "What are you basing this on?"

"I'm not going to detail the sources."

After a pause, Tennett responded, "You know my secretary has been disgruntled with the firm and me. I don't think I'd rely too heavily on what she has to say. Besides, she couldn't manage my time and schedule if she had to. I could be sitting in my office on Friday afternoon, and she wouldn't be able to find me."

"Jerry, there are multiple sources. You need to get control of the situation, okay. I like sex as much as the next guy, but let's leave it to our own time, not the firm's time."

Tennett stiffened and grinned. "With the billable hours expectations around here, it looks like it's all firm time. If that were true, then we'd all have to be celibate, wouldn't we?"

"That's absurd, obviously."

Tennett continued, "Besides, what difference does it make if I'm screwing during the afternoon, assuming I come back here at night and bill hours? It's all the same, isn't it?"

"No. In the afternoon, there are clients, lawyers, and staff who need to be able to reach you. The demands are different."

David waited for some sort of comment from Tennett. When none was forthcoming, he added, "I'll have to talk with Trish Osbourne as well."

"Why stop with her?" Tennett chuckled.

"There are more?"

"Sure."

"Then I'll have to talk with them too," David replied with a sigh and shrug of his shoulders. Was Tennett pimping him?

"You don't really think this is all that rare in the firm, do you?" Tennett smiled. "I won't say the firm would be crippled if everyone involved were fired, but it would make a dent."

"We have no intention of firing you or anyone else. I just want it to stop."

Tennett stood next to his chair, his frame rising toward the ceiling. "David, let's be frank. Just last week, I saw you on tape, leaning back on a wall getting a blow job from some gorgeous, long-haired beauty. The story has it that it was in the elevator of Hill & Devon's building. At least we go to the Palace and take a private room."

David was stunned. It felt as though he'd been deposited in a vat of ice water and couldn't get his breath. He wasn't sure how much time was elapsing as he tried to regain his composure, but he knew he had do it quickly. "I don't know where you got that."

"I saw it. On the net, man. It's not like a porno film with bright lights and audio and close-ups, but there's no doubt it's you and no doubt what's happening."

David felt he could now get out more than merely a handful of words. "Internet? What are you talking about? There's some mistake."

"There isn't. It's you. Look at it yourself if you don't believe me." Tennett volunteered how to access the video web site.

It was sinking in. He'd become a fun time spectacle for all the lawyers in his firm, and at Hill & Devon, to satisfy their voyeuristic pleasure, so easily accessible right at their fingertips on a computer. Oh God. He looked out the window, swallowed, and then, with some composure, closed the conversation. "Well, I'll have to get to the bottom of that. But whatever, if anything, happened at Hill & Devon years ago doesn't have any bearing on the here and now at our firm. I want your cooperation. End it with Trish and whomever else. I don't want to have to go further."

"I'm sorry. I assumed you already knew. I didn't think I'd be the messenger." Tennett left the office.

David turned to his computer, went to the web site, and found the video. He watched it, the whole thing, all five minutes of it. He was mesmerized. It was sick. Sick to watch it. Sick to have done it. What in God's name had he been thinking? Every physical and emotional reaction was etched on his face as he looked up and down, gritted his teeth, smiled, spoke unheard words. Now those facial expressions were spread across a computer screen, no, screens everywhere that people were sneaking into their offices and closing their doors to watch. He leaned to the side and vomited his breakfast into the waste basket.

Later, David stood at the window, looking down at the crowded traffic below. His mind raced with thoughts and questions, but the one that he returned to was what he might do to keep this from Ellen? He knew, of course, he couldn't. He had to tell her before it got to her from another source. He couldn't let her get hit by surprise. But she had been so fragile, ever since he'd had to pick her up at the shrink's office. Withdrawn, depressed, indolent. Now, the videotape horror had been raised to a whole new level. Without a doubt, it would result in an earthquake with a seven on the Richter scale.

He also knew he couldn't keep it from McGarey. He dialed his extension. McGarey answered with an abrupt, "Yes." This cold greeting was his trademark. It left many associates and staff afraid to contact him at all by phone. It was different in person. Looking a bit bedraggled, often with a grin, a wink, or a pat on the back, McGarey in person was not seen as intimidating at all.

"Gates, I have something we need to discuss. It's about Ramsey. You won't believe what the master of perversity has done now."

Before the news from Tennett, David had always recognized that word of the tape could spread. He had worried about the possibility that its existence might come out at the court hearing. If it did, he had known what would follow. The judge's two law clerks would tell their friends. Copies of the transcript would be ordered and passed around among lawyers who collect unique courtroom drama; they would tell others, "You've got to read this. It's incredible." That had been bad enough to contemplate, and he thanked God that it had not happened. It had never ever, however, entered his head that the tape itself would end up in the public domain.

David waited for the right setting to tell Ellen about Ramsey's latest dirty trick. On Saturday morning, they walked to the street market in Cherry Creek, as they often did on weekends when he wasn't working, to pick up fresh fruits, vegetables, and flowers. When they returned home, he had her sit down, and he told her.

At first, she was silent. She rose and walked to the wall and started hitting her head lightly against it. "David, David, David." She turned back to him. "I've been telling you all along it could become public. 'Oh no,' you said. 'I quit, so there's no need for Ramsey to use it.' Night after night, I've lost sleep over it. Every time I think about it, I almost feel like I'm going to get sick." She shook her shoulders and pressed her hands to her stomach. "And now the fear is a reality."

He decided not to tell her of his own physical reaction to the news. "Ellen, I can't tell you how sorry I am. I didn't think even Ramsey would do something like this."

"But you've gone right along prodding and testing to see how far you can push him. You and Gates. Well, now you know, don't you?"

This time it was David who faced the blank wall. He put his hands to his forehead. He wanted to fight back. He wasn't alone. There were two of them. But he knew that wouldn't get him anywhere. All he could think of to say was, "Thank God you're not identifiable."

"You always say that. How do you know?"

"I've seen it."

"Oh God."

"Unfortunately, I am identifiable."

"No, no, no, no, no." She held her hands to her ears. "I don't want to hear about it." She walked to the front door and out to the sidewalk where she turned back toward Cherry Creek. He decided not to follow her. Let her have some time to absorb it. When about an hour elapsed, he became concerned. Going on a walk by herself was not her pattern. He put together a small dinner and read the papers as he waited for her to return. After two hours, he heard a click at the door. She came in and said she didn't need anything to eat and was going to go upstairs to read. There seemed to be nothing further to be said.

27

Ellen had been so tense at dinner the night before that it had felt almost as though she were gripping the table. She had not been communicative, not really responding to comments that normally would have been counted on to produce at least some discussion. It had been pretty much like that ever since he had told her several days before of the videotape being on the net.

David had tried to sort it out during his morning run, but the effort was to no avail. He returned to the house with nothing but an accelerated heart beat and a body mildly wet from the workout. He walked into the kitchen and punched his secretary's speed dial number into the phone. He had struggled with the decision whether to go into the office at his usual hour that morning and had decided the clients would have to wait; the firm too. He'd checked his BlackBerry earlier and found nothing urgent, but he still needed personal reassurance from a live voice that there were no emergencies requiring his presence downtown.

He raised the receiver to his ear. What he heard was not the expected ringing of the phone. It was a high-pitched hissing noise, not quite human it seemed until the sound was punctuated with slowly, deliberately spoken words interspersed with long periods of silence. "You told me...those afternoons in your office...you'd always be there for me...

didn't you, Elliott? Again…again. 'Come to the couch,' you said…'it will be good…you will feel better. Let me put my hand…'" The words were followed by a staccato, yet quiet, laughter, one reflecting darkness, not humor. "Elliott, this message will go on forever…you will never receive another message from any other human being in your life…no more appointments for afternoon delights…poor Elliott." Then, the pitched laughter again.

The voice was subhuman, witchlike. Yet he knew it. There was enough to it and to the laugh to know it was Ellen's voice out there somewhere a million miles away. He quietly hung up the receiver and ran through the dining room and up the stairs two at a time to the master bedroom. He turned the handle. The door was locked. "Ellen, let me in!" There was no answer. "Ellen, open the door." He went to the door to the connecting bathroom. It was locked as well. Returning to the bedroom, he bent his knees and thrust his left shoulder up and into the door. It pushed in slightly and then sprung back. There was no sound from the room, no response. Again and again, he tried. Finally, the door splintered. He pushed away pieces of wood and reached through the hole, turned the lock, and entered.

The bedroom was dark, but the morning sun was seeping through the slats in the shutters. He looked at the bed. It was completely torn apart. No Ellen. He turned to the dressing area. There she was, sitting at the makeup table in front of a lighted mirror, holding a phone, speaking slowly and softly, pausing, and cackling. Her face in the mirror was unrecognizable. Her beautiful long hair matted. Huge black circles painted around her eyes. Her chin and mouth covered with a thick purplish lipstick. A vision passed through his mind of the bag ladies he saw downtown, pushing shopping carts that held all their life possessions, tattered skirts flowing, their faces made up in blacks, reds, blues with looks of desolation. Ellen? A bag lady? He shook his head in disbelief. It can't be.

"Ellen, what's wrong?" he asked quietly. There was no answer, just the continuing soft voice and hysterical but quiet laughter into the telephone receiver. Not until he put his hands on her shoulders did she seem even aware of his presence, no matter that he had rammed through the door to get there. He bent down and looked her in the eyes: "Ellen, you must come to bed. Don't worry now. It will be all right." He took the receiver from her hand and placed it in the cradle. "I'll straighten up the bed, and you can get in."

He moved back toward the bedroom, letting his hand linger for a moment on her shoulder. A bedside lamp was on the floor. He placed it on the table and turned the switch. Then he opened the shutters to let in the morning light. Normally, doing that filled him with a feeling of warmth or goodness. Not today. The light just made the reality of that morning and that room all the more hideous.

It was then that he saw it above the bed. Written on the wall in the same purple lipstick that distorted her face were the words, "Loose lips sink ships." He stared. What did that mean? But he didn't have to ask who wrote it. It was clearly her writing, identifiable despite its magnification. He pulled the mess of sheets and blankets to some sort of order and half carried Ellen to the bed. She didn't speak, just stared blankly, a few tears tracing along her pointed nose and down her cheeks. Did she even know he was there?

He picked up their telephone book and dialed, only to reach an answering machine. "Dr. Gordon, this is an emergency," he said in the message. "This is David Fox, Ellen's husband. Something is very wrong. She's totally disoriented, moaning into the phone, grossly made-up, writing on walls. I don't know what to do. Please call." He returned the phone to the dressing table.

28

David was standing at the front door, having just returned by taxi from the psychiatric ward at Presbyterian/St. Luke's, where Ellen had been taken by ambulance. He had ridden with her there and seen to her admission. The events of the morning, so unexpected, had left him stunned. The mumbling into the phone, the writing on the walls in lipstick, the hideous black makeup, having to break down the door. All of it.

As David was opening the door, a black Lexus entered the driveway and pulled to a stop. He looked at his watch. It was already almost noon. The driver got out of the car and walked up to him. "Mr. Fox, I'm Gwendolyn Gordon."

He extended his right hand to hers without speaking.

"I'm sorry I couldn't say hello to you the day you came to the office. I was with another patient."

"I just got back from the hospital. I called an ambulance. Frankly, I was afraid to drive her, that she might open the door and jump out or something."

"You were wise to do that. It could have been too much for you to handle on your own."

David didn't respond. He thought vaguely that it hadn't often been suggested that something would be too much for him to handle physically.

She continued, "I'm headed to the hospital too to be sure Ellen is taken care of. But before I go, we need to talk."

David looked at the doctor. She was not at all what he'd expected. She did appear to be the age Ellen had estimated, about sixty, but she didn't look motherly or kind as Ellen had described her. In fact, she conveyed no softness. Her eyes were dark and narrow, her almost white hair was swept back in a bun, and her broad shoulders were only partially masked by an open sweater over a flowered blouse. She didn't look as if she ever smiled. But then, did psychiatrists smile? The only one David knew professionally didn't, but he was a creep. He thought it could only be in Dr. Gordon's voice that the softness Ellen had often described was conveyed.

"Come in. We'll go to the garden in back. I'll get some ice water," he said. "I'm sure the neighbors are already hot on the wires with the ambulance pulling in and out this morning." He was uncomfortable as he realized he was unshaven and still in the gray sweats that he had put on for his early run.

They sat down in the iron chairs at a matching table on the terrace overlooking the garden. David removed a stale cup of coffee and the morning *Denver Post* he had perused quickly before his run. The doctor scanned her eyes over the garden. "It's beautiful. Ellen says how much you love it. I can see why."

David nodded but didn't respond.

She began, "I'm going to do something that some might argue pushes the profession's ethical standards, but you will come to understand the reasons. There are a number of things you need to know."

"That's not exactly an encouraging introduction, doctor." David sensed that the feeling of impending doom, with him for months now, was about to become a reality. His knees trembled. Was it in response to what he'd been through? Or what he feared was coming?

"I realize," she responded, "it will be difficult."

"For someone who's supposed to know how to ask questions," David said, "I'm pretty much at a loss." He sat forward and looked directly into Dr. Gordon's eyes. "But I guess it all gets down to this—what in the hell has happened to Ellen?"

"It sounds like she's had what we call a 'psychotic break.' I can't be sure, of course, until she's examined."

"And that is?"

"She's had a total break with reality."

"She was blabbering into the phone, writing on the walls, and God knows what else." He paused. "It feels like a dream."

"Unfortunately, it's not," said Dr. Gordon. She turned her glass in a circular fashion, causing the ice to scratch against its sides. "She certainly couldn't have made any sense to whomever she was talking to on the phone."

"It didn't seem like she was even trying. She referred to Elliott, the office, things I couldn't understand between hissing sounds and a sort of cackling laughter. She kept saying something about tying up the phone forever."

Dr. Gordon said, "What was the writing on the wall?"

"It said, 'loose lips sink ships,' whatever that's supposed to mean."

"Hmm. Shall I try to explain?"

Deferring his response as long as he thought he could, David replied finally with a resigned, "Let's go."

Dr. Gordon straightened her tweed skirt and arranged her purse on her lap. "She had secrets, David. On the day you had to come to my office, we had had a difficult conversation."

"Like?" David muttered, head and eyes down.

"She had been living a lie, a secret life. The secret began to control her, to trap her, and finally drove her to the psychotic break. She's had a relationship with Elliott Asher, who, as you know, preceded me as her psychiatrist. From my discussions with her, I doubt you knew of the affair."

David started to say, "That's true," but the words wouldn't come out. He felt as if he were reeling, riding his chair from side to side, up and down, like in the earthquake he'd experienced in Los Angeles some years before.

Not waiting for his answer, she removed her glasses and continued, "Asher was backing out of the relationship. She wanted to stop but didn't know how. She loved you and feared she'd lose you. I told her that I couldn't work with her if the relationship continued, that she was ruining her life and her marriage. It took me a long time to get to that decision, I'm afraid. It was very difficult for me."

"And..."

"I realized there was risk to it. That she might not be able to comply. You know, she didn't like what she was doing. She does love you. But Asher has a terrible control over her, knowing her as he did after the psychotherapy. He knew her weaknesses and stepped right in to take advantage of them. She was on the edge. I thought that I could sway her. Sadly, under the pressure of it all, she snapped."

"For Christ's sake," David said, "aren't there laws against psychiatrists having sex with their patients?" He threw his head back as if to acknowledge his own stupidity. "I knew there was something wrong, but that? No, that really hadn't occurred to me. Sure, we fought, but we loved each other."

"I probably wouldn't have stopped our sessions if the other party hadn't been one of my colleagues, if I have to call him that. It's absolutely an outrage," she said, pushing her palm against the top of the table. "It's the most elemental violation of the ethics of our profession. I was losing my objectivity I was so angry. Without objectivity, as you know from practicing law, you can't be effective."

David stood and walked in a circle. He wanted to ask what the weaknesses were she referred to, but he'd had too much. His shoulders curved forward, quite unlike his self-confident, ramrod appearance in court. Was it that he hadn't wanted to know about Asher? That he was not really in a position to do anything about it?

Gordon continued with her explanation, "I was also anticipating being asked to testify before the psychiatric society on the charges that have been brought against him by others. Ellen wasn't alone. I know that through other sources, not from Ellen. But she resisted my efforts for her to file a charge too. I knew that if Asher were permitted to continue in practice, he would go on ruining the lives of his patients and their families.

David shook his head. "I can't believe this. I really can't." He paused, seeming to summon himself up for the occasion. "As for your profession—this fucking bastard, excuse me—"

"You have them in your profession too unfortunately."

"Yes. I know that all too well."

Dr. Gordon pushed to the edge of her chair, again pulling at her skirt. "I feel that I know you. Ellen has been complimentary of you in many, many ways. She makes constant reference to your high standards."

"Apparently that isn't mutual."

"I understand your being angry."

David looked at her. How nice. She understands I'm angry. Christ, my wife has been fucking another man, and I'm supposed to smile and be polite. But he didn't lash out. Instead, he said, "If the truth were known, my standards are not always as high as I would like them to be." He paused. "But I try."

"Your wife will need a new psychiatrist. But I'll stay with her in the interim."

"What's the prognosis?"

"Good, in a case of this type. Thirty days, and she ought to be well enough to be released from the hospital and return home."

He raised his shoulders. "Is that where I should want her?"

She stared at him. "Only you can decide that. If you have more questions, we'll talk again. In the meantime, with a shock like this, you should be getting help as well. You do have a psychotherapist, don't you?"

"Oh yes, I do. It's the psychiatrist I was referred to a few months ago by the great Dr. Asher. Indirectly, that is. Ellen got the name from him. I wonder now if there's been a conspiracy between Asher and my psychiatrist, and I'm a dumb chump they've been having fun playing around with. It's Dr. Milton, Dr. Theodore Milton."

"I know him," Dr. Gordon responded coolly, her body seeming to tighten with the words.

"What do you think of him?"

"I think that if there's any reason why you feel you can't trust him, then you need someone else."

"Excuse me, Dr. Gordon, that wasn't my question. I'd like to know what *you* think of him. He was recommended by Asher because, supposedly, he understands business types, as it was put. Frankly, though, he's a creep. I don't see how any businessperson could relate to him. I sure as hell can't. When I meet with him, I feel like he's a mouse sitting on my open palm." He hesitated, smiling slightly in recognition of the absurdity of the description. "Obviously, he's not very big. His eyes bulge out and seem to swirl around in their sockets. I feel like he's trying to hypnotize me." David thought he saw the slightest smirk on Dr. Gordon's face.

She rose from her chair. "Let's just say, I think you could do better."

As they walked through the house to the front door, David shook his head, the tears he was trying to hold back about to break. "I don't understand it. We're crazy about each other. Believe it or not, our sex life is creative and fun."

"The issues are deep-seated, going back before your marriage. One might even ask why the two of you took that step with the conflict that existed in your relationship. You know what I mean, all that business about the tension—"

"You mean the competition between her grandfather's firm and my firm?"

"Yes. The impact of all that on your relationship has been very real. It all added up...the videotape that she talked about incessantly, Asher. She couldn't cope with it any longer. The tension became too much for her."

At the door, the doctor extended her hand and smiled. "David, there's no point in your coming to the hospital for a couple of days. She'll be heavily sedated, and the visiting restrictions are tight. I'll let you know when the time is right."

David walked her to the car. She opened the door and, with a glance back, drove out of the driveway.

He returned to the house, walking at a much slower gait than his norm. It was a beautiful, blue, crisp day, but he wasn't taking in the surroundings. His thoughts shot backward, forward, in every direction. Logic, always a part of his game, was nowhere apparent. How could this possibly have happened? Yes, things weren't always blissful. They had their disagreements, but not about the way they lived or money, the things that most people quarrel about. There was the issue of their having children. But their real stumbling block was her goddamned grandfather's law firm. It had gotten to the point where they couldn't go more than a couple of days without it being the subject of a fight.

He thought back to their early days together. What intensity there had been in their love and their relationship. They had been together on everything. She had supported his decision to move to the law firm that later became the focus of all her anger and frustration. Now, she hated that firm and Gates McGarey. And she was so different. The lightheartedness was gone. There was depression that had not been apparent in the early days. What had happened? Now, he guessed he knew.

They loved each other. At least, he loved her. Who knew anymore if the feeling was returned. But he was beginning to feel that he loved her more than he wished he did.

29

Three days passed before David received the message that he could see Ellen. He had waited day by day, hour by hour, for the call, each ring of the phone raising his anxiety level. He wasn't able to concentrate on work at all. What would she be like? What would he say? What explanations would she have? How could he talk with her at all if she were like the apparition he'd last seen? He didn't want to see her; no, he felt guilty because he wasn't with her. Would it be like *The Snake Pit*, which, unfortunately, he'd happened to have seen on late night television a few weeks before? How would he get retribution with Asher? His emotions were at the edges—anger, sadness, fear, guilt—his thoughts roaming unfiltered, without any semblance of discipline.

David entered the psychiatric unit at St. Luke's. No resemblance to *The Snake Pit*, thank God. In fact, it was much like a normal hospital environment, but locked doors had to be opened, and he had to show identification before being admitted. A nurse led him down the hall to Ellen's room, past patients who moved slowly when they moved at all. He was surprised that they were dressed in street clothes, not in gowns. The hospital personnel, whose pace was only as quick as their ministrations to patients would permit, were in uniform. Ellen was sitting at a small table under a window obscured by partially drawn curtains. Her hands, at which she appeared to be staring, were folded on the table.

The nurse said in a soft voice, "Ellen, your husband's here."

There was no response.

The nurse extended her hand and touched Ellen's shoulder in the calmest way. "Your husband is here, Ellen. David is here."

She raised her head slowly. Her eyes were glazed, her face sallow, her hair combed straight down to the sides. At least the purple lipstick was gone.

She reached her right arm in his direction, moving almost mechanically and at half speed. She clasped her hand around his forearm, her fingers digging in. Then her head was on her crossed arms on the table, and she wept. She looked thin. Her upper body shook.

David sat down opposite her and rested his hands across the table on her arms. "It's okay, Ellen."

She continued to cry.

He glanced out into the hall. The patients passing looked as though they were swimming underwater. Their pace was slow and their movements jerky. Their hair stuck out comically in unintended directions. He'd been warned that while somewhat better than the day of the break, Ellen's improvement was only marginal. She was being administered Haldol, a heavy antipsychotic drug to bring her out of the manic condition in which she'd been locked. It had the effect of slowing all her reactions. He stroked her arms. "It'll be all right, Ellen." Silence. "Things will be okay."

Eventually, she raised her head slowly and looked through those vacant eyes. "Dav...I am sorry."

"Don't worry, Ellen. They're going to get you well and back home again."

"I...fucked...you...over...Dav...sorry...so...sorry." Her head moved back to the table.

The nurse bent toward his ear and whispered that it was enough for now and he should leave.

"I'll be back soon, Ellen," he assured her. He didn't know if he could take this. But she was so helpless. He did know then and there that we would stay with her to see her through this, to see her return to health.

He wanted to, but couldn't, add, "I love you." He was leaving with no answers to anything.

30

David awakened with a staggering headache. He squinted as he tried to remember the events of the night before. He had only vague impressions. He'd been out drinking with George Jenkins, his closest friend, on whom he could and regularly did unload. They'd been friends from their freshman year in college and had both ended up in Denver. It was a ritual for them to have drinks on Friday night after work. George was a stockbroker and handled what little funds David had managed to save and invest.

Why hadn't he and George been able to find their cars after they left the bar last night? How had they ended up in the back seat of a black-and-white, being driven around trying to find their cars? How was it possible that, with the help of the police, the cars had inexplicably turned up in full view, one on the street and one in an underground parking garage? And, most importantly, why in God's name, once they were successful, had the police been so irresponsible as to let them drive off anyway? In the condition they were in?

He pushed his face into the pillow, chuckling at the absurdity of it. He placed his palms over his ears, as if to keep the world at bay. Last night had been bad. David knew that he'd rambled on for hours about all his troubles. One mojito had led to another and another. George now knew everything. Other than George and McGarey, he had kept all the sordid details about Ellen's other life to himself. People knew she was in the hospital, that she'd had a nervous breakdown, but that was it. At least, he thought that was it.

Ellen was returning home that morning. He'd seen her frequently in the hospital, and she seemed pretty much back to normal. But there were long periods of silence when they met, both of them knowing that they had to discuss what had happened but having been warned not to rush into it. As a result, their conversations were forced. Sometimes, the nurses would come up and chat and help them get through their visits. Part of him said, "Leave." Part of him said, "Stay, at least until she's stronger." But what would define that? For how long? He was so denigrated by what Ellen had done that he was not at all sure that he could stay in the longer term.

David climbed out of bed. With a slight weave, he dragged his pajamaless body into the bathroom. He had only two hours to get the house in order and be at the hospital. The idea of running that morning was out of the question, but his anxiety level was high, and he was sorely tempted. He shaved, showered, and thought about what he should wear. Why did he care how he looked? He made the rumpled bed, an act he hadn't regularly undertaken before leaving the house everyday even though he hated the look and feel of an unmade bed on returning home at night. He opened the windows wide. The light fell directly into the room and on the bedspread. Making love with Ellen in the sun had especially excited him. It squared the warmth. Or did it square the sex? But that wouldn't be happening today.

As he had done every day over the last month, he glanced at the wall above the bed where she'd written those words in purple lipstick. The wall had been painted and the shattered door replaced. The painter had recommended "Swiss coffee." David hadn't cared what color. He'd just wanted the memories eliminated. But, he wondered, would he ever *not* see those words emblazoned on that wall? Would he ever open that door without remembering how he had walked right through its remnants that morning?

The doorbell rang. It was a neighborhood florist with the bouquet of white roses he'd ordered. Where to put them? The bedroom? No, he couldn't quite imagine the two of them going back there. The living room? By default, yes. He placed them on the large library table at the entrance to the room. She loved flowers, especially white roses, and often put them on that table. How did she know about the many things that made their home warm and comfortable? Things, frankly, he'd never thought about until, in her absence, he had been required to. It all seemed to come naturally to her.

He quickly checked the house. Happily, the housekeeper had been there the day before, and everything seemed in order. He walked out the front door and headed for Cherry Creek to pick up a double latte to steel himself for their meeting. He was more apprehensive about this day than almost any other he could ever recall.

Ellen looked at him with a slight smile as he entered the waiting room outside the psychiatric unit. The only thing he could think was that she seemed so shy, so afraid. Her hand rested on a small suitcase on the chair next to her. She was in the dark gray wool pants and red cashmere sweater he'd delivered a few days before for her return home. Her appearance was transformed. She looked attractive and healthy and, most particularly, alert. No one would ever have spotted her as someone who had just spent thirty grueling days in a psychiatric hospital. Her new psychiatrist had said it was time for her to return to the world, that she could handle it. Ellen was now on her third psychiatrist. David on his second. He made a fair amount of money as a young partner at Sperry, but not enough to afford two shrinks and full-time residence in a psychiatric ward. These expenses were only minimally covered by the firm's medical insurance. George was selling securities as needed. Stephen had sent word that he would help, but David had no intention of letting him.

The hospital staff sent Ellen off with a warm good-bye. People always seemed to like Ellen. Her attractiveness and warmth drew them to her. The nurses had seen her at her worst, heavily sedated, zombie like, but they seemed genuine in their positive expressions for her future. David carried her suitcase and a few other possessions, thinking what a contrast it was with her suitcase requirements for trips they had taken together of far shorter duration.

The drive home passed mostly in silence. Ellen seemed to be absorbing everything around her, turning from side to side, almost as if the familiarities of Denver were new to her. She commented on the attractiveness of a low-rise office building she'd driven by on several occasions in the past. She referred to the barren aspen trees and the piles of leaves chasing their way across the streets to rest in gutters and on sidewalks and wherever else they found a stopping point, but otherwise she said little. Neither did David. It was awkward.

She got out of the car in the driveway and stood studying the house and garden. The fall weather had robbed the bushes and trees of their leaves. The lawn was turning brown and wouldn't have to be mowed for the rest of the year. Feeling the scene was a bit depressing, David took her by the elbow and entered the house. She saw the roses on the library table and beamed at him. He smiled back. She walked into the living room and looked slowly around and then proceeded through the French doors to the terrace. She stood for some time with one hand on the glass table, saying nothing.

Finally, she turned to David and said, "I've never been so happy to be anywhere in my life." She spoke with such depth of emotion that it came as no surprise to David to see her eyes were filled with tears.

He looked away. "I bet, after what you've been through."

"That's true, but it was really pretty civilized by comparison to *The Snake Pit* version, don't you think?"

"You're not kidding, but whatever, it was tough for me to see you there."

Ellen put her hand on his arm. "I am so sorry I put you through this. I won't ask you to forgive me now, that would be too much, but someday, somehow, I hope you'll be able to."

"We have a lot to talk about, Ellen."

She walked back through the open doors and stopped at the library table. She turned to him, put one hand on his neck, kissed him lightly on the cheek, and said, "I know, but no matter what, David, however this turns out, I will never forget coming home to these roses."

David couldn't respond. He put his arms loosely around her shoulders, and they stood together for a long time. Her arms then dropped, and she turned and walked toward the stairway up to their bedroom. He did not follow.

31

For a couple of weeks following Ellen's return, there was a sort of unstable calm on the surface. She and David danced around the issues, biting into the edges from time to time as one or the other gained enough courage. There was so much to talk about, so many questions. She was depressed. She apologized repeatedly. But she really couldn't explain, in any sort of a logical way, why the affair had started or why she hadn't ended it. She didn't even say how she felt about Asher now. She wrote David a letter in which she told the whole painful story.

David tried to establish sort of a state of emotional hibernation; he was so intimidated by the tenderness of her condition. But he didn't always succeed, the calm on occasion giving way to pleas and tears and anger. For some inexplicable reason, he was masochistically driven for details. Where? When? What? She fed him little, particularly after his emotional reaction to the place and time being Asher's office during regular office hours. Why not his office? There wasn't a chance of being caught in that insulated atmosphere. David didn't know whether to be outraged or consoled by the fact that the setting hadn't come complete with romantic candlelight dinners in exotic places. It all seemed so grimy, so beneath her or what he had thought she was. He forced from his mind memories of his own sexual encounters in office settings—the conference rooms at Hill & Devon, to say nothing of the supposedly secret elevator experience, which now he would give anything to take back.

He ran and reran his relationship with Ellen through his mind. He didn't want to be cocky, but he saw himself as reasonably intelligent and attractive. Why would she have been with another man? It's not as if he played around, or beat her, or starved her of money or emotion. He liked to think he was a pretty good husband and provider. Did he have to accept that she had fallen into the hands of charlatan? How responsible could she be for what had happened? He wished that somehow it could be clearer, that he didn't always have to balance his feelings against hers.

There was at least one rewarding thing for him. He was getting solace from the fact that the pompous asshole was in extremis. Ramsey's name was spread across the *Denver Post* in connection with the Grathway matter. Mr. Clean Cut on the take. These weren't the words used but the meaning conveyed. David thought, *maybe I can't sue the bastard over the video, but he's getting his ass kicked everywhere else.* The negative publicity would be excruciating for a person of Ramsey's stature in the community, at the bar, in his firm. David warmed when he thought of how Ramsey would be received walking into the Denver Country Club, even more walking down the halls of Hill & Devon.

Not only had Ramsey screwed Grathway's shareholders, he had cheated his own partners. There had been no offer to share the ten million dollars with them as required by the Hill & Devon partnership agreement. "All fees are firm fees" had always been the accepted firm principle, and it was beyond outrage that that principle should be violated by the firm's chairman. David learned from inside sources at Hill & Devon that Ramsey's resignation from the chairman position, and indeed from the firm, was imminent. He had been given the option of stepping down or being forced out. Ramsey's ego would not permit the latter, so it was assumed he would resign. And it was juicy to contemplate what the IRS would do to him for the ten million dollars in unreported income.

"Resign" would be the public face put on Ramsey's leaving Hill & Devon. Yet, it would be known on the street as an act of defenestration.

The firm conceivably could implode. It had continued to lose partners, almost at a staggering rate. Ramsey's departure might accelerate the process. The media can't be kept out of gory stories. They would probe and dig, and out of it would come a story of the Titan Law Firm and the Upstart Law Firm and how their fighting led to the Titan's fall. Ellen would bleed for her beloved grandfather, who had built the Titan, and would blame David. The crevasse between them would widen and swallow them both. There was neither a way to keep this from her nor to explain it. It was like watching someone fall—in slow motion. You knew the outcome, but it seemed to take forever for it to happen. And there was nothing you could do about it.

32

David knew that the cards were stacked against him in his desire to sue Ramsey over the video. The potential fallout on Sperry, Reid & Hutchins was too great. Some partners of the firm would be mad as hell getting dragged into a noisy, public fight. It would be David's suit, true, but the two law firms would be right there scrapping in the middle.

It had become increasingly apparent in any event that a lawsuit over the video would provide at best a Pyrrhic remedy. The attendant publicity would just have produced more viewers. The press would be all over it. Imagine the headlines: "No Holds Barred in Fight between Big Law Firms." But it was about as fundamental an invasion of privacy as could be imagined. Obviously, David hadn't consented to the video. Maybe he should have been smart enough to figure a recessed camera might be there. But it wasn't exactly as if he were thinking at the time. No way could it be argued that there was implied consent—that anybody who gets on an elevator is offering to be filmed, much less to have that film blasted over the Internet.

David worked to convince himself that no one really watched it. After all, he read that there were one hundred million video viewings on the net every day. How many of those could be his? Not many. He'd finally gotten the video killed using the web site's published procedure for challenging inappropriate postings. He had argued successfully that the video violated the web site's rule that prohibited the posting of material that was obscene, pornographic, or sexually explicit. But he was embarrassed to walk the halls of the firm. He found himself closing the door to his office, which was not his style. He felt as though people smirked as they passed by him. He even thought he saw one of the paralegals give him a provocative wink. Entering a courtroom was excruciating. As he rose to make an appearance, he was sure that the lawyers behind him in the gallery were inclining their heads to one another, with knowing looks and whispers, saying, "That's David Fox, star of stage, screen, and home movies." But nothing was ever said—by anybody.

David decided finally against suing Ramsey and wanted to convey that decision to Ellen. He thought she'd be relieved, yet he didn't know how to start the conversation. They hadn't discussed the video since her return to Race Street three weeks earlier. And for good reason. Whenever the subject had come up before her break, it seemed to push them further into a state of emotional agitation. There had been an effort on both their parts since Ellen returned to continue in the regular pattern of their lives as much as possible. They ate meals together, watched TV, read in the same room. Ellen was back at work, apparently dealing effectively with her marketing assignments.

David was sitting in the den watching a Denver Broncos game when Ellen walked in to ask him something. The den, which was more like a small library with dark paneling and bookcases, was the room in which they spent most of their time. The living and dining rooms of their newly acquired home went largely unused. He tried to start in as casual a way as he could, with a practice development issue he was dealing with at the firm concerning an important client. He thought he might be able to engage her with a question in her area of expertise. She knew the client who was involved. She listened, but didn't offer much in response.

David doused the sound on the TV. "Ellen, there's one subject we need to discuss."

"One, David? They're a lot more than that, aren't there?"

"True, but there's one that I'd like to get out of the way."

"My conduct undoubtedly."

"No, Ellen, not your conduct. If anyone's, it's mine. Ours, really, I guess."

"It must be something pretty important for you to silence the beast with a football game on." She looked toward the large-screen TV. On more than one occasion, she had said how much it annoyed her that they had spent all that money on the tube and not on furnishing the room. "Go ahead. We've got to get to this sometime, don't we? It's surreal sitting around here with all the problems we're facing not really addressing them."

David cracked another beer. He knew he was fortifying himself. He offered Ellen one too, but she shook her head negatively.

"It's the video," he started.

"Imagine that," she said, feigning surprise. "What else would have you dancing around this way?"

He started, "Ramsey should be held accountable—"

"How do you know he did it?" Clearly, she was ready for the subject. "It doesn't say *Ramsey Productions*, does it?"

His voice rose. "Hardly. He's too smart for that. But he had possession of the tape. And he was crazed enough to do it."

"What are you going to do about it? Sue him? Sue Hill & Devon? Or, here's a great idea, sue Granddad." She threw the book she was holding across the floor. It slammed against the foot of an antique table.

"Ellen, stop. Your grandfather wouldn't stand for it if he knew what Ramsey had been up to. You've got to get over the idea that Stephen Hill and Hill & Devon are one and the same. They aren't and haven't been for years."

"I disagree about that. He may not be practicing anymore, but he built the firm. His ego is totally tied up in it."

He looked at her for a long time and then dropped his voice. "This affects us both, and I thought we should try to make a joint decision about what to do."

She looked down and paused. "I'm sorry."

"Anyway, I don't think we should file suit against Ramsey or anyone else. I'm worried that a lawsuit might just publicize the whole mess." He smiled to underscore the importance of the point.

"So, what do you do?"

"You know it's no longer on the Internet?"

Ellen nodded her head slowly. "I'm afraid most of my friends know about it anyway. Some even saw it before it was pulled. I've gotten calls saying, 'Did you know?' or 'How embarrassing.' They're nice enough not to speculate about the person with you, but imagine what they are saying to each other—'either it's Ellen, or he's getting head from someone who looks a lot like her from behind.'"

"I'm sorry."

"Great, isn't it? Just great."

David dropped his head and looked at his beer. There had been two of them, but he felt responsible. Why should he? She had freely participated. It had always been that way for him—assuming, for some inexplicable reason, the role of female protector. It had started when his dad died, and he'd felt it necessary to take on responsibility for his mother. The funny thing was that his mother didn't need it. She was an intelligent, strong, and centered woman. She'd gone back to work at age forty-three, first starting a wholesale ceramics business that soon failed and then going into the retail stationary business. She, his brother Brian, and he had lived modestly but well enough. Somehow, she had made and saved enough money to help put them both through college. It turned out that she was the real strength of the family.

Ellen blurted out, "What about our family? Who knows, maybe even kids some day?"

He moved toward her on the couch. She quieted. "The point, Ellen, is...it's Ramsey who has done this to us. But you won't accept that."

"And you can't prove it." Ellen sat, arms crossed. After a period of silence, she said, "There's more, David. There's the Elliott thing. Where are we going? Are we ever going to be able to heal the wound?"

"I don't know. It's hard for me to accept that you were with another man. I wasn't the greatest husband, I suppose, but I don't think I was that bad either. And I thought we had a good sex life."

"We did. That wasn't it."

"How can you say that? Your relationship with him was sexual."

"I still don't know what all it was about. I only know he suggested it, and I responded."

Impatiently, David said, "Well, isn't that something you need to understand? If you don't, how do you know it's over? How do I know?"

"It is over. I've been a fool, but I don't need to continue to be."

"I'm sorry I had to ask for that." He gazed at her. "Tell me, as this was going on, what did you think was going to happen to us?"

Ellen opened her mouth more than once, but no words came out. Then she said, "I figured you'd never know."

"Oh really? That dumb? Which I was, of course. But what if I figured it out?"

She hesitated again. "I didn't think you'd leave me."

This time it was David's turn to pause. "And suppose I had?"

"Then I would've married Elliott." She did not look at him.

David was astounded. It had all been logically thought out. This hadn't been an irrational, emotional act. It'd been calculated and self-centered. "What?" His face turned a reddish cast. "You don't give a good goddamn what you've done to me." He'd tried to hold it back for weeks but couldn't any longer. He yelled, "You've ruined my life. You've ruined my life."

She raised her head. "I do. I love you very much. No one will ever love you as much as I do. I can't explain it—even to myself."

"Am I supposed to say, 'Well, fine, let's just forget it and move on'?" David's forehead, damp with sweat, wrinkled in an expression of skepticism.

She sat forward and took his hands in hers. "Not as easy as that. It'll take time, understanding, patience, but we can do it. It's worth trying to save, isn't it?"

David stood and walked to the fireplace, his back to her. He didn't speak.

Ellen flashed. "You'll never forget, will you? Never, no matter what I do. I can see that." She stomped out of the room.

David stared at the TV. The Broncos/Bengals game played out silently on the screen. He wasn't really following it. At one level, he wanted to go up to her. At another, he couldn't possibly. He went down the hall to the guest room. It had been his home ever since she'd gotten back from the hospital.

33

After deciding that filing suit against Ramsey would be a futile act, David resolved to go after Asher. In part, he was propelled by Ellen's disclosure that throughout the affair, Asher had been racked with fear over what David might do if he found out. In part, it was his outrage that a professional would so blatantly violate his fiduciary responsibility; he couldn't be permitted to get away with it. More than anything, though, David had been denigrated. Without wanting to admit it to himself, he required revenge.

In reality, what he wanted was to go after Asher with a baseball bat. His obsession sometimes went as far as killing the son of a bitch. David had to force out of his mind the slow tortures that would be administered to Asher on his way out. But that was ridiculous. He would just end up in jail himself. There were other, more civilized ways to deal with him, even if they didn't produce the same adrenaline rush.

Ellen wanted to "let bygones be bygones. Can't you forget it, David? It's in the past. It's done. It's over." But he couldn't and wouldn't. Asher would pay. The question was, in what form would that payment be extracted? Whatever was dearest to him. Money? His license to practice? His freedom?

It was David's decision, but he needed Ellen's cooperation. There were a number of alternatives that could be available. The most obvious was a civil action for damages for malpractice and for loss of consortium. Proving malpractice shouldn't be difficult on the facts of this case. Loss of consortium was another matter. The problem was that a civil action was on the public record, and he didn't think there was any way Ellen could be talked into it. She would do nothing that risked the story getting back to her grandfather.

Colorado law criminalized sexual conduct by a psychiatrist with a patient, but that would be defeated for the same reason. A criminal action required proof beyond a reasonable doubt, and that tough standard of proof couldn't possibly be met without Ellen's cooperation.

David began to prowl around for other less obvious remedies. The Colorado Board of Medical Examiners controlled the licensing of psychiatrists. It had procedures for dealing with complaints and revoking licenses. The benefit of this forum was that, to a certain point, the proceedings were private, not public. That way, they wouldn't come to Stephen Hill's attention.

The problem, though, was that the standard relative to sexual conduct between physician and patient applied by the Board of Medical Examiners was not a stringent one. Engaging in a sexual act with a patient was prohibited only during the term of the physician/patient relationship and for six months thereafter. After six months, no holds were barred according to this curious rule, even if the patient had become dependent on the psychiatrist during their professional relationship.

David found McGarey not in his office, but in a war room, preparing for trial. The place was a mess. Files were stacked everywhere, on the scuffed pine conference table, on tattered swivel chairs, and on the floor lining the walls. Tools of the trade abounded. Yellow pads, clamps, paper clips, rubber bands, yellow liners, pencils, pens. Post-its affixed at the edges of documents, hundreds of them, served as telltale signs of significance. Waste paper baskets were overflowing, with trash cans having been brought in for backup.

David sat down and outlined the options for McGarey. "That doesn't make any goddamned sense," McGarey said in his customarily vociferous way. "You mean to tell me that one day before the six months is up, the doc's undue influence is operational, but one day following the six months, it ain't?"

"Yeah, it's totally arbitrary," David answered.

"Would that be Asher's argument—we waited six months before we started?" asked McGarey.

"I'm guessing it would be." David pressed the palms of his hands to his temples. "There's so damn much pointing to the affair that I don't think he could deny that it had existed."

"When did the professional relationship end?"

"It hasn't." David smiled and looked up as if to say, "Get that, will you."

The smile turned into a grimace.

"What?"

"His bills stopped coming months ago, but I've found prescriptions for depression and antianxiety pills he issued as recently as in the last sixty days. Can you give drug prescriptions to a nonpatient? I don't think so."

"Of course not."

"Also, the affair was carried on in the professional environment she was used to when he acted as her psychiatrist...in his office during regular business hours."

David took a long sip of soda. "But there's another remedy, not as dramatic or final as taking his license away. Still, it's interesting. A complaint could be filed with the Colorado Psychiatric Society. It's part of the American Psychiatric Association. This could result in removing his membership in the society."

"But it doesn't get him where it hurts enough," said McGarey. He looked shorter sitting at the table, peering over stacks of files. "It wouldn't be his license, just a membership."

"But, Gates, that's the kiss of death. Try getting hospital privileges if you've been kicked out of the professional society. It doesn't happen."

"What's the advantage of going that route?"

"One advantage is that the proceeding is completely private and confidential. Then maybe I could talk Ellen into filing, though Dr.

Gordon wasn't able to. Even if I'm not successful with her, I can file as the wronged husband."

"Okay."

"And the other advantage is that, under the rules of the society, sexual conduct between psychiatrist and patient is prohibited for life. None of this bullshit about an insulated period of only six months after the professional relationship ends."

McGarey stood and walked to a board on the wall on which all sorts of illegible writing appeared. "But if Ellen won't go along and testify, how do you prove it? Asher will deny it if he thinks he can get away with it. And he will think that if Ellen won't appear and testify."

"I've got a letter from Ellen in which she tried to explain how it all happened in the first place. She wrote it when she came back from the hospital. I don't want to go into it, but it leaves no doubt what happened."

"Yeah, but how do you get it in evidence at the hearing? Obviously, it's hearsay."

"Hearsay is accepted in these proceedings. Normal evidentiary rules don't apply. Everything is pretty relaxed. There's other evidence that becomes important too. There are rumors that other women have complained against Asher. I first heard it from Dr. Gordon. If I could get a lead on a couple of them, we might be able to show a pattern. There are also the articles he's coauthored for the American Psychiatric Journal on the subject of sexual conduct between psychiatrists and their patients. Now it appears obvious that these are based less on scholarly research than on personal experience." David paused. "Real-life couch time that is."

McGarey didn't respond. David opened a file he'd carried into the room and took out some papers. "Let me read this from *The Principles of Medical Ethics* of the American Psychiatric Association to give you a flavor of what I'm talking about. 'A psychiatrist shall not gratify his or her own needs by exploiting the patient. The psychiatrist shall be ever vigilant about the impact that his or her conduct has upon the boundaries of the doctor-patient relationship, and thus upon the well-being of the patient.' I think he's violated that, don't you?"

David put the papers down. McGarey looked at him. "Fortunately or unfortunately, I'm sure as hell not the one to advise you on what to do with this one." McGarey threw his right arm skyward, adding with a guffaw the first light touch to be heard this heavy afternoon, "Look at my track record with women." He pointed to the photographs of the two different families that David had noticed and wondered about before. McGarey didn't talk much about his first family, and David decided not to acknowledge his partner's apparent reference to his then status as a twice-married man.

Perhaps the biggest problem in David's mind was whether, in seeking to punish Asher, he wasn't risking alienating Ellen altogether. But he had to wonder whether the damage already done to their marriage wasn't beyond repair. He couldn't get the thought out of his mind that if Ellen still loved him, if it were really over with Asher, she'd be behind him. It sent a shudder through him to think that he too might soon be making his entry into the ranks of the divorced right along with Gates McGarey.

34

On Saturday afternoon, David suggested to Ellen that they go for a walk in Cheesman Park. She asked what he wanted to talk about. She always seemed to anticipate him, but maybe it wasn't all that hard to figure out why. Cheesman Park was one of his habitual running spots, but not a place he had ever invited her to walk. And most all of his approaches to her these days led to talks about serious subjects.

He chose the park because it was a refuge, a rectangle of green in an urban setting, surrounded by high-rise condominiums. It was a place for those who wanted to stroll, lots of them with dogs, or sit and contemplate, or play with children. Or to run, as did he, its almost two-mile perimeter. More recently, it had also become a venue for gay and lesbian rallies.

It was several minutes into their walk, basically minutes of silence, when David cleared his throat.

"Okay, what do you want to talk about?" She smiled. "You know, David, you're a dead giveaway when there's something serious you want to discuss. Plus, a stroll in Cheesman Park? Not exactly our usual Saturday afternoon fare."

"How is it that I'm a dead giveaway?"

"Because you clear your throat before you start. I know you're a great lawyer, but sometimes I wonder how you can conduct those heady negotiations when you telegraph your seriousness that way." Ellen added, "I know. Maybe it's balanced out by the confusion created when you smile over nothing funny."

"I'm afraid this isn't anything to smile about—even for me. I've filed against Asher." He had done it. He hadn't wanted to be talked out of it.

"David, no." The "no" stretched and hung as she looked at him frozen.

"Yes."

"I don't deserve a lot of consideration, I know. But, God, this can't be just your wounded male ego."

David clenched his teeth and looked forward. Just a fucking wounded male ego. He wanted to walk off, but he knew he couldn't. "You're assuming more than I've said."

"Oh yes, 'assuming facts not in evidence' as the great litigators say. You know, David, when I married you, I didn't think you were like the litigation assholes I'd been around. You weren't full of yourself. You weren't pompous. You seemed understated. But now?"

"Ellen, there won't be a public hearing. There won't be any publicity. Your grandfather will never know." He looked at her, waited for a reaction.

She hesitated and then calmly asked, "What kind of lawsuit is ever private?"

"It isn't a lawsuit. It doesn't involve criminal charges though he has committed a crime. It doesn't seek a monetary award though we could. It doesn't even challenge his license." David reasoned that by starting with all the things it wasn't, he'd diminish the seriousness of what it was.

"What is it then?"

"It's a complaint before the local psychiatric society that could affect his membership, but not more."

"If that's all, why do it?"

"He's a threat. He violated the most elemental rules of his profession. He can't be permitted to get away with it. If his membership is taken away, his practice will die."

"But, David, he's no longer a threat to us," she said, almost pleading.

"I wish I were confident of that, but even if he isn't, I'd proceed. There are other complaints against him before the society. You weren't alone." A smirk spread over his face announcing this startling accusation. "You did know that, didn't you?"

She didn't respond, but she paused in stride a moment, enough to make him wonder if that news was a shock to her. Or was she silent because he had questioned whether anything continued between her and Asher? Maybe both.

David resumed, "Most of the complaints filed with the society, I'm told, involve some sort of sexual misconduct by psychiatrists. I have a feeling that people, you, expect me to say, 'Hey, it happens. This is the way the dance is danced. Relax.' Well, I can't go along with that."

"You can't do it on your own. And if you think I'm going to testify, you're wrong."

"Then how can I believe it's over? If it were, you'd be there with me. Maybe even in front of me." They passed the children's carousel. He felt even more demeaned, begging her, in effect, to support him.

"We can't make it with this, David. I think you know that. The only conclusion I can reach is that you've chosen to fight him over making it work for us."

He answered as though he had not heard her. "Ellen, your grandfather will never know."

"It's more than that. I made a terrible, terrible mistake. I want to regain my dignity. I don't want to be reminded of this for the rest of my life. I want it to end, now." Her voice wavered as she turned her face away.

David gazed at two Frisbee players maybe one hundred yards apart in the center of a huge field of grass. They were making near perfect throws to one another. A golden retriever fruitlessly chased the missile back and forth between them, leaping in the air for a successful catch only on those rare occasions when the Frisbee went astray. Why couldn't he and Ellen connect the way those two players did? But he almost had to laugh out loud at the thought. They weren't even close. It was Ellen and Asher who were the players. He was the dog, running back and forth, panting and getting nowhere.

They continued walking, circling the park a second time. Finally, Ellen said, "David, I'm going to leave. I'll take an apartment." Her face cast a look of bleakness, but she turned and smiled. "We'll have to see how it goes."

David's head jerked back in surprise. He had known it could get to this. At some level, he had wanted it to. Still, he was shocked. Was it in response to her up and leaving? Or was it that she hadn't asked him to leave? Maybe that would have been easier. Why had she decided to move? Maybe she's punishing herself. Or did it mean something else? Was she going to Asher?

⚖️

Two weeks later, David was still questioning his decision to go after Asher. Why did it matter? The marriage was over anyway. Ellen had moved from Race Street into a condominium nearby. They'd had sparse contact since. But he always came back to the same feeling. He was degraded, diminished as a man, a husband, a lover. It did matter, goddamn it. And he would make Asher pay, pay so that he would never stop feeling the pain.

David increasingly spent his time planning for the hearing before the psychiatric society. He stayed at his desk late at night, researching what was available online about the society's rules and procedures. He visited the offices of the society and met with a staff member. In ninety-eight cases out of a hundred, he was told, the victim was the complaining party. It wasn't that the spouse of the victim could not file; it was just that it was rare. David had the impression that he was being vaguely discouraged from proceeding on his own without Ellen, but no one was standing in the way. McGarey was a reliable confidant and a flexible boss as this aspect of David's life drained him of the full strength required for his responsibilities at the firm.

The complaint was a document he refined with care. He was as specific as he could be based on Ellen's admissions to him in their conversations and in her letter detailing what had taken place, and based on Dr. Gordon's statements months ago. He also alluded to the rumors of other complaints, but he hadn't, up to that time, been able to verify them.

Under the society's rules, the initial review of the complaint was conducted by an ethics committee. Reason to go forward must have been found because a hearing date was scheduled. The hearing would be before a small panel of psychiatrists selected from the ethics committee. Witnesses would testify under oath. Asher would appear, most likely with counsel. David debated whether he should retain a lawyer. McGarey advised against it. Doctors hated lawyers. Besides, McGarey said David was as good a strategist and litigator as anyone around. "But how about my objectivity, Gates? There's none."

"You can talk with me along the way. You can do it," McGarey answered. David was filled with self-doubt, but down deep he thought McGarey was right.

Thank God that hearsay was permitted, or David would have no case at all. Still, he'd be facing Asher, who would lie despite the oath, and deny that the affair had ever occurred. David couldn't really prove him wrong without Ellen's assistance, which it appeared he wasn't going to get. But he planned his cross-examination of Asher carefully. It ought to be satisfying no matter what the result. Who knows, he might be able to trip him up. All he needed was a break.

Dr. Gordon's testimony was critical. David had sought to reach her on several occasions, only to end up each time conversing with her answering machine. He wondered if she was deliberately dodging him or if she was out of town. She would be aware, because of her leadership role in the organization, that the society had no subpoena power to force her or anyone else to testify. He could only hope that her hatred for Asher was such that she would decide to appear voluntarily.

Eventually, she returned his calls and asked him to come to her office. They passed small talk for a short while. David started, "Your testimony about Asher before the psychiatric society is very important."

"I cannot testify," she answered deliberately. Clearly, she had been ready for the question.

"You must, doctor."

"Ellen can tell the whole story."

David raised both hands from the elbows and extended his arms sideways. "But she won't." A half-smile of desolation passed his face.

"Mr. Fox, I'm under pressure through the society to have nothing more to do with this matter. I shouldn't have come to you in the first place. There are threats of disciplinary proceedings against me for having done so."

"What are you saying? We're just going to let the good Dr. Asher go along fucking up other people's lives, like he has Ellen's and mine?"

Gordon didn't answer. A minute passed with no words being spoken. There was absolutely no noise in the room. David rose and opened the door opposite the one he had entered. "I guess this is what they call 'the conspiracy of silence.' What a lousy stinking profession."

35

David had not had much time to spend with Ted Goldstein since his arrival at the firm. They passed in the hall one afternoon, and Ted asked if David had a minute. The library was nearby, and they walked to an empty table in a quiet corner. It used to be that law libraries were busy places, heavily trafficked by younger lawyers on research assignments. In today's world, the library was sparsely populated thanks to electronic access to the library database from the individual lawyer's office.

Goldstein looked around to see if anyone was near and spoke quietly. "I feel like I'm getting the cold shoulder from some of the women. They don't speak. They turn their heads away or down as I pass. I think it's calculated."

"Sure you're not imagining it?"

"Sure."

"Who are you talking about?"

"I don't want to name names."

"One of the firm's steadfast rules, Ted, is that no matter how we've disagreed or even fought, once a partnership decision is made, we all get behind it. In your case, we made that decision, and it will be supported. As soon as you show them that you're not some sort of lecher, they'll come around."

"Like proving I've 'stopped beating my wife'? How do I prove a negative?"

"Time. It'll take a little time."

David thought about what a nightmare it had been getting the partners to agree that they should stick with Goldstein in the face of Ramsey's public accusations. Many of the female partners hadn't wanted him there once they'd learned that he was supposedly a sexual harasser. What had finally turned things around was the fear that Goldstein and his cohorts would sue the firm if it didn't honor the letter agreements affirming their hiring. Goldstein had implied as much to David, information that didn't need to be shared with the others for them to realize that a lawsuit was a real possibility. It also influenced the partners that Goldstein had committed to taking the offensive by filing a libel action against Ramsey. Since truth is a complete defense in a libel suit, they'd figured Goldstein must be confident that he could prove the harassment charges were false. Most important was the seven-million-dollar practice, which would add to everyone's wallets from day one.

Only David and McGarey knew that Goldstein had a secret weapon. At about the same time that Goldstein had been charged with sexual harassment for allegedly groping a female associate at a Hill & Devon Christmas party—a charge he'd convinced the Equal Employment Opportunity Commission not to pursue—Ramsey himself had also been charged. His case was quite different. Ramsey had apparently had a relationship with a female partner. He'd dropped her, and she claimed that, after that, her work responsibilities and compensation didn't progress along with the other partners. Rumor had it that Ramsey and the firm had settled the charge quietly, and the woman left the firm. That might come in handy to Goldstein in pursuing his case against Ramsey.

Goldstein shrugged his shoulders. "Now that we've established that there isn't any bad news to discuss, shall I proceed to the good news?"

"I'm all ears."

"It's about Hill & Devon. A press release will be issued later today announcing that the firm is disbanding."

"No!"

"Yes. It's definite. And Ramsey won't be the spokesman. He's out. The announcement will be vague enough about the disbanding, lots of general reasons. We know that it's basically that they've been hemorrhaging partners and clients. As for Ramsey, it will simply say the usual, that he resigned from the firm to pursue other opportunities, without identifying what they might be. As if anybody would want him."

David was unable to repress a smile. He hadn't thought it would happen this fast, or at any time this dramatically. An implosion had not really been in his mind. He'd never anticipated more than a persistent undermining of Hill & Devon's base with a commensurate building of Sperry. What would it do to Stephen Hill? How would Ellen take it?

His negative feelings were directed at Ramsey, not at Hill & Devon. After all, it had been Ramsey, not really his firm, who had played with his future, who had threatened him, who had destroyed the possibility of his partnership, who had wantonly invaded his privacy. David still had friends at his former firm, at least he liked to think he did. And there were plenty of alums of that firm now at Sperry. Hill & Devon had been a fine law firm with outstanding lawyers. Had it been destroyed by one man? Maybe that gave Ramsey more credit as a pillar of the firm than he deserved, but David was sure it wouldn't have ended in the same way had the Great Man not been at the helm of the ship.

"We've got to see Gates."

David and Goldstein appeared at McGarey's open door and knocked. McGarey waved them in. He used their entrance as an excuse to get off a call. "I've just had two high-priced lawyers walk in here" was a line he often used to bring a telephone conversation to an end. McGarey's office gave the feeling of complete disorganization. One had to wonder how he could operate in it. McGarey's assistant bustled in, sighing heavily as she, yet again, had to move files, books, and papers from the chairs to find room for people to sit.

David delivered the news of Hill & Devon's demise. McGarey raised his right arm bent at the elbow, hand clenched in a fist, dropped the arm with a jerk, and drew out the word "Yes."

"I've received four calls already this morning from partners who want to bail out," said Goldstein. "Of course, they're too late to avoid the liabilities they face in a blow up like this. They just want to find a stable home as soon as possible so that they won't skip a beat with their clients."

"Why now? What was the catalyst?" asked McGarey, almost panting.

"I think it was when they realized the depth of Ramsey's problems that they decided they couldn't hold it together. There's my defamation suit. A lot of people around there think Ramsey went off his rocker to respond to my leaving that way. I mean, we all know that no matter what is felt or said in-house about a partner leaving, the official response for public consumption is neutral at worst."

David interjected, "You can't take all the credit for it, Ted. There's the fraud charge on the ten-million-dollar payoff to Ramsey. And the partners being after him on why the payment wasn't disclosed and shared with them."

"And don't forget the IRS. They'll want to know why the money wasn't declared and shared with them too," added Goldstein, his eyes blinking rapid fire.

McGarey tipped back in his chair, clasping the fingers of his hands behind his head. "You know, I always thought Ramsey was a 'suit,' not really very smart, not really very classy, not really any of the things that he appeared on the surface. He looked good, handled himself well, strutted around a lot. He managed to cover up for a long time what was really there. But you can't get away with that forever."

There was silence. Goldstein didn't offer his view of Ramsey's reality. David sat silently waiting for something more. "We need to sit down," said McGarey, now hunched over his desk, pen poised above a yellow pad, "with a list of names and figure out which of their partners we want to make a pitch for. They have some great people. It's a golden opportunity. But first, let's celebrate. Today, we're going out to lunch. The club. And it's on me."

36

David's assistant Amy, who had loyally followed him to the Sperry firm, came on the intercom. "There's a Chet Deaver here to see you. Says he's a private investigator and wants to speak with you about the Asher matter. I've told him we don't have a case with that name, but he won't take no for an answer." David hesitated and then replied, "That's okay. I'll go out and see him."

"Don't say I didn't try," and the intercom clicked off.

Two men were waiting in the reception room. One was sitting and reading the *Wall Street Journal*, and the other standing at the window facing the Rockies, his back to the room. David said, "Mr. Deaver?"

The man at the window turned.

"I'm David Fox. Please come in." David escorted him back to his office, shut the door, and motioned Deaver to sit down in one of the chairs facing the desk. David sat behind the desk.

"Thank you for seeing me. Here's my card. I'm a private investigator looking into a matter involving a Dr. Elliott Asher. I think you might be interested."

"Why do you think that?" parried David. A shiver ran through him.

"Because I believe you have a case before the Colorado Psychiatric Society against him."

186

David struggled to be cool. He wasn't about to admit anything, yet he wanted all the information he could get. This could be his break. To slow things down and give himself a chance to think, he asked if his visitor would like a cup of coffee. Rather than asking Amy to get it, he went across the hall to the coffee room and returned with two cups. He found Deaver standing at the wall, ostensibly looking at the plaques hung there that reflected David's degrees and court admissions. Immediately under them was a table stacked with files. It suddenly struck David that this man might have looked down at the loose papers sitting on the files. When David had been a private detective, he was trained to absorb everything he could get his eyes on, even acquiring in the process some helpful skills in the art of reading upside down.

"What makes you think I have a case there?"

"I'm not at liberty to disclose my sources, but I will say there appear to be multiple people with claims against Dr. Asher. He was a busy fellow. The claims have a common thread…Asher had sexual relationships with his patients or former patients. There is at least one charge subject to criminal investigation. There's another before the Colorado State Board of Medical Examiners to revoke his license. The others I'm aware of are before the psychiatric society, as I have reason to believe yours is, or are brought as civil actions."

"My understanding, Mr. Deaver—"

"Chet, please."

"—is that proceedings before the society are private, not public. If there were a charge filed there by someone other than your client, like me, you wouldn't have any way of knowing that, would you?" David smiled with apparent satisfaction over his point.

"As I said, I have sources. That's really what I'm paid for, to access information. And I'm pretty good at it."

David looked at Deaver and thought, *I can see how you would be.* He was, in a way, disarming, looking nothing like your classic gumshoe. He had on a dark suit, white shirt, and a conservative tie. He looked more professional than most lawyers in the office did.

David wondered how many costumes Deaver must have. When he was wandering into a bar looking for information, the attire was probably a sweater, sport coat, or leather jacket, certainly no tie. David remembered the drill. Being a private detective during summer vacations from college had been fun sometimes, but more often, it had been dull. He recalled being on a stakeout for hours, waiting in a car to photograph a subject as he came out into his front yard to work in the garden. The subject had claimed that he was unable to reach above his shoulders because of injuries suffered in an accident. David, who represented the insurance company being sued by the subject, caught him on film reaching up and cutting the low branches of a tree. In that case, he'd been successful but had spent a boring day sitting there with a camera, waiting. Being a private eye sounded much sexier than it really was. There was, however, something to be said for it in the sex department. Girls found it fascinating that he was a detective and were unusually susceptible to his stories, embellished or not. The work had been essential to his getting through college. Less critical but still important, it had been helpful to his getting into a bed or two along the way.

"You'll have to tell me what you think you know about my involvement. If that checks out, I'll want to know what information you have that could be helpful to me."

"What helps you will help all of Asher's victims because yours is the first case that will be heard. The other complaints are only under investigation at this point."

"What does the underground tell you about my alleged case?" David fiddled with a rubber band, wrapping it in and out between the fingers of his left hand.

"That your wife fell into Asher's web, but she won't file against him. That she had a nervous breakdown over it. That she's left you. That you're proceeding against him. That's the general outline. Correct?"

"Before I answer, I have a question. Assuming I had a case, would any of these other women, not their husbands but the victims as you put it, be willing to appear as witnesses and testify?"

Deaver leaned down and took a file from his briefcase on the floor by the side of his chair. "Quite possibly. What do you have in mind?"

"A coordinated effort is always better than a series of solo performances, don't you think? Their experiences aren't directly relevant to my supposed case, but could tend to show a pattern on the doctor's part. We might be able to get that pattern in evidence. The society's rules are lax." His thought, not expressed, was that Ellen might be angry enough if she had proof that Asher was working both sides of the street that she would be willing to go after him.

"Do you know where your wife is now?" asked Deaver.

"Of course."

"Do you know she has had contact with Asher?"

David stood and paced behind the desk. He didn't answer.

"You see, part of my job has been to keep him under surveillance, and I see the comings and goings at his office and condo. She has been to his office, though not in about a month."

David sucked it in. He did the math. That meant she'd been there after her return from the hospital. He wanted the conversation to end. "Why don't you find out whether the others would stand up in a hearing and let me know?"

"Am I to assume then that you have filed a complaint and have a hearing set?"

"Don't assume anything. But I'm willing to talk if there are others who will provide support."

"I don't need to find out anything. I know the answers for four other complainants. Unlike your wife, they're champing at the bit to go after him. The cases have common threads. All of them are women. One is divorced. One is in the process of getting divorced. The other two are still with their husbands. All of them were seeing Asher for multiple problems they were experiencing, including marital issues. They had been patients of Asher's long enough for him to know their personal lives and relationships in intimate detail. Again in each case, he ostensibly ended the professional relationship before the sexual relationship commenced. In all cases, the affair was carried on in his office. Does any of that sound familiar?"

David decided to give up the parry. "Quite."

"All four have authorized me to disclose their names to you and have indicated they would be willing to consider testifying in your case."

David didn't need to think long. This was the break he'd been praying for. It ought to be enough for Ellen to rise up in anger. It would present a pattern. Asher would be portrayed as a serial violator of the most fundamental ethical standards of the society. "Let's set up meetings with them to prepare. We don't have long. The hearing is just two weeks off."

Deaver nodded. "I know."

David escorted him to the elevator. When he returned to his office, the distinct spicy scent of Deaver's cologne still lingered in the air. This was one incongruity he found in Deaver. David had been taught in his detective days not to leave tracks. Apparently, Deaver had gone to a different school.

37

As David walked the short distance to his meeting at Elizabeth Chenny's office on Eighteenth Street, he felt relief that they didn't know one other. The last thing he wanted was for anyone he knew to learn of the sordidness of his life. Chenny was a well-recognized divorce attorney who represented prominent and wealthy parties in high-profile divorce proceedings. More often than not, she represented wives in their attempts to balance the wealth scales with their successful husbands.

In this case, she was representing a wife, yes, but one with different motivation. Alice Fenn's quarrel wasn't with her husband. Their property interests were not huge and that part of the unraveling of their marriage had been resolved. Her fight was with Dr. Elliott Asher. Alice was one of the women whose names had been brought to David's attention by Deaver. The meeting between David and Fenn had been arranged only on the condition that they meet in Chenny's presence.

He entered the reception room and introduced himself. The building was an older one in downtown Denver that had been remodeled and was populated by lawyers, architects, and other professionals, but not by the large law firms that were housed in the high-rise buildings nearby. The offices were plain. The operation was a small one, as was typical of lawyers with narrow specialties such as domestic relations. A secretary led him from the reception room to a conference room down the hall, outside the sight of the public areas of the office. Confidentiality was particularly essential in a domestic relations practice.

David's second thoughts about playing both lawyer and witness in the hearing rumbled through his mind during the introductory sparing that was typical of such encounters. Like dogs staking out their territory, he and Chenny said what they were there about and what they were willing to do or not do. Chenny explained that her client had filed a civil suit against Asher, which was at an early stage with no pretrial discovery scheduled. She looked tough to David, short, clipped dark hair, glasses, no makeup. He pictured her as a competitive swimmer. David explained the nature of his complaint with the psychiatric society and the upcoming hearing.

Fenn sat silent and motionless through the opening exchange. When it finally came to her turn, however, she gushed information, unfiltered, as though once having started she couldn't stop. Chenny's efforts to keep her on track were to little avail. She would be hard to control as a witness, a nightmare at trial. The story she was anxious to tell was in some respects what David had anticipated. She and her husband, who had been married twenty years, had experienced marital difficulties that grew more serious. They'd also had discipline problems with their teenage son. She'd felt the need for counseling and had been referred to Asher. At first, she found him professional, concerned, and empathic. As they explored her marital relationship in greater depth, he asked questions that caused her slowly to look at her husband in a different light. She had to face her own actions and motivations, which was frequently difficult.

The only thing Fenn spared were explicit details of the sexual relationship that evolved. Somehow, David couldn't quite picture it. She didn't look the type. She was plain and proper-looking. She wasn't young, and she had a bit of a stutter. But some facts came out. At one point, out of the blue in a session, Asher said that he'd like to make love to her. He added that, of course, he couldn't because of his professional relationship. He said there were studies published in professional journals on the subject of sexual relationships between psychiatrists and their patients. He reached in his drawer and handed her a copy of a study, suggesting that she take it home to read. He cautioned her to treat it confidentially. She read the piece and found that he was one of its coauthors.

As Fenn was spilling out her story, Chenny kept glancing at her BlackBerry. She tried to be subtle, but it was disconcerting. She appeared bored, distracted. Undoubtedly, she had heard the story before, probably in excruciating detail, but her focus on other matters while her client was speaking was rude. David took mental note of his reaction, recognizing that he too was prone to sneaking squints at his BlackBerry and needed to be more sensitive to the appearance that habit created.

Fenn went on to explain how she returned for the next visit with Asher after devouring the article and fantasizing about making love with him. She entered the office. He embraced her and had her undress herself and then him. They became lovers, then and there in his office. She continued her twice-weekly appointment schedule, which consisted now of passionate encounters on his couch. She received no more bills.

Eventually, she answered her husband's incessant questioning by acknowledging the affair. He exploded and sought counseling himself, a step she thought he would never have been willing to take. Then, suddenly, he moved from their longtime high-rise condominium and filed for divorce. When her husband left her, Asher seemed to change. His ardor weakened; he was less responsive. Ultimately, he said they couldn't continue, that he feared her husband would sue him. He couldn't take the chance. And that was that.

Alice Fenn was the third of the four witnesses referred by Deaver whom David had interviewed. The pattern was pretty clear, leaving a trail of Asher's own outrageously irresponsible professional DNA. All were women in their late thirties through mid-fifties. All were presentable, if not attractive. They were or had been married. Each was troubled in some way. Each had insecurities. All were vulnerable. The action always took place in Asher's office. Big spender he wasn't. Several of the affairs overlapped. Asher made sure not to leave any tracks. All ceased to be billed when the affair commenced.

38

David asked Ellen to meet him at Amore, an Italian restaurant in the Cherry Creek shopping district. He chose the small, quiet restaurant as the place where he would make one last attempt to talk her into testifying at the hearing, which was now only days away.

Ellen was there when he arrived, sitting in the back room at a corner table. The place looked and smelled authentically Italian. He bent over and kissed her on the cheek and then sat down.

Despite all they'd been through, her uneven smile, her sparkly eyes, her fresh smell still caused him to quicken. In her naturalness, she was almost, not quite, beautiful. His attraction to her remained strong. But as soon as he began to feel that, countervailing feelings arose—of having lost his confidence, of simple hopelessness. He wanted her back at home. Yet he couldn't be sure that she'd given Asher up, particularly after what Deaver had told him. And what if she were to say she had or would, could he trust her? He veered from one set of feelings to the opposite, all in the space of seconds. He never reached resolution.

Ellen started, "The waiter's already told me about the specials. From his size, it looks like he must consume all the leftovers." She threw her head back, her laugh culminating in a snort, but it seemed forced. She gazed around the room. The other tables were not yet occupied. "It seems like there are more specials than they're likely to have customers tonight."

They were silent for a minute, and then Ellen tried to smile, her lips tight. "Is there some significance to the name?"

"What name?"

"Amore? A hangout in your new bachelor life?"

David pushed back in his standard restaurant-issue, hard-backed chair. The selection had been stupid. He hadn't thought of the name. But the way she said it made him mad. "Hey. You were the one who left." He paused, assessing, as he always did, his words to be sure that what he said was not hurtful. Too often, however, the assessment came only after the utterance. Always lingering in his mind was her tender mental state. "Some bachelor life, living in a barn on Race Street. No, it was recommended by someone at the office. I've never been here before."

"I know you have an agenda," said Ellen. The flames from the candle jumped as their words and breath crossed the table.

"Unfortunately, the usual," replied David, his husky voice falling to its ultimate low. He had thought of many ways to start this conversation. He had added, deleted, and still it seemed he wasn't ready, probably because he knew there was no way to soften it. This might even be the most important argument of his life. "Let's order first."

They looked at the menu and selected a bottle of Chianti Classico and bruschetta and carpaccio con parmigiana to start.

There was no way to glide around it any longer. "The hearing starts on Thursday."

"I know that."

He hesitated to ask how. Probably he had told her the date. But he wasn't sure and didn't want to ask. That old rule of cross-examination—never ask a question you don't know the answer to—protruded beyond his professional life even into nonadversarial situations. Or was this nonadversarial?

David girded himself. Her answer could mean so much, whether they could ever be together again. "I'm still hoping you'll attend." He smiled with the plea.

She was motionless. Not a muscle in her face moved. She looked straight at him. He knew it wasn't a look of love, but was it a look of hatred?

"You know the answer to that. No."

"I can only take that to mean that you're defending him."

"That's not the only answer."

"Well, I know it can't be that you're protecting your grandfather. He'll never know about it."

"That's not it." Ellen looked down impatiently. David noticed how thin she was. She must have lost ten pounds.

"I just want it over. We can't erase the facts." She ran her thumb along a ridge in the tablecloth. "Let's move forward with our lives. It doesn't do us any good to destroy his."

"I can't accept that, Ellen. He's a disgrace to his profession. He's totally unethical. It wasn't just you, you know. There are others." She showed no recognition of what he had said. He couldn't stop. This was his last chance. "All the while he was making love to you, he was with others too. Not one other, or two. No, there were four. At least four. Do you get that, Ellen?" There it was; he'd said it.

She put her fork down and sipped her wine for what seemed like a minute. "What's the purpose of telling me this, David? To make me feel even more a fool than I do? I told you this was never rational. It was emotional. It wasn't even sexual, at least that wasn't the reason for me."

"Ellen, four other women have talked to me. The pattern is almost identical. They have problems. They see him. He learns everything, every intimate detail, every weakness, every vulnerability. He knows where their husbands fail them. He gets their confidence. He strokes their egos, pretends to feed their intellectual curiosity. Ultimately—"

"I don't want to hear it." She ran her hands up through her hair, holding it just a second or two before releasing it to fall back.

He continued nonetheless, "And he tells them he loves them, that he wants to have sex with them, but that to do that they must end the professional relationship. He gets them into bed, actually on the couch. It all happens right there in his office. Their lives begin to collapse.

They've got to tell their stupid husbands, or the smarter ones figure it out. He ruins their lives. Then he departs. Sound familiar?"

They had eaten almost nothing, but they tore through the wine, gulping down the contents of their glasses.

"What's the physician's motto, 'First, do no harm'? Isn't that it?"

She didn't speak. She was pale. Her eyes glistened, looking vacant. Had he gone too far?

"At least some of the women are prepared to testify. Please, won't you come and testify to what happened?"

Ellen rose to the question. "Even if I were willing to do it, do you really think I could detail all that in front of you? Would you want that?"

"I could leave the room." David paused. "Maybe Gates could sit in for that part."

"What? I'm supposed to talk about the most intimate details of my life in front of Gates McGarey? The guy who has killed off Granddad and the law firm he built step by step? You've got to be kidding."

"Well, Gates doesn't have to be involved. You can appear on your own and tell the reviewing panel what happened. I can be out of the room."

"David, I could say I'll think about it, and I will, but I'd surprise myself if I really ended up doing it."

"You know what that tells me." He dropped his head and paused. "I won't repeat it again." He had said things he didn't want to say. He had lost control. Still, he couldn't stop. "How can you protect a guy who is fucking all sorts of other women at the same time he's with you? Don't you have any pride?"

She didn't answer. She took the purse from the chair next to her and stood. Turning to walk toward the door, she looked at him. Her face was white. She said, "David, I don't think you'll ever understand. You want revenge, and you're going to get it, no matter what." She walked out the door.

David finished the wine and paid the check. They had picked at the antipasto. The waiter came up, arms bouncing, his voice rising and falling. He wanted to know what was wrong: wasn't the food good? David tried to explain, but he knew that the best excuse he could come up with was lame—his wife was not feeling well, and he had to leave to get to a meeting. He asked for a doggie bag for what was left, knowing full well that he wouldn't get around to eating it.

David was sorry he had his car. He wished he could walk home, but he had driven there from the office. He thought best when walking or running. He wondered if he should proceed with the case. Would he look like an idiot complaining about something that had been done to his wife when she didn't care enough to act herself? Was he motivated by vengeance as Ellen claimed? Hardly a laudatory motivation. Yet, taking a miscreant like Asher out of action could be rationalized as being consistent with the focus of his father's letter on the importance of integrity. Because Asher had none.

39

The doorbell rang demandingly, interrupted by the door knocker clanking, until David was able to get up, put on a bathrobe, and go downstairs. He opened the door. It was Ellen. He looked at his watch. It was half past eleven. He'd gone to bed early in anticipation of the start of the hearing the next morning. Ellen's visit was completely unexpected. There had been no communication between them since their dinner a few nights earlier.

Her car was idling in the circular driveway, its lights shining beams through a mild rain. She was dressed in sweats and tennis shoes, her hair uncharacteristically piled on top of her head. The rain left her slightly wet but not dripping. He'd barely closed the door behind her when the words spilled out rapid fire. "I've changed my mind. I will testify." She said it less with resentment than with resignation.

He didn't know how to respond. He hadn't expected a change in heart after the firmness of her position at dinner. All he was able to come up with was, "Thank you. I'm glad."

She responded tersely, "It's not because you want me to." She was frazzled but seemed in control, in fact more determined than he had ever remembered her.

"Why then?" As soon as the words exited, he knew that he shouldn't have asked.

"Don't ask why. Just leave well enough alone."

David debated how far to go in trying to determine what she intended to say when she testified. He asked, "Do you still not want me to be present in the hearing room when you testify?"

"That's right. Will Elliott be in the room?"

"I assume he will."

She opened the door and walked back out into the rain. When she got to her car door, she yelled back, "You were right about him, David. That's why I'm doing it."

He watched until she had pulled out of the driveway and turned down the street.

David roused to the sound of the alarm. He pressed the snooze button. *Thank God for that device,* he thought. Actually, it was amazing he needed it. He'd spent most of the night after Ellen's stormy visit awake, staring at the dark ceiling. He always slept fitfully before a hearing, rehearsing what he would say, the questions he would ask, the hurdles he would have to overcome. In this case, it was magnified by his tenseness over confronting Asher and by his concern over Ellen's condition. He'd struggled before telling her of her competitors. At one level, he'd wanted to underscore what a fool she'd been. At another level, for some strange reason, he hadn't wanted her to be hurt by the knowledge that she was not Asher's only lover.

Why the hell did he care? It was his persistent goddamned need to protect the important women in his life. Was it an old tape from his mother? "Remember, Dave, sometimes women need love the most when they deserve it the least," he could hear her say. He'd had to apply this advice often in his marriage. He wanted to go to back to his mother and ask why the advice didn't apply in reverse, why he didn't need love too, maybe even when he deserved it the least. But somehow he couldn't bring himself to do that. His mother had reacted with sadness when he told her of the separation. She liked Ellen. Thankfully, she didn't probe what had happened between them.

He was even more nervous about this hearing than those in which he filled his normal role of advocate. Here, he was the client. How could he act with any objectivity? Objectivity was, after all, the most important quality that counsel brought to a representation. Could he deal with the emotion of the situation? Could he be smart enough to handle Asher when he hated him as much as he did? He was violating the age-old admonition: "Only a fool has himself for a client."

The hearing was scheduled at the psychiatric society's offices. David arrived early and was asked to wait in the reception room. As he sat there, several people entered and then were quietly ushered from the room. David assumed they were the doctors who made up the panel that would hear the case, and they were being taken into the room where the hearing would be held.

Some of the people who arrived he did know. Two of the women David had interviewed, Alice Fenn and Meredith Hendricks, were there to testify in support of his complaint. Their lawyers were present to protect the record and learn as much as they could for their own cases, which were upcoming. "Free discovery" they called it in the profession. The other two women he had interviewed would have been good witnesses, but they'd declined at the last moment to appear. David wondered how many others were out there whom Deaver's investigation hadn't uncovered.

David knew he'd have a hell of a fight as to whether Alice and Meredith would be permitted to testify, but he thought the pattern-of-conduct rationale for their testimony was a reasonable one. In other words, the panel would be asked to resolve the anticipated conflict between Asher and Ellen by reference to similar conduct engaged in by him with others under similar circumstances. Whether their lawyers would be permitted at the hearing would be another question that would not be easily resolved.

David felt uncomfortable in the crowded reception room with the others waiting to be directed into the hearing room. Small talk didn't feel appropriate. He was nervous, made all the more so by the fact that

Ellen wasn't there yet. What if she'd changed her mind again? He paced nervously. He decided to walk into the hall. As he pushed the door outward, Ellen pulled the door open from the outside. Neither smiled. He placed his hand gently on her arm to motion her back into the hall, but she brushed by him and walked into the reception room. He was relieved she was there but concerned that she was so cold. Had her anger at Asher the night before now been transferred to him?

At about a quarter past nine, a woman came into the reception room and announced that everyone who was there for the Asher matter should proceed down the hall. The room to which they were directed was a large, windowless conference room in the interior of the suite. It was furnished with multiple tables to accommodate a variety of configurations surrounded by modestly upholstered chairs with arms. For this occasion, the tables were organized in a U. At the head of the table were three men and one woman all dressed in business attire. One of the four identified himself as Dr. Byard Rosen, chair of the panel. He acknowledged those entering the room and invited them to take seats.

A man and a woman were already seated at the table. David had not seen the man before. He guessed from vague descriptions he had heard that the man was Asher. He had not been informed in advance who Asher's lawyer might be, so he presumed the woman was there in that capacity. He had seen her face before but couldn't recall her name. He associated her with sexual harassment cases. Clever of Asher to be represented by a woman given the nature of the complaint.

Asher looked to be many years older than Ellen, probably in his mid-fifties, balding with long wisps of black hair combed straight back from the front of his skull to the back of his head. He had bulging brown eyes and an arched nose He was slouched in his chair and so it was hard to tell, but he appeared short, maybe five feet eight. He was thin and fit as a runner might be.

David knew how difficult it would be seeing Asher for the first time. His instinct would be to grab him at the neck and watch him sputter. It was David's invariable custom on entering a room for an informal hearing such as this to introduce himself and shake hands with all present. In this case, he couldn't bring himself to acknowledge

Asher, so he skipped the shaking of hands, knowing that he would have the opportunity to introduce himself to the group as a whole. He felt himself flush. He couldn't keep his eyes from darting to Asher, who appeared equally reluctant to look at him. Asher gazed straight ahead or chatted with members of the panel, making it clear that he was on a friendly basis with them. That might answer why Asher had not been seen in the reception room. He'd probably arrived early and been taken into the conference room. It was hardly a comforting thought that this was Asher's ground, his professional society, and that these were his colleagues. Would this just be a kangaroo court?

Asher gave off an aura of cockiness, as if this whole proceeding was no problem at all, other than being a waste of his time. This perceived attitude raised David's temperature. He felt even more diminished as he came to see just how unattractive this man was. What was the appeal? David was no Adonis, he knew, but this? Good God.

Dr. Rosen opened the proceeding by identifying himself and the other three members of the panel. All were practicing psychiatrists who were serving on the case as a service to the profession and the public. Given their patient commitments, the hearing would adjourn at one o'clock that afternoon. Dr. Rosen then proceeded to his left, asking for introductions. First was Asher's lawyer, Adelaide Unger, who introduced not only herself but Dr. Elliott O. Asher as well, treating her client with great deference. In order around the table, each of the two female witnesses was introduced by her lawyer. Ellen's turn was next. David left it to her to introduce herself, feeling that she might take umbrage if he gave even the slightest impression that he was representing her. Finally, he introduced himself as the complainant in the case.

No sooner than David had finished, Unger objected to anyone being present in the hearing room who was not a direct party in the proceeding, asserting this was a private matter. Argument followed as to the nature of the testimony of the other women. Unger predictably took the position that their testimony would be irrelevant. If these women had claims, they should assert them through their own complaints before the society. David replied that the other women would demonstrate that Asher's conduct with respect to Ellen followed a pattern that rendered him dangerous to his patients, to the profession, and to society.

Dr. Rosen whispered with the other members of the panel and then announced that all potential witnesses and their counsel would be required to remain outside the hearing room while testimony of the first witness was being taken. Only Mr. Fox, Mrs. Fox, Dr. Asher, and Ms. Unger could be present with the panel throughout. The panel would rule with respect to the relevance of each witness's testimony as that witness was called to appear and would swear each witness separately. Asher had won the first round.

It was left to David, as the complaining party, to begin. He still hadn't acknowledged Asher's existence, nor had the reverse occurred. He had seen Asher give what appeared to be a slight nod and smile to Ellen, but he couldn't see whether she reacted. David had never sensed a tighter atmosphere. In all the highly stressful professional encounters he had experienced, he had never felt more on edge.

David asked to be sworn as a witness. He commenced to tell the story of the relationship Asher had had with Ellen as he understood it. He related what had transpired in Ellen's psychotic break and what she'd told him thereafter about the affair. He also offered in evidence the letter she'd written to him, attempting to explain what had happened. These efforts met with strenuous objections from Unger that all of the evidence offered was hearsay and inadmissible. Dr. Rosen overruled the objection, stating that the strict rules of evidence were not applied in this informal proceeding and that the hearsay character of the evidence was for the panel to weigh. Unger became particularly vehement when David started to testify as to what Dr. Gordon had told him about Ellen's relationship with Asher. Unger raised cries not only of hearsay but of violation of the physician/patient privilege between Gordon and Ellen Hill.

Rosen inquired whether Dr. Gordon would testify. David answered that she would not voluntarily appear, and since he understood that the panel didn't have subpoena power, he had not requested that a subpoena be issued. Rosen then ruled that he would not be permitted to testify as to what Dr. Gordon had said to him about Ellen. Rosen didn't amplify on the reason for the ruling. David speculated that it might reflect more the panel's disapproval of Gordon having supplied him with this information than the obvious hearsay character of the testimony.

When David concluded, Rosen asked whether his wife also would be testifying. Deferring to Ellen's ambivalence about appearing, David looked toward her without answering. Ellen, who had been looking down at her hands folded on the table, raised her head, stared straight at Asher, and nodded affirmatively. It looked as though Asher sagged in his chair.

Unger's opportunity came to question David. She was calm and quiet, in contrast to the death grip approach in her evidentiary objections. She asked simply whether he had ever seen Asher before that morning and whether he had ever personally observed any contact between his wife and Asher. The answer was that he had not. Unger also asked whether it wasn't true that his wife had been in a mental hospital for thirty days and that her story had come out at that time, the implication being that under those circumstances her story was unreliable. David replied that Asher could hardly hide behind Ellen's psychotic break when he had been the cause of it. Unger's motion to strike the answer, yelled across the table, was granted.

Unger concluded her questioning. It was noon, and rather than proceed then with Ellen as the next witness, Rosen directed that all parties return at nine o'clock in the morning.

Ellen had been so cold that morning on entering the society's offices that David wasn't sure whether to approach her. She walked straight out of the suite. He followed her into the hall. "Ellen, can we have lunch?"

"Oh, you want to know what I'm going to say? Or tell me what to say?" Ellen frowned and pursed her lips. Her anger was patent. She could only be blaming him for the fact that she was there.

"No. I thought we could grab a bite together." He smiled. "There's a little coffee shop down the street."

Ellen turned toward the elevator. He followed. They walked down the street in silence. Often, it had been the case that Ellen would take his hand when they walked. She didn't today, nor had she for some time. When it happened in the past, it was warm. Part of him wished that could be their way again.

They sat at a table on the sidewalk under a festive umbrella. She ordered only an oatmeal raisin cookie and coffee. He followed her lead. He wasn't hungry despite his suggestion for lunch. His stomach felt like it was calcified.

"Ellen, I hope you agree I got my facts straight in there."

"As far as you knew them, you did."

As far as you knew them, he thought. *Was that a teaser? To make me wonder what really happened? Wasn't it bad enough the way it was, for Christ's sake?* He didn't respond.

His face must have registered surprise because she added, "I didn't mean that the way it sounded. I meant that what you know, you know only from me and Dr. Gordon. I can't tell you how much I resent her having gone to you about this. Talk about a breach of professional ethics. How could she tell anyone my innermost thoughts, feelings, and, yes, actions? And that, after she fired me."

David had the same thought but hadn't posed the question to Dr. Gordon. He was sure that the doctor had no malicious intent. He felt that under any other circumstances, ones not involving her "brethren" in the profession, she wouldn't have disclosed the confidences. She did because she was so mad about Asher's destructive, unethical conduct, but was she right in telling him? Would he have been happier not to know? No, that would have been the ultimate degradation.

"Anyway, David, there is more. I lived it. That's why I didn't want you present when I testified. I didn't want to hurt you even more."

"Thank you," he replied in a facetious tone.

"But," Ellen added, "I've decided you should be there. I want you to hear my story from me. The worst thing would be for you to think there is more that you don't know."

David swirled the coffee that remained in his cup and looked at her quizzically. A cold sense of fear spread through him. Could he take what he would hear? "Tell me, last night you said I was right about Asher—"

"What?" The lunchtime street traffic was heavy and noisy, forcing them to speak at a level that was uncomfortably loud for such an intimate conversation.

"What did you mean last night when you said I was right about Asher?"

"He is not a good person. Why should I protect him? It's selfish really. There's no grander purpose, like keeping him from doing the same thing to others. I'm not sure that anything we can do, or the psychiatric society can do, will ever stop him. For him, it's all about Elliott, not anybody else."

David thought about affirming her conclusion, but what would that add? He pushed his chair back and went to the register to pay the bill. They walked back to the parking garage and left.

40

Ellen rubbed her palms on her knees. Her hands were uncharacteristically damp. Not just a fitful night, she hadn't slept at all. She'd spent the hours practicing for the umpteenth time the story she would tell on the stand that morning. She had thought a lot too about David, the pressures he was under before an important hearing, how well he always seemed to handle the tension. She had never appreciated that as much before.

She was dressed in a brown wool skirt and jacket, a selection to which she'd given more than passing thought. She knew David had seen her in it before and had liked it. It wasn't all that often that he commented on what she was wearing. She had never worn it in front of Elliott.

Dr. Rosen began, "I believe the next witness is Ellen Fox."

"Before she testifies, Dr. Rosen, my wife has asked that she be permitted simply to tell her story without my questioning her."

"All right. You may proceed, Mrs. Fox."

"Well, first I'd like to confirm my husband's statements about what I said to him concerning Dr. Asher and myself." She could hear her voice quavering and was trying her best to control it. The voice was just a reflection of the shaking that was rocking the rest of her body.

"Objection. She's here. She can testify, not adopt someone else's story." Unger emphasized the word "story" as though to ridicule David's testimony.

"Ms. Unger, again, may I remind you this is an informal proceeding," said Rosen in a deliberate cadence. "We do not follow the rules of evidence. She may proceed as she wishes, and you may ask questions when she concludes. Go ahead, Mrs. Fox."

"Also," she looked directly at Asher, "the letter my husband submitted was written by me, and it is all true." Unger squirmed but didn't interject another objection. Ellen couldn't believe that she had ever been with the person slouching across the table from her. He held no appeal for her. How could she have been such an idiot?

"As to Dr. Gordon, I want to say that I don't approve of her having talked to my husband." She bristled, "I can't believe that is acceptable under the rules of the society."

Rosen moved forward in his chair but then pushed back. "Please go on, Mrs. Fox."

She looked around, her eyes landing last on David, on whom they lingered. He was expressionless. She knew this part was going to be rough. Could she get through it without crying? "Just that Elliott, Dr. Asher, I do feel took terrible advantage of our relationship." She paused, again looking directly at him. "He told me that he loved me and that he wanted us to have a sexual relationship. He didn't tell me he was doing the same thing with other patients as well. I wonder if he also told them what he told me—that it would be helpful to his understanding of the 'efficacy,' I believe was the word he used, of psychiatrist/patient sexual relationships? He said there were many cases where the kind of sensitivity and tenderness that a psychiatrist could provide had a beneficial impact on the patient." She paused and smiled derisively. "It did not with me. I ended up in St. Luke's."

The palm of Unger's right hand hit the table as she said, "I object. There is no evidence that anything my client did had any impact on this witness going to a psychiatric hospital."

"Ms. Unger," Rosen responded impatiently, "she's entitled to her opinion, whether it's supportable or not. If you have evidence that there was no relationship between Dr. Asher's conduct and Mrs. Fox being admitted to the hospital, you can present it." Turning to Ellen, Rosen said, "Anything more, Mrs. Fox?"

Ellen was flustered, exactly the reaction that Unger had undoubtedly hoped for. "No, I don't think so, doctor."

"Thank you. You may ask your questions now, Ms. Unger."

"Ms. Fox, it is true, is it not, that you were a willing participant in the alleged affair with Dr. Asher?" With a sort of flourish, Unger removed her glasses and waved them in her right hand.

"He didn't rape me if that's what you're asking."

"You knew what you were doing and made a conscious decision to have an affair with him, isn't that right?"

Ellen sighed. David had warned her that it would be tough on cross-examination. Why had she come? Had she made a mistake in not letting David represent her? "Looking back, I didn't know what I was doing. I wasn't thinking, but yes, I did go along with it."

"And Dr. Asher told you, didn't he, that he would have to end the professional relationship between the two of you if you were to have sexual contact?"

"Yes, he did."

"And that, in fact, happened, didn't it?"

"Well, he didn't bill me, and I didn't pay him. That was really the only difference."

"Yes and—"

"But," Ellen interrupted, "he did continue to prescribe drugs for me." It looked to her as though Elliott and Unger both jumped in their chairs. David nodded his head up and down knowingly. She was smart enough to understand that the drug thing should be an impediment to Asher's claim that there was no continuing professional relationship.

"And we did continue to have discussions in his office about me, how I was feeling, how I was reacting, my problems, etc."

"And you discussed all the same things about him in your meetings, his problems, his concerns for example, did you not, Ms. Fox?"

"To an extent, yes."

"So, the psychiatrist/patient relationship didn't continue? Or are you saying that you acted as his psychiatrist too?"

"No, of course not. But he had his own problems. He was scared to death of my husband. Not so much that David would hurt him physically, I don't think, but that he would sue him, try to 'ruin him' as Elliott put it. He talked about that fear constantly."

"And what did you say?"

Ellen looked at Asher, who was sitting low in the chair, head tilted down, apparently looking at his lap. "I tried not to discuss it. I knew what we were doing was wrong. It was unfair to my husband, but I didn't seem to have control of what I was doing. Sometimes I felt almost as though I was hypnotized in Elliott's presence. It was weird."

"You're not saying he hypnotized you, are you, Ms. Fox?"

"No, I can't really say that, but I felt hypnotized."

"I have no further questions." Unger closed her leather notebook and placed her pen on the table before her.

Without first permitting David to ask further questions, Dr. Rosen interjected his own. "I have a question or two. Tell us about the medications he prescribed for you, Mrs. Fox."

"All the same medicines I'd been taking all along—antidepression, antianxiety, you know all those things. Zoloft was one, Serequil another."

"This continued after you ceased seeing Dr. Asher as, shall we say, a paying patient?"

"Oh yes."

"And when did it stop?"

"It hasn't." Asher stirred. Unger looked at him. The slap of a file falling to the floor came from somewhere in the room.

"You still have the pills and are taking them?"

"Yes," Ellen replied almost offhandedly.

Rosen turned to Unger and asked if she had further questions.

Unger leaned to her right and held a whispered conversation with her client. "I do," she replied. "Ms. Fox, aren't these medicines based on prescriptions that go back to that time when you were a patient of Dr. Asher's?"

211

"No, not all of them. I know he gave me another prescription for Zoloft after I stopped seeing him professionally."

"Do you have that prescription, Ms. Fox?"

"No. But the pharmacy does."

Unger leaned toward Asher again. "No further questions at this time." Rosen sat up in his chair and said there would be a break before the next witnesses.

David and Ellen talked in a small conference room with a glass wall to the hallway. The other walls had no adornment, not even a cheap poster. He told her that her testimony on the prescriptions was of huge importance to the case. He asked her if she would return. She didn't answer. The last thing she wanted to do was to listen to what the other women would say. What a miserable human being this alleged "healer" was. What huge advantage he had taken of her—and, she supposed, of the others. Why couldn't she have woken up earlier?

41

David dropped by McGarey's office early the next morning, knowing it was likely that he'd be there. "Gates, do you have any time?"

"Are you kidding? I'm waiting for a blow by blow. Let's take a walk and get some fresh air."

This was a role reversal. Normally, McGarey wouldn't get up and leave his office if he could possibly avoid it, and David would opt for exercise in any form. But David asked to pass. He closed the door and sat down.

"How far did you get?"

"Ellen testified. She was effective, even though I could tell she was plenty nervous. Next, the other women testified, in each case outside the presence of the other at Unger's insistence. They were helpful. Meredith Hendricks was nice, sweet, cried a little. You could easily see him taking advantage of her. The other, Alice Fenn, was mad as hell and aggressive, maybe too much so. I mean, it seemed like it would have been pretty hard for Asher to run her around. It was the same basic story. He told them how attractive they were, how desirable, and before long, they were on the couch with him. Nothing really changed after that, except the bills stopped. One of his pitches, unbelievably, was that they could help him contribute to the important body of knowledge on psychiatrist/patient sex that he and his colleague were developing. Christ! I can't believe Ellen fell for that bullshit."

"What about Asher?"

"I haven't gotten to him yet. He won't make eye contact with me. Gates, he's ugly, ugly as hell and old." He stopped, realizing what he'd said, and smiled broadly, "Sorry, not really that old, maybe mid-fifties, but too old for Ellen." He shook his head. "I can't understand it."

"David, he was working on her mind. It didn't make any difference what he looked like. If looks were what it was about, do you think you'd have a lot of competition?"

David ignored the question. "His lawyer is Adelaide Unger. Have you run into her?"

"Haven't had any cases against her, but I recognize the name. A media fiend, right?"

"Yeah and tough as nails. Lots of objections, but the panel isn't listening to them. You know, 'rules of evidence don't apply here,' and 'we'll take it for what it's worth,' etc. But she wasn't really able to break down their stories."

"Good. What's on the schedule now?"

"I assume Unger will call Asher this morning. Monday will be reserved for other witnesses Unger puts on and for my rebuttal."

"How are you going to handle him?"

"I intend to make him squirm, and I pray Ellen comes back to see it." He paused. "Unger's questions imply they won't be challenging that the affair took place. But what worries me is that we've got a kangaroo court here. Asher is friendly with the panel members. Dr. Gordon won't testify. There may be too much to break through." He smiled. "Whatever, I can't wait to cross-examine the son of a bitch."

On arrival at the society's offices, David was relieved to see Ellen. He thought he understood how difficult it must be for her after sitting through Hendricks's and Fenn's testimony. The pattern of Asher's conduct was so clear that she undoubtedly could compare notes with those women exactly. It was important that she was here for Asher's testimony. He would have to meet her accusations head on.

David had been looking at Asher, trying not to blink or avert his eyes. He wanted Asher to feel the pressure, to fear what was coming. He sensed that Asher did and had been trying to direct his attention elsewhere, looking at the door as people had entered, commenting to members of the panel, whispering to Unger.

The hearing started. "Please call your witness, Ms. Unger."

Unger requested that, before beginning with the testimony, Ms. Fenn and Ms. Hendricks, together with their counsel, be excluded from the hearing room again. David's position was that if Dr. Asher would be testifying as to the accusations of the two women, they should be permitted to be present to hear what he had to say. Unger replied that her client did not agree that the two women, not complainants in the proceeding, should have been permitted to testify in the first place; therefore, it was not Unger's intention to answer their testimony here.

Rosen huddled with his fellow panel members, who leaned toward one another whispering, until finally he nodded to each of them as if to confirm their consensus. He announced that the witnesses would be permitted to stay in the hearing room to hear Asher testify.

The beginning of Asher's examination by Unger consisted of a tedious review of his education, history, and experience. There was no doubt that he had all the requisite credentials and had enjoyed a distinguished career. He was a member of the faculty at the university while also engaged in private practice.

Unger then turned the questioning to his professional relationship with Ellen Fox. "Did there come a time that you no longer maintained a professional relationship with Ms. Fox?"

"Yes."

"What occasioned that?" asked Unger.

"Mrs. Fox let it be known that she wished to have an intimate relationship with me." Asher looked up, not at Ellen, as he said this.

Oh here it comes, thought David.

"And?"

"I said, of course, that wasn't possible. The mere existence of that desire made it quite impossible for me to continue as her psychiatrist. We could no longer make any progress with those feelings on her part. I told her that she would have to see someone else." Asher was sitting up straight in his chair, delivering the words with apparent authority.

"How did you feel about that?"

"In part, I was disappointed that I would have to cease as her psychiatrist. Without going into the nature of the problems that she brought to me, which wouldn't be appropriate, we had been making progress. I felt I was being of help to her."

"And then what happened?" asked Unger, asking the question with a tone that made her sound vaguely bored. Her glasses were again being used as a prop in her hand.

"I referred her to another psychiatrist, a female who I thought would be most appropriate for her."

"And who was that?"

"Dr. Gordon. Dr. Gwendolyn Gordon."

"Did you have any further contact with Ms. Fox?"

Asher glanced at Ellen and then looked away. "I didn't see her again for some weeks. But she telephoned me often. She wanted to see me. I explained that I couldn't. She would cry. Then she started turning up at my condominium in the middle of the night, knocking on the door, later banging on it. It was embarrassing." Asher's confident manner in testifying was beginning to feel like a highly practiced presentation.

"Yes?"

"On one occasion, when this was going on at ten at night and I was concerned that she was bothering the neighbors, I opened the door and told her to come in and be quiet. She did."

"Then what happened?"

"She threw herself at me."

"And?"

"And I wasn't able to resist. That was the beginning of the sexual relationship she had wanted. She is a very attractive person. I was not strong enough to continue to resist, I'm afraid."

Two of the members of the panel looked at one another in apparent discomfort.

There it is, thought David, *the admission. But, Jesus—she went after him?*

"Did you meet with her again?"

"Yes."

"Where?"

"At my condominium."

"Ever elsewhere?"

"No."

"What about your office? You have heard her testimony."

"No, never in the office."

"Did you at any time send professional statements for services rendered to her after you ended the relationship?"

"No."

"Did you, after that time, ever issue prescriptions for medication to her?"

"No, I didn't. In fact, I instructed her that she should obtain new prescriptions from Dr. Gordon and not continue on with what I had given her."

"No further questions at this time," said Unger.

David looked at Ellen. Her head was tilted slightly forward. Her long hair hung down masking her face. He couldn't see her expression. He needed time to work through this surprise. He requested a fifteen-minute break before commencing cross-examination. He left the room, rode down in the elevator, and walked out into the sun to gather his thoughts. Asher's story was not at all as he had understood it from Ellen. According to her, he was the aggressor. The lure of the fight with the bastard in that hearing room was fading. He didn't know if he could go on. He should have had McGarey there. But he didn't, and he had to pull himself together. "Be confident. Stand tall," he repeated and repeated to himself as a mantra.

The heat of the sun was comforting. Cars rolled by, horns honked, signals changed from green to yellow to red, people walked by in animated conversation. Everything seemed so normal in the world. Why was his life fucked up?

When he returned to the society's offices, he saw Ellen and Asher standing a few feet apart in the hall outside the glass-walled conference room. They weren't speaking, but they looked tense, maybe even angry, as if words had passed between them. David walked on into the hearing room. He looked back. Ellen was following, her eyes dazed, her head shaking from side to side. He knew what Ellen's answers were to all the questions he planned for Asher, except one—whether their relationship continued? That one he hadn't been able to bring himself to ask her explicitly. On the others, he had no choice but to proceed on the assumption that she had told him the truth and that Asher was lying.

When the hearing resumed, David started his cross-examination of Asher. "Does your, shall I say, personal relationship with Mrs. Fox continue?"

"No."

"When did it end?"

"It was in October of last year. She called my office, hysterical, making no sense at all, and that was the end."

David rose from his chair and stood facing Asher. "Did you inquire about her condition at that time?"

"No."

"Why not?"

"She was no longer my patient." Asher twisted in the chair.

"Were you at all interested in what happened to her?"

"Oh yes."

"But you didn't inquire?"

"Not of her. I did learn somewhere, probably from Dr. Gordon, that she had been admitted to St. Luke's at about that time."

David rose, walked to the wall and then back to his chair, where he rested his hands. "And what did you do about that?"

"Nothing."

"You had been her psychiatrist, but you did nothing?" The edges of David's mouth widened and held as he looked at Asher, underscoring the unmistakable tone of condemnation in his question.

"My position as her psychiatrist had ended."

"And you had been," David hesitated, "her lover?"

"Only after the psychiatric relationship ended."

"Oh yes. But you didn't care enough about her—your former patient, your former lover—to do something about it when you learned she was in a psychiatric hospital?"

Asher crossed his right leg over his left knee and looked down. "There was nothing appropriate for me to do." He could not meet David's eyes. The earlier signs of confidence in delivery were gone.

"Did it ever occur to you that you may have had some responsibility for her being in St. Luke's?" David had assumed that he'd get a frantic objection from Unger to this question, but she didn't move. Apparently the strategy was to let her client fend for himself in the hope that he'd look more credible to the panel.

"Of course not. I helped her greatly."

"Do your regular rounds take you to St. Luke's?"

"They do," answered Asher, displaying evident pride.

"And even though you were there on a regular basis, you didn't stop in to see how she was doing?"

Asher looked at one of the panel members, as if to ask for help.

"Again, it wouldn't have been appropriate. She was no longer my patient. It might have been seen as meddling by Dr. Gordon or whomever."

"Have you ever had a friend at St. Luke's?"

"Yes."

"Whom you've visited?"

"Yes."

"But not Ellen Fox." David bowed his head and smirked. The muffled ring of a phone in an adjacent room interrupted his flow of thought. "Dr. Asher, do you maintain a calendar of office appointments?"

"I do," Asher answered with a note of relief to apparently be through with a line of questioning that had made him squirm.

"Then I would ask you, Ms. Unger, if your client will produce his calendar for this year and last for examination?"

"Why?" asked Unger abruptly.

"The witness has testified that he didn't meet with my wife at his office after their professional relationship ended, that their meetings were at his home. My wife's testimony is to the contrary. His calendar may shed light on that conflict."

"As I'm sure you anticipate, counsel, the answer is no," Unger almost spit. "The calendar would disclose confidential patient-privileged information, specifically the names of patients."

David was prepared for that argument. "I would have no objection if the calendar were inspected by the panel in camera. That should satisfy counsel's concern."

"The term, Mr. Fox? We're not lawyers," said Dr. Rosen.

"I'm sorry, doctor. In camera simply means that you, the panel, review the documents yourselves without anyone else, including me, seeing them. That way the names of other patients are protected from disclosure." David had returned to sit in his chair. His legs ached, a condition that undoubtedly resulted from his habit in tense trial situations of bouncing his legs up and down on the tips of his toes under counsel table. The bouncing he had done in that conference room was probably equivalent to miles of running. It was a bad habit but not a visible one, so he had little incentive to tame it.

"Is that acceptable, Ms. Unger?" asked Dr. Rosen.

"No, the privilege is the privilege." She never conveyed even the slightest sign of softness. "It's not any different because the viewers of the evidence are fellow psychiatrists. It would still violate the privilege."

The ploy was obvious. Since the panel didn't have subpoena power, Unger knew that the production of the calendar could not be forced. Still, the request had been worth the effort. The panel couldn't help but think that Asher had something to hide.

David opened a file on the table in front of him. He turned to another subject. "Dr. Asher, do you maintain files for each of your patients?"

"I do."

David felt that Asher was trying not to look at him. When he asked a question, Asher looked up or away. When Asher answered a question, he looked down at the table in front of him. His eyes strayed upward and at David only on infrequent occasions when he brought his answer to a conclusion.

"Do the files contain information about the diagnosis and course of treatment of the patient?"

"Yes."

"Do you maintain a record in the files of medicines you have prescribed?"

"Yes."

"You have testified that you prescribed no medicines for my wife after the time that your professional relationship terminated, is that right?"

"Correct."

"Ms. Unger, will you produce Dr. Asher's file for my wife so that we can resolve the discrepancy in the testimony on this point? No other patient names would be disclosed since it's her file."

"No, the files are privileged information as you well know."

"Then, again, I would suggest that the file be reviewed only by the panel so that the confidential nature of the information will be protected."

"The answer, Mr. Fox, is the same. No."

"Then, Dr. Asher, I will show you a prescription drug container purporting to contain sixty Zoloft tablets issued on December 1 of last year for my wife under your name. Could you explain that?"

Asher stared at the container, taking off his glasses to read the print. "I don't know. This may be the same pharmacy she used for the same prescription when I was her psychiatrist. It probably was issued by Dr. Gordon, and the pharmacy just continued my name on the label in error."

David leaned over to Ellen and whispered. David then said, "Dr. Rosen, my wife has something to say." Rosen looked at his fellow panel members and at Unger. No one responded.

Ellen began, "I wish to waive the psychiatrist/patient privilege. I am prepared to have my file examined by the panel."

Dr. Rosen looked at Unger and said, "Your position?"

Unger and Asher exchanged glances. She replied coolly, "We'll take that under consideration and get back to you." Asher grimaced as he rubbed the palms of his hands along the sides of his head, patting long strands of hair against his skull.

Since it was then almost one p.m., David suggested an adjournment to the following Monday morning. "That will give counsel and her client adequate opportunity to decide what position they will take as to my wife's file and to reconsider making the calendar available, again for review by the panel only."

Rosen seemed relieved. "We will adjourn until Monday morning, nine a.m. Thank you."

David packed his files into his briefcase. Usually, his cases were heavily document-oriented, and he needed multiple litigation briefcases and a cart to move them. Not in this case. The few documents that were there rattled around in his litigation bag. People were leaving the room. Ellen continued to sit.

David asked if she wanted to leave with him. She didn't answer but rose and started to walk out of the room. David followed her. She didn't speak to anyone as she left the suite. She passed right by Fenn and Hendricks without even acknowledging their existence.

They rode down alone in the elevator to the parking garage. David asked, "Will you be here Monday?"

"I don't know. Maybe since I've come this far, I ought to see it to a conclusion. But it's not easy."

The elevator door opened. "I understand. Not for either of us."

She looked at him as if to say something but then turned and walked toward her car. He looked after her. He had always loved that walk. He didn't know anymore what he thought. This whole thing was all so unnecessary in one sense. Yet it didn't seem like he could help himself. He saw Asher, and it was like he went blind. The bastard, the fucking bastard. He had to have him. But it hurt so much. He knew it hurt Ellen. It couldn't help but erode whatever chances they might have together. Why was he putting them through this?

42

David ran into Ellen on Monday morning down the street from the society's offices. He'd arrived early to review some papers, and she was making a stop at a nearby bank. She had called him Sunday morning, leaving a message that she was in Colorado Springs at the Broadmoor, where she'd gone to get "a little space." The call had come in while he was at the drugstore finding remedies for a bout with the stomach flu.

He told her that he'd returned the call and was sorry they hadn't made contact. She said not to worry, that the question had passed, so she hadn't called him back. It didn't look to him like Ellen had gotten any R & R over the weekend. She seemed tired and distracted. Of course, what must he look like after spending the weekend hugging the toilet? He noticed that she was wearing the same conservative brown suit she had worn on the two previous days. *Why?* he wondered. It wasn't her style not to have changed outfits.

Unger was the only one present when David entered the conference room. She was sitting at the table in her usual spot, looking through files. *Good,* David thought, *she's brought Ellen's file and the calendar.* He said, "Good morning." She said nothing, but nodded a silent acknowledgment. She was one of the more unpleasant adversaries David had met in the practice over the years. She featured a gruff exterior, unfriendly, with zero femininity.

After meeting Unger in the hearing room on the first day, he had done some investigation, which had confirmed his impression that she had a high-profile practice. She was sometimes on television and radio and in the papers, playing her cases and causes in the press. Usually, her clients were females pursuing sex discrimination and sexual harassment claims against company executives. It had been a surprise to find her representing an errant male psychiatrist charged with bedding a female patient. Why would she have taken such a case, particularly one involving a nonpublic proceeding that wouldn't offer the type of publicity opportunities on which she thrived? The answer must be that she was waiting for the court litigation to get underway. That would present a feeding frenzy for the media with a prominent psychiatrist maintaining sexual alliances with multiple patients in clear violation of the ethical standards of his profession. It was hard to imagine that she really sympathized with his position given her traditional gender representation.

David asked, "Did you bring the calendar and the file?"

Unger looked up again and said simply, "No."

Okay, so they're going to fight. The inference he would urge the panel to draw based on that refusal was obvious—that the calendar and file weren't being produced because they would support Ellen's credibility and undermine Asher's.

Others entered the room. Alice Fenn and Meredith Hendricks came in with their lawyers and took their seats. The panel sat down. Ellen arrived seconds before the appointed hour. Asher had not arrived. They waited for a few minutes, and then Dr. Rosen turned to Unger and said, "We're ready to begin. Do you expect Dr. Asher shortly?"

Unger looked up, removed her glasses, and answered, "No." Her second statement of the morning—both one word negatives.

"His cross-examination was to be continued this morning at nine o'clock," said Rosen. Looking at his watch, and with a tone of mild exasperation, he added, "It's after nine."

"Dr. Asher is dead. He died over the weekend." Her words were like a tsunami, sucking the air out of the room. No one moved. "His body was found yesterday afternoon." Unger's eyes traveled the length of the table, surveying the witnesses and their lawyers. "He died of a gunshot wound. The authorities do not believe the wound was self-inflicted. They will be conducting an investigation."

David looked at Ellen. She emitted an almost noiseless "oh" and averted her eyes from him. Meredith gasped and rested her head on her arms on the table. Alice's eyes looked as though they were extending outside their sockets. No one spoke. Dr. Rosen began to converse with his fellow panel members in hushed tones. Finally, he said, "Obviously, this is shocking news. It would appear that there is no need for this proceeding to continue under the circumstances. The only question was Dr. Asher's continuing membership in the society. That, of course, is no longer an issue."

David moved the files on the table in front of him, playing for even the briefest amount of time as he considered how to respond to Dr. Rosen's statement. He knew he needed to be cool, to show no emotion. It couldn't end this way. There needed to be a conclusion. It would be a long shot. "Dr. Rosen, may I respectfully suggest that some action be taken by the panel based on the evidence you do have. I recognize that the record is not complete because Dr. Asher's testimony was not concluded, but the case shouldn't be permitted to evaporate as far as the society is concerned and be a blight on its high standards."

"It isn't just a question," interrupted Unger, "of Dr. Asher not having been able to complete his testimony. What about the witnesses we would have called? There is nothing Dr. Asher would have more sincerely wanted than vindication by the society of these scurrilous charges." *She might as well be preening to the television cameras*, thought David. "But an incomplete record is an incomplete record, and no conclusions can be drawn from it. That's elementary. Mr. Fox's complaint must be dismissed." Unger finished with a wave of the hand as if she were tossing the complaint away.

"The proceeding will stand adjourned," said Rosen. "We will advise you, Mr. Fox, and you, Ms. Unger, of our disposition. Our thanks to all of you for your time and attention. Without implying any conclusions from the evidence presented, we want to express how sorry we are for the complainant, the witnesses, and their families for any injuries they may have suffered. The society supports the highest ethical standards for its members." Rosen closed his file and started to stand when he added, "And we want to express our sorrow for the death of our colleague." Rosen stood for a moment, head bowed, and, with the panel members, exited the room. The others remained seated until the doctors had left.

David and Ellen walked through the society's offices together, again without speaking. He could hear excited whispering between Alice Fenn and her lawyer, but no words were audible. Meredith Hendricks appeared to have tears building in her eyes as she removed a cell phone from her purse. For a moment, David wondered if there would be cameras and reporters on the street. But of course not, he reminded himself, they don't even know that this proceeding is in motion—supposedly.

As they exited the elevator in the parking structure, Ellen said, "David, you said this would all be private. Is that still true?"

Ellen appeared to David to be surprisingly calm in the face of such shocking news. Could he have been wrong all along in thinking there might have been some continuing relationship with Asher? "It shouldn't change that."

"But they'll start asking questions. Won't they turn up the fact that the proceeding was under way and then they'll want to know all about it?"

"Who is 'they'?"

"The police. And once they get it, so will reporters."

"I don't know. You're too far ahead of me. I'll have to think it out. Needless to say, neither one of us will talk to the press. God knows about the others."

"You understand why I need to know?"

"Yes," he responded, knowing of course that her reference was to Stephen Hill.

"David, maybe, just maybe, this can all go away now. Be over finally." She reached for his coat lapel. "Do you think?"

43

David arrived at his office early Wednesday morning after picking up a steaming latte and a cold bran muffin at the Starbucks across the street. He never could quite understand how a company that knew so well how to present hot brewed coffee could deliver its baked goods in stone-cold condition. What did they have against microwave ovens?

Arriving at the office at seven o'clock assured him of at least an hour, maybe an hour and a half, of relatively uninterrupted time at his desk. He was far behind in his work after all the time spent on the Asher case, and he hardly knew where to turn. He looked at his e-mail, which he hadn't taken the time to scan on the BlackBerry before leaving home. There were twenty-two messages, many of which were routine firm memos that he would save for another time. Numerous messages were from clients. Even a relatively young lawyer in David's position could remember when clients didn't expect the instant access that e-mail now afforded. It didn't matter anymore where you were or what the hour was. No longer was there the luxury of time for thought before a preliminary response was expected.

What piqued David's interest was an e-mail which read simply: "David—I have information about our case that I think will interest you. Please contact me. Chet." David had not talked with Chet Deaver since the hearing concluded. David replied, immediately suggesting he come to the office for lunch.

David's attempts to concentrate on the tasks that had brought him to the office early were not effective. He could respond to e-mails, return calls to answering machines, which were to be expected at that hour, read a letter or memo here or there. But his mind kept jumping back to Deaver, and therefore to Ellen and to Asher. What did Deaver have now?

Again, the PI was dressed more formally than the lawyers they passed walking down the hall to David's office. David asked what Deaver would like for lunch and then called Amy with the order. Files neatly arranged in stacks on a small table by the window were pushed to the side to make room for the two to sit down.

"What's the information, Chet?"

"It's about Asher. The society proceeding is academic now as I understand it."

"The panel implied as much," replied David with a scowl, "but hasn't ruled yet. I suspect, though, that they'll be happy to have a way out of making a decision."

"I have contacts in the police department," Deaver said, "with information on their approach to the investigation."

"I thought it might be something like that."

"Asher was apparently elk hunting in the Indian Peaks Wilderness. A bullet entered his left back below the shoulder, passed through the aorta, and exited the body. The bullet was found lodged in the trunk of a spruce tree a few feet away. The bullet casing was on the ground nearby. There was no weapon found at the scene other than Asher's own hunting rifle. There's a test that's done with a binocular microscope to see if a bullet or a casing has come from a particular rifle. They've determined this much…they were not from his rifle."

"You're saying that it couldn't have been a suicide?"

"Right. Or, obviously, not an accident with his own rifle."

"Was he with anybody?"

"If he was, the police aren't letting on whom. He apparently was out there frequently on weekends in elk season. Whether he normally hunted with other people, I don't know."

"Who do they think did it?"

"They don't know." Deaver raised his eyebrows in an exaggerated manner and lowered his voice. "David, you're on the suspect list."

"Me?" David stopped and then continued, "Because I filed a complaint against the asshole to remove him from the psychiatric society? Come on."

There was a knock at the door. David walked over to open it. It was an office messenger carrying a tray with sandwiches, chips, and bottled drinks. David told him, somewhat brusquely, to put the tray on the table. Without so much as a thanks, he closed the door behind the retreating messenger.

"It's not an exclusive list," said Deaver. "You might say the case is virtually teeming with suspects."

"Who?"

"Besides you and Ellen—"

"Ellen?" David threw his head back. "She couldn't kill a thing."

"Then," Deaver continued, "there's Meredith Hendricks, and her husband, both of them, and Alice Fenn. There are others too, some of whom I'd heard of, but a couple not. There are any number of people who might have been interested in seeing him dead."

Deaver unwrapped his brisket on rye and took a bite, while David paid no attention to his lunch.

"How did the police find out about my complaint? It was supposed to be a private proceeding."

"Well, these things have a way of getting out. Look at all the people who knew about it."

"What's their timetable? When do you suppose they'll contact me?"

"The investigation will move right along. It's an important case. I assume you'll have counsel present in the interview."

"I don't need counsel. I've got nothing to hide." David bypassed the sandwich and started nervously digging into a bag of chips. The spicy smell that pervaded the room thanks to Deaver was not an aid to his appetite.

"Well, think about it. These things have a way of taking strange twists and turns, but I don't need to lecture you about lawyers, do I?"

"Thanks for the heads up. I sure as hell wouldn't have wanted them showing up here out of the blue. It's funny. Asher reaches out, even in death, to fuck up my life."

44

There was no way he was going to have them come to the office. What if they were in uniform? He had the feeling that everyone at work watched him anyway. Imagine if there were police swarming around. He didn't want people to know about Asher's intrusion into his life, certainly not to have reason to associate him with Asher's death. Only his college friend, George Jenkins, and McGarey knew anything, and it was safe with them. The other option was to ask the police not to come to the office in uniform, but that would show vulnerability. Anyway, investigators have a look about them, and someone would end up being suspicious even if they weren't uniformed.

Instead, the interview was arranged for the house. He made coffee and had mugs, sugar, and cream on the breakfast room table. Ellen would have used cups and saucers, but these were, after all, police. He emptied the dishwasher of probably a week's worth of dishes to make room for some that had piled up in the sink. He wasn't around all that much, and when he was, the fare was light. There were never visitors at Race Street anymore.

He was nervous about uniforms, even here. If they did come decked out in black uniforms with pistols and cuffs, it would set the neighbors talking. They had talked, he knew, when Ellen was carted off in an ambulance and then when Ellen moved out, leaving him in an empty house.

Sitting atop the table was an article from the prior day's edition of the *Denver Post*. Headlined "Death of Psychiatrist Investigated," the article reported that Dr. Elliott Asher, a noted psychiatrist, had died of a gunshot wound in what appeared to be a hunting accident and that the death was under investigation.

The doorbell rang. David placed the article in a drawer and went to the front door. A man and a woman, both in street clothes, introduced themselves. He guided them into the breakfast room. They didn't want coffee. They sat down and exchanged comments about the beautiful sunny morning and the misfortune that they all had to be inside, rather than out in the fresh morning air.

David asked for their cards. They also displayed their badges. Donovan was an African American, about fifty, with grey hair against a dark complexion. He was striking. Hull couldn't have been more opposite. Apart from their gender and racial differences, she was in her late twenties or early thirties, of medium height, and quite thin. She hardly looked as though she was physically capable of handling the requirements of a police officer in an emergency.

Lieutenant Donovan started, saying, as he had on the phone the day before, that they were there to meet with David in connection with their investigation of the death of Elliott Asher. "You knew him?"

"In a way," answered David.

"For how long?"

"One week."

"What occasioned your meeting him?"

"He'd been my wife's psychiatrist."

As Donovan asked the questions, he looked down at a spiral notebook that rested half on the table in front of him and half on his lap. The page contained notes in handwriting. David wasn't able to decipher anything from his vantage point. Hull, Donovan's sidekick, wrote in an identical spiral notebook. She smiled slightly whenever David's glance turned toward her.

"How long had he been?"

Not wanting to get into the ins and outs of how long he had technically remained her psychiatrist, David answered, "Nine months, a year, I don't know."

"And you just met him a week ago?"

"That's right."

"How did you meet him?"

David questioned how much he could or should divulge about the psychiatric society hearing. Even though it was a private proceeding, he was talking to the police. He didn't want to risk an obstruction of justice charge by being anything less than truthful. "There was a hearing before a professional society where we were both present, and I met him then."

"Who introduced you?"

"We weren't introduced exactly."

Donovan sighed. "Well then, how did you meet?"

"Let's cut to the chase, Lieutenant Donovan. Do you know about the Colorado Psychiatric Society hearing where we met?"

"A little bit, yes."

"Then, I would ask, how? It was a private proceeding, not open to the public. How is it that you know anything about it?"

At this point, Lieutenant Hull interjected, "We're not free to give you that information, Mr. Fox. There are people who've talked to us on a confidential basis, and we have to respect that."

Thinking that they probably knew quite a bit about the hearing, David decided that it would look better for him to be more forthcoming and not make them drag each little detail out of him piece by piece. "There wasn't exactly an introduction, but I knew who he was and he knew who I was."

"How was that?"

"Because his attorney introduced him to the assembled group at the commencement of the hearing, and I introduced myself in the same way."

"Did you shake hands?"

A chill ran through David to think of the prospect. "We did not."

"Did you talk to each other?"

"No, not in the conventional sense. But I did ask him questions on cross-examination, and he answered the questions."

"Mr. Fox, this hearing was last week, right?"

"Yes. It was adjourned Friday afternoon to recommence on Monday morning."

"What was scheduled for Monday morning?" asked Donovan.

"My cross-examination of Dr. Asher was to continue."

"Did you see Asher after the close of the hearing Friday afternoon?"

"No."

"Did you talk with him by phone?"

"I did not." Coincidentally, the phone rang in the den. David considered getting up to answer it, but decided to let the caller leave a message.

"Do you know anyone who did see him or talk with him?"

"Like who?"

"Like your wife for example?"

"I don't know. I have no reason to think that. I heard she was at the Broadmoor. But you'd have to ask her. We're separated."

"Yes, we know."

"Can you tell us what you did over the weekend, Mr. Fox?"

"Not anything very exciting. I was exhausted from the week. On Saturday, I came down with the stomach flu. Other than a trip to the drugstore, I spent the entire weekend right here nursing the problem."

"Yeah," Lieutenant Donovan said, pushing his bottom lip down and out. "Was anyone with you?"

"Unfortunately, no." Immediately realizing how that might be taken, David grinned and added, "I'm afraid I wasn't very desirable under the circumstances."

"Mr. Fox, you filed a complaint against Dr. Asher, which is what the hearing was about, right?"

"That's true."

"What was the nature of the complaint?"

"He had been fucking my wife if you want to know the truth." He turned toward Hull, "Excuse me, Lieutenant."

"No problem. In this line of work, it isn't the first time I've heard the word," she answered, deadpan.

David continued, "He'd been my wife's psychiatrist and ended up having an affair with her. That's completely against the ethical standards of the Colorado Psychiatric Society, and I was attempting to have his membership revoked for violation of those standards."

Donovan cleared his throat. "You can understand why we're talking with you, Mr. Fox?"

"Well, you're barking up the wrong tree. Hate the bastard, yes. Shoot him, no."

"We're making no accusation. We're simply trying to find out the facts."

"Then you should know that there are a lot of other people who weren't terribly fond of dear Dr. Asher either, but that doesn't mean that there were a handful of killers running all over the countryside looking for him."

"As a reassurance to you, we are talking to others as well."

"Does that include my wife?"

"Yes." Donovan continued, "We're not at liberty to discuss the details, but the circumstances pretty much rule out either suicide or accidental death. By the way, do you hunt?"

"For elk, but rarely."

"When did you last go out?"

"A couple of years ago."

"Do you have a rifle?"

"Sure."

"May we see it please?"

David hesitated. "I'll get it. As I said, it's been a while since I used it."

He left the room and climbed the stairs to the bedroom. He opened the door to his closet and stepped to a smaller door at the back of the closet accessed by a brass knob. He pulled on the knob, entered, and turned on the light. The closet smelled dry and musty, likely reflecting the mice droppings he saw on the wooden floor. His rifle, which normally rested in a leather case on a shelf across from the door, wasn't there.

He returned to the breakfast room and said, "It isn't where I used to keep it. I'm not sure where it is. I must have loaned it to someone."

"Does anybody else have access to it?"

"Anybody in the house would, I guess. But no one else has used it. With the exception of my wife, who has borrowed it a few times in the past."

"When did she last use it?"

"I'm not sure. A long time ago. She didn't hunt. She'd sometimes take it as protection when she went hiking or mushroom hunting in the backcountry."

"Protection? From what?"

"Bears, mountain lions." The sudden realization that Ellen might be viewed as having access to the rifle and having used it that weekend caused David's stomach to flip. *But no,* he thought with relief, *she was at the Springs. The Indian Peak Wilderness, where Asher was found, wasn't anywhere close.*

Hull asked, "What kind of rifle is it, Mr. Fox?"

"It's a Winchester. I don't really remember the details about it. It belonged to my uncle, and he left it to me when he died."

"When you locate it, will you call us?"

"Yes."

"We may have other questions as we get into this, Mr. Fox," said Donovan. He rose from his chair and shoved his notebook into his jacket pocket.

"You can call me anytime," David replied. He escorted them to the door.

45

David and McGarey went to the Palace Arms for a drink after work one night, the setting for their occasional outings when they wanted a change of scene from the office. McGarey asked whether the police had resurfaced after the interview the week before. They hadn't. David didn't bother to report that he hadn't located the missing rifle. He was obsessed with the thought that Ellen could possibly have been involved in Asher's death. Why was it that he couldn't discuss this, his greatest worry, with his closest confidant?

"I've never understood why you didn't follow my advice and have counsel when you talked to the police," McGarey said not for the first time.

"Gates, I told you my feeling that if I were to waltz in with some hotshot criminal lawyer, it would look like I had something to hide, so I didn't."

"I know, but why should you care what the hell they think?"

"You're probably the last guy who'd have brought someone along." Grinning, he added, "You would have just blasted in and given them a piece of your mind about what an asshole Asher was."

McGarey laughed. "You're right, but Ellen's was really a different case."

"I tried to get her to hire someone with criminal law expertise, but she wouldn't hear of it." David was not more specific about the conversation with Ellen, but he remembered it vividly.

"Ellen, don't you think you should have a lawyer when you meet with the police?"

"So you think I did it. Is that it?"

"No."

"Did you use one, David?"

"No, but I think I'm a little better equipped to handle this kind of thing than you are, you know, given my training. I'd be willing to pay for it."

She looked at him for a long time and then said, "I can take care of myself."

"Ellen, the Winchester hunting rifle is missing. Do you have it?"

"No."

David searched her facial expression for a clue. Was she telling the truth? He couldn't read her. "Did someone borrow it?"

"Not that I know of."

"Do you have any idea where it is?"

"No, and I don't want to talk about this whole subject anymore."

"What she finally did, I don't know, Gates."

McGarey moved his martini glass from side to side. "I gather there's no repair activity underway in the Fox family?"

"Are you kidding? None. She's in another place. She's secretive about what she does, who she sees. The only good thing is that she seems to be together emotionally. I don't have the feeling that she is on the verge of another visit to St. Luke's, thank God."

"What do you know about the investigation?"

"I have a good source of information from the inside," David answered. "I'm sworn to secrecy, but the police talked to seven people. All were patients or former patients and/or their husbands. They had plenty of suspects." As he spoke, David wondered once again, how Deaver got this information. *Legally? Hell, is it my worry how he gets it?* The answer, he knew, was that it was.

"Then you're not alone on the suspect list."

"Hardly. The problem isn't finding motive. Lots of people had that. The issue is that no one has been identified as being at the scene, so there are no witnesses. There's no DNA material. There's no weapon. They scoured the place, every inch of it. They found the bullet and casing, but not what it came out of. Now it's impossible to continue the search with a blanket of snow on the ground."

David continued, "You want to know how this makes me feel?" The bar was crowded and noisy with people celebrating the end of another day. He dropped his voice and leaned forward. "Part of me says good riddance. You can understand that?"

McGarey tipped his glass to David's, nodding his head.

"But part of me wishes it never happened." David's voice now rose to challenge the din. "If I could replay it, would I still file? As it turned out, I got nothing. With the panel's dismissal because the hearing couldn't be finished, the whole thing is as if he were never charged. Intellectually, I understand it. But at the same time, I hate it. Basically, he got away scot-free."

"With the exception that he's dead."

"Well, yes," David shrugged, "with that exception, but he's not here to suffer. I wanted him to suffer. It's that simple."

"Pretty understandable. The guy ruined your marriage. But this police investigation could drag on forever. It may never be closed. They might not find anything more to move on, or they might. My advice?"

"What?"

"Move on with your life."

David smiled briefly. "Thanks, Dad. I know." He sipped his mojito. He loved that drink. "But I'm finding execution on that idea to be pretty daunting."

The focus of discussion changed to their former favorite subject, Jim Ramsey. Former because he seemed to have disappeared from the scene in which he had occupied such a significant space. He had plenty of troubles. He was still a named defendant in the Grathway Corp. shareholder suit and was under investigation for securities fraud. The latest development was that he'd been indicted for tax fraud for failure to report the ten-million-dollar finder's fee. His former partners at Hill & Devon had sued him for fraud as well for not having shared the payment with them.

As for Ted Goldstein's libel suit against Ramsey, it was rocking along with depositions being taken. Goldstein reported to David regularly on developments. The most interesting report was how Ramsey had squirmed when he was forced to admit that a sexual harassment charge had been filed against him by a female partner and settled quietly. Goldstein was adamant that there would be no settlement in his case; he wanted a final resolution and vindication from the court.

To some extent, David and McGarey could only speculate about what was going on with Ramsey. Even though the speculation was appetizing, some of the spice had been removed for them. There was no longer any plotting to be done. Thanks to Ramsey, the unprincipled but smooth-talking suit, Hill & Devon was no more. Sperry was now one of the ascendant firms in the city. The satisfaction they took from that was something the two of them, unfortunately, could only really talk about together. Their elation would be viewed as bad taste, involving as it did, the death throes of a once-great law firm and the fall of its leader. What they really wanted to do was to scream it to the tops of Denver's high-rise office buildings.

46

There were no developments in connection with the Asher investigation until the next spring when McGarey received a call from David asking him to come to his office right away. McGarey knew from David's voice and the request that he come downstairs that it was important. He dropped what he was doing and took the elevator down one flight. He knocked. David opened the door, gestured him in, and closed the door quietly.

"Gates, these are two officers from the Denver Police Department." David walked to his desk chair and sat down. He was pale. There was a slight tremor in his arms and hands. His voice broke slightly. "They are taking me into custody in connection with the death of Elliott Asher. I want you to represent me."

Girard Donovan and Loretta Hull stood and showed McGarey their identification. They were not in uniform. McGarey, not indicating that he had any prior knowledge of the death, asked why they were taking David into custody. The officers proceeded to relate the circumstances surrounding Asher's death the preceding fall. At the time of the death, the investigation turned up only a bullet and a bullet casing. The autopsy had determined that the bullet went through the decedent's aorta. There had been no other evidence. Then, with the spring thaw,

241

a hiker found a rifle at the base of a large, old blue spruce that had recently split just above the ground and been uprooted. The tree was fifty feet from the location of the body. The stock of the rifle was found sticking up out of a hole at the base of the trunk, apparently having been forced out when the tree uprooted.

The rifle was a .270 Winchester. Binocular microscope tests showed that the rifling on the weapon was a match for the evidence that was found at the scene. From the serial number on the gun, it was traced through the manufacturer to the dealer, whose records showed that it was sold to a Chester Fox some years ago. Donovan explained that David had not been able to locate his rifle when they met at his house, but had said that he had a Winchester that he'd inherited from an uncle. This development explained why they came back to David. Hull added that Chester Fox was being traced as they spoke.

McGarey asked for a minute with his client before they left. He opened the door to let Donovan and Hull step out. Amy, David's assistant, sat at a cubicle across from his office, talking with another woman. They both looked at McGarey as the door opened. Amy appeared surprised. McGarey seldom came to David's office; it was always the reverse. And there were the two strangers.

McGarey closed the door and turned. "Jesus Christ, David. You never told me about the rifle being missing."

"Gates, believe me. I didn't do it. I want you to call Ellen and tell her what's happened. I see you looking at me. Yes, I'm trembling, but not for myself. My worst fear may be coming true. Ellen shot him. She borrowed my rifle and shot the fucker."

"Who is Chester Fox?"

"My uncle."

"Shit." McGarey paused. "Don't say anything until I've talked to Ellen." He shook his head and then opened the door to invite the two officers back in. He told them that Mr. Fox would not be answering any questions at that time. The officers agreed that handcuffs would not be used. The four left the office for the police station. Amy was wide-eyed as they walked by her without speaking.

47

It was ten p.m., late for her phone to ring. She picked it up.

"Ellen, it's Gates. Sorry to bother you at this hour."

Ellen hadn't talked with Gates McGarey for months, at least since she and David separated. He was maybe the last person she expected, or wanted, to hear from. "Yes?"

"I'm afraid it's bad news. The police have taken David into custody."

"What? David?"

"Yes."

"Why?"

"For the murder of Elliott Asher."

"What are you talking about?" The phone half slipped from her hand.

"David called me to be present when the police came for him. Seems that a rifle just turned up in the vicinity of where Asher's body was found. They traced the bullet to the rifle and the rifle to David, or actually, to his uncle."

Ellen couldn't respond. She moved to the edge of the bed, her hand gripping the phone, her head almost at her knees. She whispered into the receiver, "No. God. No. God."

"Ellen, are you alright? Would you like me to come over?"

"No." A long period elapsed. "I'm okay. It's just such a shock. David, in jail? He's the most centered guy in the entire world."

"I'm getting him the best criminal lawyer in town. I'm sure he'll be out on bail in no time."

"It's impossible. It can't be David," Ellen said, her voice rising. "What's the evidence? I mean, surely they have to have something more than a rifle that matches a bullet."

"That's why we need the right lawyers. I imagine you'll be getting a visit from the police as well. You know, Ellen, you should have counsel. I'd be happy to help find someone."

"Let me think about it, Gates. I appreciate it." She hung up the phone.

The earliest light was beginning to filter through the windows of her bedroom. The room was spacious for a condominium, at least its closets and bathroom were, but she had never felt any comfort here. It was her retreat after she and David had split. Like the space itself, the furniture was leased. Her possessions were still in residence on Race Street. She missed them. She had thought that the move would be temporary. David would want to put it back together. But as the months slipped by, that hope had begun to fade. David didn't seem to want a quick reconciliation. She realized more with each day what a fool she had been. Asher meant nothing to her by comparison to David. David was everything. But she hadn't been able to remove Asher from her life.

She had always known it could come to this. That she might end up being implicated in Asher's death. She had in her mind a plan of action should that happen. But she had never thought David would become involved. She couldn't permit it. She had borrowed his rifle. He wasn't there. She could go to the police and get them off David's back. But the public spectacle of a murder trial would be too much for her grandfather, if not for her. She would have to leave. Someday, she could come back and face it. Not now.

She lay tormented through much of the night, eliminating, adding, substituting words. What she would say to the police, to David, to

Granddad. She moved to the desk, turned on the light, and began to scratch out the words.

Dear David,

I will be leaving. You won't be able to find me. I will not put Granddad through a long-drawn-out and very publicly embarrassing trial, which is inevitable if I stay. I am giving the enclosed letter to Gates. I think it will protect you. That's all I want—desperately. What is happening to you is unfair. It's all due to my weaknesses and fears. You don't deserve it. I love you. Ellen.

She looked at the words. Usually, the first words were not good enough. Here they seemed right. She took another piece of paper and started, "To Whom It May Concern." She labored until the light was pouring in the room. She revised and revised, playing carefully with the words she chose. She would have both letters delivered to Gates.

She then started to pull together her things. She had thought it out so many times she knew exactly what was necessary and what wasn't. There wouldn't be room for much of her life. She took what she needed from a small safe hidden in the middle drawer of her dresser. She'd decided and wouldn't look back. She wasn't scared, but felt alone, isolated. Would that feeling mark the rest of her life, she wondered.

She dressed in cotton pants and a blouse, with a lightweight cotton sweater. Casual, unobtrusive, just another traveler. She wouldn't need warm clothes, so they could be left behind. She rolled two suitcases to the door and looked back into the living room. *Just as well*, she thought. David had had no life there with her. In fact, he'd never entered the place. Nor had much of anyone else except neighbors and a couple of close friends.

She shut the door and walked out to the street, pulling her roller boards behind her around the corner to the Guest Suites Hotel, where she found a cab. She directed the driver to her bank and then on to the Denver International Airport, American Airlines. She felt surprisingly upbeat. Was it that she had known all along that this is what she would do and so was relieved to be doing it? She had read about people who decided on suicide and turned upbeat simply because they had made a decision. Here there was no longer the decision to wrestle with. Just the execution. And that was what she was doing.

48

That afternoon, McGarey met with David at the jail. They were permitted to use a small room, occupied only by the police standard-issue steel table and two chairs.

McGarey began, "I reached Ellen last night and told her what had happened. She was distraught to say the least. She sounded shocked. I offered to go and see her, but she said no. She didn't say whether she'd done it. Just kept repeating that it wasn't fair to you. Then I received these notes from her by messenger this morning." McGarey handed him two envelopes, one opened and addressed "To Whom It May Concern," the other unopened and addressed "David."

David turned first to the envelope addressed to him, opened, and read it. He stared at the paper, looked up at McGarey, and then opened the second envelope.

My husband David Fox is being held in connection with the death of Dr. Elliott Asher. I am writing this letter to state that he had nothing to do with Dr. Asher's death. I was present when he died. My husband was not. My hunting rifle discharged accidentally, and Elliott was hit by the bullet in the back left shoulder.

David felt as if he were whirling, positioned horizontally, legs out-stretched and turning in a circular motion. He'd feared that she had done it, but to see it in black and white in her hand was such a stark reality. He couldn't permit himself even to think of it. He said nothing to McGarey, who sat there looking uncomfortable.

> I am very sorry, but it was not my fault. I tried, but I couldn't do anything for him. His death seemed almost instant. I panicked, hid the rifle, and left. The rifle belongs to my husband, but I used it on this occasion without his knowledge.

David tried to grasp what he had read. An accident? Who will believe that? He was conflicted. Maybe she went hunting in order to pull off exactly what occurred. Instead of wanting to be with the bas-tard, she hated him enough to see him dead. But maybe the meeting was her last reach out to him, and it *was* an accident. Would he ever know? Did he want to know?

"If it was an accident, why hide the rifle?" asked McGarey. He was somber, his usual playful look nowhere in sight.

David sighed. "And what about not reporting it if it was an acci-dent? It doesn't figure."

"No."

"Have you given the note to the police?" David asked.

"That's the next step."

"They'll arrest her."

"If they can find her."

David looked at him quizzically. "What do you mean?"

"I've tried to find her. I can't. She's not at her condo. Can't be reached by phone." He paused. "David, she may have run."

David was stunned by the suggestion. Ellen? A feeling of relief for himself was quickly counterbalanced by despair for her. His head sank to the cold metal table.

49

On his release from jail, David started trying to locate Ellen. He made calls to some of her close friends, but they fired back with so many questions that he couldn't or wouldn't answer that he was discouraged from continuing. He thought briefly of calling members of her family. He didn't know how much they knew from her about the circumstances of their separation. He feared their questions. He was sure they wouldn't be open-minded on the subject. There had been too much ill will engendered from the law firm fight to think that they could possibly be approachable. No, it was better not to open that door.

The obvious choice was to hire Chet Deaver to see what he could find out. It turned out to be little. Ellen had left from Denver International Airport on an American Airlines flight to Miami early in the day on which he was released from jail. The trail ended there. She could still be in Miami. She might have left the country with a false passport. From Miami, she had easy access to the entire Caribbean and all of Central and South America, lots of spots that could provide more or less anonymous shelter from the authorities. He found that she had withdrawn nine thousand dollars cash from their joint checking account. The amount was selected probably because it was just below the ten thousand dollars that requires special reporting by the bank.

David's efforts continued for almost two months with no word as to her whereabouts when he checked his voice mail on arriving one morning at the office. There was a message from Ellen on the machine.

"David. It's four in the morning your time, the way I figure it. Surprised you're not there. No. Needless to say, I didn't expect you to answer. I just wanted to leave a message that I'm okay. I'm a long ways away. I've gotten a job of sorts and have a small, very small, apartment. A bit different than Race Street, but it's cozy. I do miss you and wonder how you're doing. And I wonder about Granddad and how he's doing, but I don't suppose you would know. Despite all that's happened, is it possible for you to call and tell him that you've received a message from me? That I'm fine and love him very, very much? There are many things about this I hate. Missing the two of you is at the top of the list. I'm worried that Granddad's getting so old and needy for companionship, for TLC, for some of the things that I, you know, I could do for him. You won't be able to find me. Don't try. When I'm ready to come back, I will. I can't right now. Take care. I hope you're well."

David sat back and hit the message button again—and again. He lingered on her voice. It was lower and more deliberate, but it was Ellen. She sounded a bit depressed but not unhappy really. He wondered whether there was some way the call could be traced, whether he needed to advise the police. He made a mental note to check. He didn't erase the message.

David hadn't talked with Stephen Hill in a long time. Ellen's grandfather had been so upset by what he saw as the ad hominem attacks on Hill & Devon that he refused to see him. David hesitated to call him now. If he did, would he hang up the phone? Ultimately, he decided to try Stephen's home-office line. After four rings, the phone was answered by a shaky, raspy voice.

"Hello."

"Stephen, this is David."

There was a long pause. The voice at the other end cleared several times. "I'm afraid to ask why you are calling."

"Don't be. I'm not calling with bad news."

"Thank God."

This was not the Stephen Hill with whom David had last talked. It was the voice of a much older and uncertain person. "I realize it's been a long time, so this must come as a surprise."

"Actually, I've wanted to call you many times since Ellen, well, since she left. I've wondered if you could possibly know anything about her? How I might reach her? I never anticipated she'd leave like this. I want her to come back, to face the problems."

"I don't know where she is. But I have received a telephone message from her asking me to call you." David proceeded to pass along Ellen's message. There was silence. David could hear a sort of sniffling noise on the other end. Was he crying? Or was he just an old man with a dripping nose?

Finally, the noise of paper ruffling against the receiver was interrupted by Hill's crackling voice. "David, let's just bury the hatchet. Maybe some way, together, we can figure out how to get her back." The voice appeared to be gaining strength, sounding more confident. "Would you meet me for lunch?"

David hesitated. He didn't like the idea, but didn't he owe it at least to Ellen? He found himself beginning to feel sorry for Stephen or, maybe more realistically, to view him for what he was and what he wasn't. It wasn't Stephen who'd been his enemy. Everything David had suffered at Hill & Devon was attributable to Ramsey. Ellen's grandfather had not directed any of it, he was sure. Nor was he aware of it. He was far too classy a guy. Why hold it against an innocent person? As David had said many times, he did not represent the firm as it existed today.

David entered the door of Palomino, a popular downtown restaurant, and recognized Stephen Hill sitting in a corner booth. He looked little different. He was a handsome man, even in his mid-eighties. He made an effort to rise in the booth, which David brushed off with the direction that he stay seated.

The beginning was awkward, with both men struggling for something more than the mundane to say. It wasn't possible, as one would normally, to check back on past happenings. They had been too closed to developments, other than negative ones, in each other's worlds for too long.

"David, there isn't much that's very important in my life anymore. The firm has been significant, but we are no more. Your firm is now in the strong position ours once was. I can't say I like it, but it is a fact." He slowed, almost halted. "And I've come to accept that the role reversal is not something for which I can blame you. We brought it on ourselves."

Could David believe what he was hearing? "As far as I'm concerned, Stephen, there's really only one person to blame."

"Jim Ramsey?"

"Exactly."

"I've learned that he didn't treat you well. His actions impugned the integrity of the firm. For a long time, I didn't want to admit that. I wanted to believe that you were digging away at us at every turn. You and Gates McGarey, but then as more came out about Ramsey, I understood better how you felt. It's incredible that the actions of one man can destroy a fine law firm. He is a despicable human being."

"What's that saying of Warren Buffett's, something like 'it takes a lifetime to build a reputation, but only twenty-four hours to bring it down'?"

"Yes, the Sage of Omaha. How true." He seemed suddenly tired. Probably, it had taken a lot out of him to say what he just had.

The restaurant Stephen had suggested for lunch was an interesting choice. Undoubtedly, he didn't want to be seen at the University Club, where he was a fixture, with a person, a relative, rumored to have been an architect of his firm's demise. The waiter approached. Stephen studied the menu. As the waiter shifted from foot to foot, David considered going ahead but thought better of it and deferred to Stephen. Ultimately, the orders were placed, and they turned to the business at hand.

"David, as I started but then got distracted, the thing I really care about most in life now is Ellen. It kills me what's happened. I can't stand not being able to see her, to help her, to communicate with her in any way. She has taken on a burden she shouldn't have. She's ruining her life. And, frankly, you're the key to reaching her. At least you're the person she's most likely to contact and who could carry a message for me."

"You do know we were separated when she left?"

"I do. Unfortunately, I know a great deal. I've made it my business to get to the bottom of what happened. I even know about the psychiatric society proceeding."

David was not surprised that the old man had found some way to access the information. "Thus far, she's played it close to the vest. There's been just this one middle-of-the-night telephone message, which, it appears, there's really not a way to trace. That's it."

Stephen lifted his head. "There will be more. This shows she wants to talk with you. She tells you she wants to talk with me. It will happen, but I'm an old man, and time is running out." His fist fell lightly to the table. "I want it to happen now."

"What do you propose?"

"Ask her to come back. Tell her I want her to return. It's time."

"Well, we would…if we could ever reach her."

Stephen's voice lowered and he looked sternly into David's eyes. "Not we, you."

"I would of course—"

"I mean come back to you, to end the separation."

"What?"

"Yes. To put your marriage back together. She'd come. I know she'd come."

David was silent and then spoke, "I'd do almost anything to get her back. I agree that she can't have a life until she returns and faces her problems, but I couldn't mislead her into coming back by holding out that we could reestablish our marriage. Too much—"

"You know," Stephen interrupted, "one of the most important things I've learned in a long lifetime—my biggest mistakes have not been in what I've done, but in what I've failed to do. Chances I've failed to take, opportunities I've failed to pursue. I don't want to make the mistake of not acting in this situation to get her back."

"What are you suggesting, that I lie to her? Get her to return by telling her that we can reconcile and then dump her?"

"No, staying with her through a resolution of the criminal charges. She'll need your support. Once that is done, it's up to you."

David was appalled. What Stephen Hill was proposing was dishonest. How could he possibly do that to someone he loved? "I can't—"

"I would make it attractive for you, David. You don't really need it. You're doing well, but I could make a difference in your life. And I will certainly take care of her lawyers. It will be expensive. We'll get the best, the very best, whether here or wherever in the country. We can get her off. I know we can. The fact that she left can be explained somehow. She panicked. Didn't use her head. Things she hasn't told anyone yet."

David folded his napkin and placed it on the table. So, it was Stephen Hill too. Not even Mr. Pillar of the Community was straight. David had given him too much credit. "I've been trying to find her. I'll continue to do that. When and if I do, I'll ask her to contact you. I'll tell her how urgently you want her to return, but I can't and won't make any commitment to her or to you about our future if she returns. I've got to live with myself." David stood, extended his hand, and left the restaurant.

50

He handed McGarey a copy of Ellen's e-mail. "I received it a couple of hours ago." David excitedly launched into an explanation of what it said as if McGarey didn't have it before him. "This is the first real clue where she is. She's worried about Stephen. She talked to him on the phone, and he sounded terrible. She wants to see him before it's too late."

McGarey's eyes turned up from the paper. "Where the hell is she?"

"Clearly, she's out of the country. On a body of water somewhere. She's working in a marina that caters to Americans, or at least English-speaking tourists. It's probably a Spanish-speaking country because that's the only other language she has any facility with."

"Any guess where?"

"She mentions a friend, Ramon, she wants me to talk to who obviously is from south of the border. We know she went to Miami. If she had been headed to Mexico, most likely it wouldn't have been via Miami. It sounds to me like she's maybe somewhere in the Caribbean."

"And?" asked McGarey.

"Maybe Belize or countries bordering the Caribbean, like Guatemala, even as far down as Venezuela. You know we were on Curaçao when I was injured. She loved it down there—except for that little incident."

"But, David, that's still a lot of territory to check out."

"I could try Deaver."

"But what if he finds her. What do you do then?"

"Exactly. It's why I haven't gone ahead. If I find her, do I have to go to the police and turn her in? I may be better off not knowing where she is."

McGarey stood and shook his head as he walked to the window. "Are you asking legally what you have to do? Or ethically?"

"I have to analyze it both ways, don't I?"

"David, what I don't get is—what do you owe her? How much respect did she show you when Asher was on the scene?"

"I know. I tell myself that all the time. But, you know, there's still a feeling there. I guess on some level I still love her."

McGarey ignored the comment. "If you do find out where she is, are you going to go to her? If you do, that must up the ante in terms of your responsibilities to the police. And what if you give her money? Up again."

"The e-mail says that she wants me to help her get back to see Stephen. Who knows what she'd do once she did that. Stephen would try to talk her into going to the authorities, but you don't know."

McGarey stepped up to the bookcase on his office wall, which was lined with casebooks, statutes, and legal treatises. He pulled out a volume titled *Colorado Criminal Code*. The books were dusty. Probably no one had taken a cloth to them in months. He brushed his hand against his pants, mumbling something about what a piss-poor job the cleaning crew did. He thumbed through the index to the word "accessory" and found Section 18-8-105, headed "accessory to crime." He read it slowly and then handed it to David, asking whether he'd looked at it.

"I know what it says, Gates. Practically by heart." David took the book "It says right here that I would be an accessory if, 'with intent to hinder, delay, or prevent the discovery, detection, apprehension, prosecution, conviction, or punishment of another for the commission of a crime,' I were to harbor or conceal Ellen."

"Arguably you would be doing that if you knew wherever in the world she was and you didn't inform the police. And sure as hell you would be if you snuck her back into the country."

David continued, "It also says I can't give her 'money, transportation, weapon, disguise, or other thing to be used in avoiding discovery or apprehension.' Now, I wouldn't buy her a wig or a gun, but money or transportation might be something else."

"Jesus, David, you're crazy to even be thinking of this." McGarey's hand hit his paper-ridden desk with a slap. In the process, he knocked some documents off the side of the desk to the floor. He bent to pick them up. "You're an officer of the court. You've taken an oath to uphold the law, and the law says that you don't help people escape the criminal court system. The federal statutes will be the same."

"They are. I've checked."

David began to pace. His voice rose above the tones that were his norm, the deep baritone of typical big firm litigators. How much of the voice timber was real, how much was forced, was never clear. Whatever, with David, it sounded good. "What if the action I took could be justified as my effort to get her to come back and face the music? For example, what if I help her financially so that she could be saving the money to purchase a ticket back to Denver? Or maybe I outright give her the money to buy the ticket?"

"Great, but suppose she takes the money or takes the ticket and disappears again?" McGarey shoved the criminal statute book back to its resting place in the bookshelf. He stuck a piece of paper between the books, probably a reminder to tell building management to get the cleaning crew off its collective ass and get busy with a feather duster. Once a year didn't seem too much to ask.

"Maybe, if I could send a message back through this friend of hers, Ramon, I could say that I'll help her return to see her grandfather, but she has to agree that she'll turn herself in."

"You know her a hell of lot better than I do, but I don't think she'll come back with the federal fugitive warrant out against her. What about bail?"

David answered, "Big Daddy Hill. He'll put up the bail. He can afford it, and he loves her enough to do it."

"She may not be bailable, no matter what the amount. She is a fugitive."

David hated the words. But he knew it was true. "Then she'd just have to sit in jail."

"Ellen? I don't see it." McGarey rose, walked up to David, and pointed his index finger in his face. "She'll sneak a visit and then run again. You've got to protect yourself, David."

"Let's see what this Ramon guy has to say. I sure as hell can't violate any law by just meeting with him." David looked at Gates. He realized how much he had come to rely on his feedback. Not that he always agreed with him, but McGarey's take on things seemed more often right than wrong. He wished in this case that McGarey's skepticism about Ellen was wrong, but deep down, he harbored the same concerns.

51

David had been sitting in the den awaiting the arrival of Ramon Cruzes. The bell rang, and he went to the front door. Cruzes introduced himself with accent-free English. He was not at all what David had anticipated. He had a fair complexion and sandy hair and was probably five years older than he was. They went into the den and sat down. David offered him something cool to drink.

David had had no more luck trying to trace Ellen's e-mail, which apparently had been sent from some Internet café, than he'd had trying to trace her first message by voice mail. He was torn whether to turn them over to the police. He finally decided that, since he hadn't been able to trace them, he was not required to do so, but he wasn't comfortable with that decision. This meeting could provide a breakthrough, but he still hadn't been able to resolve the conundrum of what he would have to do with information as to her whereabouts were he to have it.

"Mr. Fox, your wife asked that I come and talk with you."

David immediately said, "I don't want to know where she is."

"That may become necessary in order for me to give you her message."

"I don't want to know unless I expressly ask you for the information. I don't know how much you are aware of her situation, but for me to have knowledge of her whereabouts might oblige me to inform the authorities here. Your country probably has a similar concept."

"My country is your country, Mr. Fox."

David was taken aback but tried to hide it. He had assumed, given where he suspected Ellen was and the visitor's name, that Cruzes was from a Latin country.

"Please call me David." The response was a bid to mask his shock, but he wondered nonetheless whether it still wasn't obvious.

"I met your wife in—well, you don't want to know that. She's in the tourism industry where she is living. I was with a group sailing, and we met her. In one of those small-world things, I learned that we had acquaintances in common. The conversation came around to the fact that I had business interests in Denver, and she asked that, when I came here, I deliver a message to you."

The contact, as Cruzes described it, seemed to David to be far too casual to explain the request for delivery of a personal message. How much did Cruzes know? David asked, "Did she explain to you why she needed an intermediary?"

Cruzes moved in his chair and took a sip from his drink. "No, not really. It was unusual. That much was clear. Now, from your earlier remarks, it makes me feel uneasy. I assume she's been charged with something."

David questioned whether Cruzes was being candid. Why would he participate in this back-channel communication scheme unless he knew why she couldn't communicate her needs and intentions directly? "I'd rather not go into that. But she's under suspicion with respect to a crime, wanted by the authorities."

"May I ask what crime?"

David didn't answer. "You can understand that, as a lawyer, I can't take the risk of becoming involved in any way."

Cruzes shrugged his shoulders. He walked to the French doors to the terrace and commented that the garden was beautiful. David thought he would lighten the load a bit. Looking out over the lawn and trees, he said, "Yes, but I don't particularly appreciate the leaves that come with the scene."

Cruzes did not pick up on the diversion. He turned to face David. "I don't suppose it would hurt you to know what she wanted me to say. She wants very much to see her grandfather. She's worried about his health. She was hopeful you might be willing to help her return."

Now it was David's turn to stand and walk to the window. "I don't even know how to communicate an answer. I get calls in the middle of the night to my office answer machine and untraceable e-mails."

"That's what I can do. I will be seeing her in the next few weeks again."

"In the same place that you're not supposed to tell me?"

"I thought we'd agreed not to discuss that."

David wondered if Ellen and this guy had a relationship. Sort of brazen, wouldn't it be under the circumstances, if she should send a lover to see him? David hadn't had any relationships since their separation and was beginning to wonder if he ever would, or could.

"What I can or cannot do depends on what her intentions are when she returns. If she's willing to turn herself over to the authorities, that would be one thing. Perhaps I could be helpful." David paused for Cruzes to comment, but with none immediately forthcoming, he continued, "If she isn't willing to do that, I can't be involved."

"I can't answer what her intentions are. All I can do is tell her what you have said. And I will."

"Do you know exactly what she wants me to do?"

"She mentioned that she needs help getting into the country and, once she's here, a place to stay."

"I think I could work on that. I would help her with counsel too if she'll commit."

"All right."

"May I have your card, so I'll be able to reach you?" asked David.

"I'd rather not, now that I know how complicated this is becoming. I have your number and address. I will call or write as developments occur."

David was surprised, but said nothing. He had never experienced a situation where a person he was meeting with wouldn't give him a business card. Cruzes's refusal made the situation all the more mysterious.

What did she do? Hire this guy out of central casting to appear on his door step, pretending to be a player?

Cruzes extended his right hand in an odd handshake, his hand moving sideways as they shook, rather than up and down. That oddity added to David's feeling of uneasiness. Why was he letting himself get involved at all in this scheme? He'd better call Deaver.

52

David felt as uncomfortable as he could ever remember. She was a fugitive, and here he was at Denver International Airport to meet her. He only had assurance through one of her stealth telephone messages left at the office in the middle of the night a few days earlier that she would turn herself in. She had asked that he not tell her grandfather so that she could surprise him. That, as it turned out, was not a problem. Stephen Hill had died three days before. David learned the news from Ted Goldstein within hours after it had happened. He had not spoken to Stephen since their lunch at Palomino and hadn't thought the old man was on the verge of dying. He felt a sense of there having been unfinished business between them. The obits in the *Post* and the *News* were glowing about all of Stephen Hill's positive attributes. Only passing mention was made of the demise of the firm he founded.

Ironically, David would be the one to have to break the news to Ellen. The funeral was scheduled for the next day. Her reaction was predictable. He'd have to wait at least until she got to the car. Maybe it was the delivery of this message, more than anything else, that brought him here. Otherwise, she might hear it without anyone to help support her.

She had said she would be traveling under a different name. Jesus, a fake passport. It so underscored the clandestine nature of what she was doing. But that shouldn't really come as a surprise since she might not have been able to get out of the country undetected without one. And now, with a fugitive warrant outstanding, the authorities would turn up her name if she tried to travel on her own passport.

Her grandfather's death had moved to the back burner David's thoughts about filing for divorce. In the months of her absence, wondering if she would return, he hadn't known how he could ever get a divorce, yet he feared he'd never be free until he did. There was little hope they could put it back together. Stephen Hill's offer of a business proposition at lunch had only served to put that in focus. To be tied to her after what had happened would cripple him. It was beyond wrestling with whether to forgive or not, whether he could forget or not. It was impossible to think that he could be married to a murderess—if that's what she was, and he didn't see how it could be otherwise given the fact that she'd run.

He waited in the baggage claim area, where her message had said to meet her at American flight 2007 from Miami. Drivers milled around holding signs with customers' names. The people-watching was interesting. He couldn't help but focus on how some people were dressed. Hawaiian shirts, short shorts, and flip flops didn't look quite right to him for boarding a plane, but maybe it just represented what was getting off a flight from Miami. The baggage from flight 2007 began to snake its way down the chute at carousel five. The crowd surged, with passengers pushing past one another to get their bags off the line. Fifteen minutes passed, then twenty. The crowd began to diminish. A few suitcases continued their circular journey with no one claiming them. After thirty minutes, another flight was posted for the same carousel. Somehow, he had missed her. The unclaimed baggage from the flight was pulled off the carousel and placed to one side. David started to check the name tags, but her name didn't appear. Of course not, she was traveling under a different name, and she hadn't given it to him.

He wondered if she were holding back somewhere in the airport, fearing to come forward. He found himself looking around, anticipating the possibility of a police officer walking on the scene. He tried to push that out of his mind. If the authorities somehow knew of Ellen's arrival, they wouldn't be sending uniformed police to greet her, he suspected. Plainclothes officers undoubtedly would be utilized. *Could she have been picked up at the gate?* he wondered. If she had, they wouldn't have bothered to bring her through baggage claim to exit the airport. He double checked his cell phone. There were no messages. There was no point in staying longer.

The headlights from David's car hit the back wall of the garage. Piles of papers and boxes almost to the ceiling served as a reminder of jobs he had to do. No matter that he was reminded at least twice a day, he never seemed to get around to tackling the projects. They were discretionary. He could live without accomplishing them. Others he couldn't, and they were the ones that occupied whatever little time he had available.

David walked to the door leading to the back porch/mud room, opened it, and flicked on the kitchen light. He threw his coat on the back of a chair, grabbed a beer from the refrigerator, and sat down at the table. He glanced at the now old news in the morning's *Denver Post*. He was tired of the international news. It was the same day in and day out. X numbers killed in suicide bomb blasts outside Kabul. It never seemed to get any better. When would it ever end? He did pay attention to the local, business, and sports news, which was enough to soak up from that paper since he also regularly read the *Wall Street Journal* and the *New York Times* for broader news coverage. He was a newspaper junkie, unlike so many people his age.

"David."

He lurched up and backward, knocking the chair to the floor. He turned toward the door to the den. There was no light on in the den, but the figure standing beyond the open door was visible as a silhouette against the light from the moon. He didn't need more than the voice and the outline of the figure to know who'd spoken his name.

His voice cracked. "Ellen?"

"Yes, David." She walked into the kitchen.

"I've just come from the airport. You weren't there."

"No, I was here."

"What?" David raised his hands to his head. "What's going on?"

"I was able to get an earlier flight out of Miami, and I was so nervous at the airport that I decided to come here."

"And you didn't call me?"

"I did call here, but there was no answer."

"What about my cell?"

"It's been a long time, David. I couldn't remember the number."

"Don't try too hard or anything." David puffed his cheeks and blew air out in a loud exhale. "I was worried about you. Surely, you must have known I would be." He sat back down at the table with a thud.

"Frankly, I thought there was an advantage to getting in and out of the airport on an unexpected schedule—just in case."

"In case what?"

"In case the police might be planning to be there."

"And what do you think would cause the police to be there?"

She looked down. "If they were told."

"How many people even knew you were arriving?"

"No one but you. And Ramon."

"And did you think I'd sic the police on you?"

"Not really."

"Then you didn't trust Ramon?"

"Please don't cross-examine me." She turned, her head bowed. "No, I trust him. And you. But you've been so adamant about my turning myself over to the police, you must admit."

He went to the refrigerator. "Do you want a glass of wine?"

"Do you have white?"

David uncorked a chilled bottle of white wine and poured a glass for her. They looked at each other without speaking. He was checking her out, and it was obvious. He smiled.

"I didn't know what to expect after all these months. You know, how you might have changed and all."

"Have I?"

266

"You're a bit tanner, and your hair is lighter, that's all. And you look pretty thin."

"You don't look any different, David. And the house is the same."

"You've been through it?"

"Just walked around downstairs. I didn't think you'd mind."

He did mind but decided to let it ride. It had been his home now for months. Nothing much in the house had really changed. It was all the same old furniture and possessions in all the same spots. The only rearrangement was that he had expanded into her side of the medicine chest and had shoved her things to one side of the closet to make more room for his. The reality was though that everything had changed—the spirit of the home was gone and had been from the day she left.

"Ellen, tomorrow is a big day."

"Oh yeah, I'm sure." Grinning, she said "You have me going to the police and then meeting Granddad in that order. Right?"

"Not exactly."

"What then?"

"There's something important I have to tell you."

She looked at him expectantly.

"It's your grandfather."

"I can't wait to see him."

"Ellen, he passed away three days ago."

She stared at him. Her eyes were wide, but there was no other expression on her face. It was as though the news hadn't registered. She hadn't heard it. She said nothing.

"I know how much you wanted to be with him. And he you. I hadn't told him you were coming. You said you wanted it to be a surprise. He was in the hospital, though only a short time. He had a massive stroke. And he was gone. It was quick and painless."

She continued to stare without speaking. Then she began to cry softly and sort of laugh simultaneously. She shook her head back and forth. "What, what are you saying? I can't believe this. I came back to be with him. And he's gone?"

"The funeral is tomorrow."

"Oh my God."

"St. John's, three in the afternoon. There's a reception following at the country club."

Ellen looked across the room, away from David. "I had so, so much wanted him to know I was back because he'd requested it, to set his mind at ease."

"I'd tried to assure him you'd do that, sometime, when you were ready."

"That's not the same."

"Of course, but it was important to him, and I believed you would. I didn't see you living as a fugitive the rest of your life. I don't think he did either."

"This is terrible. I can't believe it." She sat, her wine glass approaching and then retreating from her mouth. He didn't know what to say. Finally, she broke the silence. "Well, I'm going to the service, appointment with the police or not. That's all there is to it."

"If you do, you'll be taking the chance of being picked up."

"I don't care."

"I mean, they're going to figure you might be here for the funeral, and they'll have people at the church."

"How do you know so much?"

"I don't. It's that I'm suspicious of it."

"That's just the way it will have to be."

"I've discussed this with a criminal defense lawyer, Royce Rollins. He's agreed to represent you. You're much better off to present yourself to the police first before they pick you up, and he will help you do that."

"I set foot in police headquarters, and I'll never get out."

"He thinks they would agree for you to go to the funeral accompanied by an officer to ensure your return."

"Oh great. Me, handcuffed to a policeman, every single goddamned person in that church staring at me. They'll be hundreds of people there. That's laughable. No way. No fucking way, David."

"Rollins thinks it can be handled in a discreet way. I've set up a meeting with him for nine a.m."

"At nine a.m., I'm going to be at Del Rio's picking out a wig. Yeah, a nice dark wig."

"Come on. That's ridiculous. There's no way I can be involved. I'm already in a compromised position by what I know." He sighed and smiled simultaneously. "I can't be taking you to church dressed in a disguise."

"I'll see the police right afterward."

"That isn't the way it'll play out if they find you. It's going to appear that you're hiding out. How will you ever convince them that you came back to turn yourself in, but decided to go to the funeral first—in a black wig?"

"David, I've got to sleep. I'm exhausted." She put her head down on the table and began to sob. It had been her first dining table. How many meals had they had there? How many talks? How many laughs? And some tears. When they'd moved to Race Street, it had been installed in the kitchen and replaced with something grander in the dining room. That something, it turned out, was seldom used, only for the rare dinner parties they had given for family, friends, or for firm-related purposes.

"Things will be clearer for you after you've slept," David said. "I'll take you to the Brown Palace. I made a reservation."

She raised her head and wiped her eyes. "No, I want to stay here. With you. Just tonight."

He was prepared for this, but that didn't help him withstand it. Maybe it was better anyway that he know where she was and what she was doing. "Okay, if you want. You can stay in the guest room."

"That's not what I mean. With you. I need to hold on to you. Desperately. Just a hug."

"Ellen, I don't see—"

"Please, David. This once. Nothing will happen. I promise."

He turned out the kitchen light and started to walk toward the stairs. Ellen followed him.

"Your bags?"

"Oh, in the den."

He grabbed her two carry-on bags, light by Ellen's past standards, and walked up the stairs. She changed in the bathroom and got into bed. He followed, after locating a pair of pajamas he hadn't worn in years. They were steel blue. He had no idea where they'd come from. He felt her rigid beside him. He lay on his back. She reached out a hand to his wrist and held it. They were silent. Finally, she spoke, "At least, this way, he won't have to go through the trial. It would have been so hard on him. That was one of the reasons I left."

Her scent and touch were so familiar. But the closeness didn't stir him. He felt no desire for her. Were his feelings gone? Or was he afraid? She didn't move. All the options raced through his mind. The last thing he should do would be to enter the church with her. Her presence with him would be a dead giveaway. He wouldn't be seen as just another person paying his respects. Many who would be there knew that the two firms had fought bitterly. They would nod to each other, and their eyes would point to him as he passed. The lawyer would help them work it out when they met with him in the morning. The silk pajamas actually felt good on his skin. He wasn't sure if she had fallen asleep. It took him a long time, but finally, he slept.

53

He glanced at the clock next to the bed. It was late. He pushed the covers back and was surprised by the pajamas. He looked to his left. Ellen was not there. The bathroom door was shut. He knocked, but there was no answer. He opened it slowly, saying her name. No answer. He went into the hall and called out. When there was still no response, he went down the stairs. She was nowhere to be found. He looked in the garage. The Saab convertible, her car, which had been sitting there for months, was gone. Christ, she'd taken the car. He ran back upstairs. One of the bags he'd placed in the corner of the bedroom the night before was not there. How in the hell had he slept through all this? His eyes traveled to the wall above the bed. The words "loose lips sink ships" still glowed there in his mind, as if they had never been covered with paint.

Had she run again? He thought of the appointment with Royce Rollins that morning. He'd mentioned the name last night but not the address or telephone number. He had assumed they'd be going together. Now, if she got there, it would be only because she'd remembered the name and had gotten the address out of the telephone book. Doubtful. But in case, he decided to show up at Rollins's office anyway.

Rollins, like many criminal lawyers, ran a small shop, with one other partner, one associate, an investigator, and a secretary. He'd been an assistant U.S. attorney in Albuquerque before setting out on his own and moving to Denver. He had built a practice case by case, to the point where he was considered among a handful of the best criminal defense lawyers in the city. Stephen Hill had said that he'd bear Ellen's fees. With his death, David decided that he would underwrite the costs. That seemed fair enough considering that she had left the marriage, at least up to that point, with nothing. No cash, other than the nine-thousand-dollar withdrawal from their joint account, and no properties. A first-rate defense would be costly.

Rollins greeted David and walked with him toward a conference room. The offices were small and somewhat rundown. David had no desire to be a criminal defense lawyer. Yet he did have some feeling of envy when he saw a small, successful operation like this, presumably without the myriad of management problems that existed in a large firm environment.

"Where's your wife?"

"I was hoping I might find her here. You haven't heard from her?"

"No."

"Shit."

"What?"

"Well, it's confusing, but she showed up at the house last night. She came in on an earlier plane and left me—well, I don't need to go into all the details. Anyway, I told her about her grandfather and our appointment this morning to get your advice in deciding how to deal with the police. It was left, I thought, that we'd talk about it the morning after she had gotten some sleep. I woke up this morning, and she was gone."

"You have no idea where she is?"

"That's right. She did mention last night going to a hair salon to get a wig for the funeral. She didn't say it like she was kidding."

"Oh, that's a great idea." Rollins threw his head back and let out a short laugh. "Is she always a drama queen?"

"Really, no. She isn't thinking clearly. It's bad enough with the criminal matter in front of her, but to have her grandfather die just before she arrived is a real blow."

"The only thing I can suggest is that you go to that hair salon and get her over here right away. I'll keep things free to meet with her if you can find her."

"I was right, wasn't I," asked David, "to tell her that she should go to the police first with you and get their agreement to attend the funeral?"

"Absolutely."

"That they wouldn't require that she enter the church chained to someone?"

"I'm pretty sure that we could avoid that, but you know, she's proven herself to be a flight risk. In fact in her case, it's a flight fact. She'd be accompanied, but I would hope it would be by a plainclothes officer and no chains. I doubt that they'd let her go on to the reception afterward, however."

"I think she'd be too embarrassed to go anyway."

David left and set out to try and find Ellen. He was not successful.

McGarey called at two thirty to see if he was ready to leave for the funeral. David had debated in his head ad nauseam when and how to arrive at the church. He didn't want to be there too early and have to hang around in front making conversation. On the other hand, he didn't want to be late and walk down the aisle with everyone already seated looking at him. Being with McGarey would give him some sense of confidence, yet that wasn't a perfect solution either as they undoubtedly would be viewed by some as representatives of the enemy that had literally pounded Stephen Hill's firm into the ground.

They climbed the steps at the front of St. John's Cathedral. David had known that this landmark event would bring a large attendance, but he wasn't quite ready for the numbers of heads he saw moving and bobbing when they entered the church. He felt more than conspicuous. He was sure that people were gazing in his direction, offering snide whispers to their seatmates about his role in the law firm battle or his relationship to the family. Whether they were aware of his brief arrest he didn't know; he had managed through Olivar to keep it out of the papers.

Despite his wish to be invisible, he walked down the aisle slowly, surveying the crowd for Ellen. About ten rows from the front, McGarey stopped and nodded toward two seats together midway in the pew. He raised his eyes, asking if these were all right. David nodded yes.

They slipped down the row to the empty seats. As it turned out, they were not that many pews behind the family. David looked around to see if he could spot Ellen. Nothing, he was sure, could have kept her away. He also looked for police uniforms or men with the unmistakable look of plainclothes officers. He saw none of the former, but many of the latter, the church being populated with younger or middle-aged men in dark suits with somber looks. The church was full, undoubtedly in the vicinity of three hundred people. He shook his head to dismiss the ridiculous thought of how many fewer there would be if this were his own funeral.

David inspected the backs of the heads in the first pews where the family was sitting. Could it be possible that Ellen was there, right in front? He didn't find a head to qualify, and he didn't really think she would be that gutsy. He couldn't see faces, except slight profiles as some of them leaned to their seatmates to whisper, but they were either the wrong sex, too old, too tall, too something. A couple of the women he couldn't identify at all because their hats blocked any distinguishing characteristics.

There was no casket. Good thing as it looked like there would hardly have been room for one amongst all the floral arrangement in front of the altar. He contemplated the irony of Stephen Hill's story—from a lifetime of successes and happiness as far as anyone knew to an end with his law firm imploding and his granddaughter on the run from the law. Despite their disagreements, David couldn't help but be sad for him.

The organ music paused. The bishop of the Episcopal Diocese of Colorado walked up to the pulpit. He was a huge man, bent by his years but who still had a sonorous voice. He reviewed the life and achievements of Stephen Hill, his career, his law firm, his good works in the city, which had been more than abundant, his roles as loving husband for over half a century and supportive father and grandfather. David waited for him to mention Ellen by name. He didn't.

Following the bishop came one nephew, who spoke for the family, and then a former chairman of Hill & Devon (thank God not Jim Ramsey—he wouldn't dare show his face here), the CEO of the largest regional bank in Denver, which had been a mainstay client of the firm, and the chairman of the Denver Art Museum, which had been Stephen Hill's most important charitable activity for the last few years. According to the program handed out at the door, at this point, the bishop was to return to the pulpit for closing remarks. As he rose, another figure, moving quickly from the side of the apse, walked in front of him. He paused, looking bewildered, as the figure, a woman, positioned herself at the pulpit.

David stiffened. Her hair was somewhat blonder and much shorter than it had been the night before. She was wearing dark red lipstick, which was uncharacteristic, but clearly, it was Ellen. Her dress was black and indistinguishable from that worn by any number of the women present, but it was the dark maroon scarf at her neck that made him realize that she had been there all along, the woman in the black cloche with tinted glasses, sitting at the end of a pew a few rows in front of him. She had removed her hat before going to the pulpit but not the glasses. She'd done it. Here she was for the taking. She began to speak.

"I am Ellen Fox, Stephen Hill's granddaughter. I came here yesterday to see him after a long absence, only to find that he had died the day before I left my home in Guatemala."

Her voice broke. She paused and then continued.

"The news was devastating for he had been my closest relative and friend for most of my life. I can talk about him from a different perspective than the others today who have spoken so eloquently."

Heads in the family pews were bent toward one another, passing whispered comments. David wondered how much they knew about her, about them, about Asher, about the circumstances of her having left the country. He was willing to bet that, with that family, they knew plenty. He noticed a man in a dark brown suit moving down the aisle on the left and then stopping next to a pillar that was even with the first pews. Another man in a dark blue blazer and gray pants moved to the same position on the right. David thought he saw a wire leading from under the coat to the ear of the man to the left, but he couldn't be sure.

"He was such a warm and loving person to me all through my life. He was an advisor to me on matters of huge importance—at least I thought they were of huge importance, and he patiently never tried to convince me otherwise. He encouraged me. He prodded me where needed. He was my first ATM machine, supporting me generously, though not lavishly—that will be no surprise to anyone here because the word 'lavish' wasn't in his vocabulary."

Muffled chuckles spread through the church. She continued, "I'm sick that I wasn't here with him these last months. Indeed, not even in communication with him due to no fault of his. But I think he knew that he was always in my heart and mind. I feel entirely sure that I was in his."

She halted again, this time unable to restrain quiet sobs. When she regained her composure, she continued, "I have always felt strength from him, and I do today, even with his departure from this physical world. With his strength, I will be prepared for whatever may come my way. There's nothing he would not have done for me, that he did not do for me. His actions in life were borne out of love. He should always be remembered for the honor, generosity, kindness, and gentleness that characterized his life. Thank you."

Ellen turned and walked back toward her seat. The two men at the sides of the church stood still. David thought he saw Ellen nod to the one standing near her pew. The bishop, no longer perfectly in control, thanked everyone for their participation and announced that a recep-tion would be held at the Denver Country Club immediately following the service. The organ began the recessional.

David watched Ellen. She stood at the edge of the pew as members of the family exited past her. Some kissed her cheek. Some shook her hand. No one lingered. The greetings were not exuberant. Two cousins stepped around and behind her and began their way down the aisle without saying anything. She looked after them. David had no desire to deal with the family from which he'd been excluded. He waited to approach her until they had passed and were walking down the side aisle. The two men who had been watching came up to her. She turned to them and said simply, "I'm ready. Let's go."

54

Girard Donovan and Loretta Hull were assigned the job of interrogating Ellen as they had her, David, and other possible suspects earlier in the investigation. The meeting took place at police headquarters in a cold, windowless room with a metal table and chairs. There was nothing on the walls to distract attention other than a large clock with a noisy second hand and an outdated calendar displaying a photo of aspen trees turning color. Ellen was accompanied by Royce Rollins. They'd been given an opportunity to talk alone before the Miranda rights were read and the interrogation began. Rollins demanded that the interview be videotaped in order that there "could never be any question as to what went on in that room." The camera was located and set up.

At Ellen's insistence, Rollins requested that David be permitted to be present. She had decided, like her testimony at the hearing, that it would be best for him to hear what she had to say firsthand. Otherwise, he was always going to think something had been withheld from him. The interrogation began.

"Mrs. Fox, tell us in your own words what happened up in the mountains that day." Donovan added, "We'll try not to interrupt with too many questions."

277

Ellen hated to think of how many hours she'd spent reviewing and re-reviewing the story in her mind. She'd always known it would have to be told someday. The day had arrived. In a way, it would be a relief to have it out. "Well, I had made a date with my grandfather for that Saturday to go mushroom hunting. There was a particular spot in the Indian Peaks Wilderness where he loved to go and that was still pretty accessible for him. He'd been a great hiker, but in the past few years, it had become difficult for him to walk very far. We strolled through the spruce and pines looking for mushrooms but didn't have any luck. After we were about a mile in, Granddad said, 'This is a bust. Let's sit down.' There was a clearing at the edge of the trees, looking out over a beautiful high alpine valley. We put our things down. I leaned my rifle against a large rock and put my pack down next to it. I got Granddad settled sitting against a tree next to the rock."

"Mushroom hunting with a rifle," Donovan said scornfully.

Ellen was cool. "Granddad was worried that I'd be mauled by a bear or eaten by a mountain lion, so he always insisted that I carry a hunting rifle on trips into the backcountry. My husband had a rifle, and I took it along to keep Granddad happy."

Ellen looked at David, wondering if he was thinking of the times they had laughed at her grandfather's self-protection strategies. David didn't return her glance.

"Where was this?" asked Lieutenant Hull.

"We'd been in that area on a number of occasions. It was late in the season, but generally, you could still find mushrooms there. It's a little hard to describe. It was the Bear Lake trailhead. I'm not too good with directions. I think we were north of the trailhead." She stopped and then started again, "It was, well, where the body was found."

"Go ahead. What did you do then?"

"We talked."

"What did you talk about?"

"Granddad said he wanted to discuss something with me. He'd been less communicative on the walk than usual. Normally, he'd chatter away about the smell of the spruce, the winds in the trees, the characteristics of mushrooms, the beauty of wildflowers. He could go on and on. I'd heard it all fifty times, but I never reminded him that I had.

"That day was different. He'd been quiet. His breathing was labored. As soon as we sat down, he blurted out that he knew about my relationship with Elliott Asher. In fact, he even knew about David's charges at the psychiatric society. I was amazed. I asked him how it was possible that he knew of the proceedings because they were supposed to be confidential."

She turned toward David with a stern look and voice. "David had assured me it was confidential." She paused and then returned to her story. "Granddad looked down, maybe a little ashamed, and told me that a doctor, a member of the society, had told him. Anyway, he said he didn't approve of my actions, not at all, even though he realized how, excuse me..." She looked at David again and, eyebrows pointed upward, said, "how difficult David was for me. Granddad was mad that he had filed a complaint and implicated me. He was much angrier, however, with Elliott because he had 'used me,' as he put it, while 'sleeping with all those other women.' He couldn't understand how a man like this, how any professional, could take advantage of a confidential relationship with a patient or client. I told him how sorry I was, that I was not proud of what I'd done, and that I hadn't wanted him to know about it."

Ellen paused and looked at Rollins as if to question whether to proceed. He nodded affirmatively. She thought how much less nervous she felt here than when she had testified at the hearing. This was a more serious matter, but she felt freer here than she had there.

"At one point as Granddad was going on, I looked out into the valley. Off in the distance, there was a figure walking, apparently alone, along the trail, heading in our direction. I didn't think much of it. I assumed it was a hunter. Elk hunting season had just opened. Granddad had insisted that we wear orange jackets as protection. The person was too far away for me to make out any details, except the walk, with a sort of hitch in the right leg, looked familiar. As the figure got closer, I realized it was a man, and in fact, the man was Elliott. I didn't know what to do. I told Granddad who I thought the person was so that he wouldn't be surprised. He replied that that was 'exactly the person he wanted to talk to.'"

"How is it, Mrs. Fox," asked Lieutenant Donovan, "that Dr. Asher just happened to show up at the exact same time and place as you and your grandfather? There's a lot of forest out there."

"Of course, it would seem odd to you, but you see, Elliott knew I'd be there. At a break in the hearing before the weekend, he'd asked if he could see me Saturday. Instead of saying no, I made the mistake of supplying an excuse. I was going mushrooming with my grandfather. Elliott knew from past discussions where my favorite spot was to take Granddad. In fact, Elliott had been there with me. It didn't take a lot of imagination to find us."

David seemed almost to blanch at hearing that she had taken Asher to her secret mushroom spot.

"I see," Donovan said.

"I walked down to the trail to speak with Elliott outside Granddad's hearing. Elliott, who was a hunter, was carrying his rifle. He said he'd spotted my car at the trailhead and knew I was up there."

"Let me interrupt you," Donovan said. "Dr. Asher wasn't wearing elk hunting camouflage gear, was he?"

"I believe you're right."

"Can you explain that?"

"I can only guess. He wasn't hunting elk that day." She stopped and then started. "He was hunting me."

No one spoke. "Or the opposite?" Hull said.

Ellen decided not to respond. "I told him I'd just learned that my grandfather knew of the situation and was very upset. I asked Elliot to leave because I didn't want a confrontation. He said, 'good' and that what was going on was 'ridiculous.' He pushed past me and walked up the trail to the clearing where Granddad was sitting next to the rock.

"Eliott introduced himself. Then he began to harangue me about David's complaint, my participation in the hearing, how we were trying to ruin his reputation and destroy his ability to practice, and on and on. He said I could make David withdraw the complaint if I wanted to. I could have refused to testify. I asked him please to stop, that it was not something to discuss in front of my grandfather. The more I protested, the louder he got. He was trying to pressure me, in front of one of the most important people in my life, to walk away from the proceeding.

"I could see Granddad's face beginning to flush. His hands shook. He said to Elliott that if he had anything to do with it, 'he would lose a lot more than his license,' that he was 'a menace to society.' I had never seen Granddad that agitated.

"Elliott looked at my grandfather and started laughing. Then came an abusive barrage against me. He referred to me as 'Ellen, Granddad's little baby' and said things like 'Little Ellen, the dirtier it got, the more she wanted.'" Ellen flushed and looked down and saw David's feet. His legs were pumping up and down under the table. He looked like he wanted to bolt.

"Granddad yelled, 'What kind of person are you, Mr. Asher? You're no doctor, Mr. Asher.' He mumbled something about 'the worst scourge on mankind since the advent of venereal disease.' He tried to stand, one hand against the rock and the other using my rifle as a brace. He got up, planted his feet, and then turned and pointed the gun at Elliott. Elliott laughed and slapped his knee, and then turned and reached behind him for his own rifle. I didn't know what was going on, but I told them both to stop. I moved toward Granddad to take the rifle. As I did, it discharged, and Elliott dropped. I went to him. Granddad fell back against the rock, shaking and talking, mostly in words I couldn't understand, except 'menace to society' and 'scourge on mankind,' which he repeated mechanically."

She looked at David and heard him whisper, in apparent disbelief, "Stephen Hill?"

"The bullet had entered Elliot's back below the left shoulder. He groaned. His eyes bugged out. There was a lot of blood. He kept repeating," she paused, her brow furrowed, "'fucker, fucker.' The words became too quiet to hear. He was unconscious and breathing erratically. I tried to speak to him, but there was no response. I didn't know what to do. Within a few minutes, his breathing ceased. Then there was nothing I could do for him."

"What happened next, Mrs. Fox?" asked Hull.

"I panicked. I wandered around and saw a hole next to a spruce tree. I got my rifle and found that if I wedged it into a gash in the trunk of the tree and then down into the hole in the ground at the edge of the trunk, it would disappear completely. I shoved it there and closed the hole with rocks and dirt." She still found it hard to believe that the rifle had been resurrected from the earth. It had been a struggle to wedge it in there and cover it completely.

"I went back to Granddad, and we cried. I told him it was all my fault. I meant that in the sense that if I hadn't gotten involved in this sick relationship, none of this would ever have happened. I said that there was nothing we could do for Elliott, and we should leave. I said that if we reported it, it would look bad for me, that there was no way the shot could be traced to me or to him. As we drove home, we went back and forth. He insisted that we had to call the police, but ultimately, he agreed to go along with my plan to say nothing."

David shook his head back and forth, distress etched across his face.

"Why would we believe you?" Donovan asked, his tone of voice rising. "If this was the truth, why didn't you tell us? Innocent people don't run."

Rollins had carefully prepared her for this tough, predictable question. "I thought and thought about this. At the beginning, right after the shooting, I felt no one would believe me because of what Elliott had done to me and because I was involved in a proceeding to see him disciplined. So I didn't say anything. Then David was arrested when his rifle was found," she looked at him, "and I couldn't let him be charged. He had nothing to do with it. I was terribly worried about Granddad. I couldn't let him end his years as a defendant in a murder trial. The publicity would be awful. It would kill him. By leaving, the blame would follow me, which is where it should be anyway. I caused the problem to begin with."

"It was you who had the rifle, Mrs. Fox, wasn't it? Tell the truth."

"No, I reached to get it away from Granddad. He had it."

"Then why does it have your fingerprints?"

Ellen shrugged. "Frankly, I'm surprised it has any. I tried to rub them off. Whose does it have?"

"Your husband's. We're checking for yours actually."

"It wouldn't be a surprise. He's used it. I have. Anybody else?"

"Like your grandfather? We don't know yet."

"Did you have an understanding with your grandfather when you left, Mrs. Fox?" asked Donovan, as he moved to sit on the edge of the table, thrusting his bulk out at her.

"Understanding about what?

"Your story."

"No. I left him a note that I'd come back in a few months, and we would go to the authorities together. That I thought it would be best if he didn't know where I planned to go. I told him not to worry, that it would be all right. I always knew I would come back and go to the authorities."

"Yeah, when everyone had died, so there wasn't anyone around to tell the real story," Donovan added, leaning even closer toward her. The room was quiet.

"Imagine that," Hull said with a look of mock incredulity. "You knew your grandfather had died when you left wherever you were, didn't you?"

"No, but I knew he was very old. I had a bad feeling about it. I knew it was time to be with him." Ellen paused.

Donovan's voice rose. "Why would we believe you? You tried to wipe the rifle. You hid it. You ran when we found it. You lied to us in the investigation. And you return to face the music only after there is no one to tell a different story."

Ellen looked helplessly to Rollins, then to Hull, finally to David. She said simply, "I am telling you the truth."

There was a long period of silence as no one spoke or moved. "Where have you been, Mrs. Fox?" Hull asked.

"In Guatemala."

"Where in Guatemala?"

"The Rio Dulce."

"How did you get there?"

"I flew out of Miami to Belize City and on to Placencia. From there, I got a ride on a sailboat through the western Caribbean and up the river."

"And what did you do there?" asked Hull.

"I helped run a marina. There are lots of Americans there. No one bothered me."

Donovan fell back into his chair at the table and removed his glasses. "Your story now isn't exactly what you told us when we met shortly after the shooting, is it, Mrs. Fox?"

"Yes and no. I had to tell you then I didn't know how it had happened in order to protect my grandfather. But the rest of what I told you was true. It was true that I'd gone shopping that morning at the Cherry Creek Mall and that later I'd driven to Colorado Springs to spend the night at the Broadmoor."

"Yeah, my notes show you told us that with all the tension of the hearing, you just had to get away to sort things out."

"That was true."

"Nothing like a little shooting to add to the tension level, is there?" Donovan glared.

"I can't deny that, but I had planned for at least a couple of days to get away by myself. And I showed you the Broadmoor bill and some slips from the shopping." Ellen felt she was handling it. She'd come a long way from her days at St. Luke's.

"That's right," said Hull. "I have them right here. Quite convenient." She returned the papers to her file and added, "What communication did you have with your grandfather?"

"None."

"To agree on your story?"

"What do you mean?" Ellen asked.

"We interviewed Mr. Hill last week."

Ellen looked at Rollins and then David. David's look seemed to communicate resignation: here it comes, the real story.

"His lawyer called and arranged a meeting in his hospital room. Mr. Hill told us that he was having small strokes, TIAs, and he wanted to talk with us while he still made sense. He said it wasn't fair to leave the implication that you were responsible for what happened, that he was. His version of what happened matches yours, with one exception. He said you two had talked."

Ellen wondered whether her heightened pulse could be heard throughout the room. Actually, the only thing to break the silence was the mechanical click of the wall clock. Ellen started to answer, but

Rollins told her not to, the first words he had spoken since the beginning of the interrogation. He asked for the document.

Donovan waved the statement in his hand. "Mrs. Fox, we don't even know whether your grandfather was at the scene at all. You could have arranged the whole story with him. Here it is. We'll be back." He thrust the paper at Rollins and got up to leave the room with Hull. The door slammed as they left.

Rollins held the statement as he and Ellen read it in silence. She ran her fingers through her hair. She was almost shaking. She wept. He had done it for her. He had taken the blame.

When they finished, Rollins handed the statement to David and looked at her. "Did you talk to him or not?"

"No. If he said we did, I'm afraid it must have been an example of dementia, from his stroke you know."

"I can tell you one thing," Rollins said, "with your statement and your grandfather's, there's no way in hell that they can charge you with murder. They'd have to have evidence, like facts concerning the entry of the bullet to the body, that is inconsistent with what you and your grandfather have told them. My bet is they don't."

David read the statement, looking up at Ellen as he absorbed each paragraph. A long period passed before the two officers returned. Donovan said to Ellen, "You win for now. You won't be detained at this time. You're free to leave." Turning to Rollins, he added, "But she shouldn't leave the city until other issues are resolved."

"Other issues?" asked Rollins.

"Obviously, there are obstruction of justice questions. The feds will be interested in the false passport use. And the unlawful flight to avoid prosecution charge is still outstanding."

Donovan raised his arm to signal the end of the interview. The videotape equipment, which had been shut down since the officers left the room, was removed.

The meeting over, Rollins departed quickly for another appointment. Ellen and David walked down the stark hallway past open doors with uniformed police at their desks, on the phone, talking, laughing.

David asked, "Ellen, why did you do this to yourself? Why did you do it to us?"

"I had to. I couldn't let Granddad pay the price for what were really my mistakes, any more than I could you."

They left the building. David offered her a ride. She asked that he take her by the house to pick up the rest of her things and then drop her off at the Brown Palace. Most of the drive was passed in silence. It was as if they were spent. There was nothing more of importance to say, and small talk didn't fit after all they had gone through that day.

They pulled into the driveway. She said, "The nightgown is on the back of the bathroom door. Throw it in the suitcase and bring it down, would you?"

"Sure, but don't you want to come in and pack the bag? I'll carry it down for you."

"I'd rather not."

Bag stowed in the car, they drove to the Brown Palace. As they pulled up to the hotel, Ellen said, "When these other legal questions are cleared up, I think I'll head back to the Rio Dulce. It's a beautiful place, and I feel comfortable there. I suppose now that I'll have the resources to stay there awhile."

The doorman opened the car door, and she started to get out. She turned and grasped his arm. "Don't worry. I'll stay out of your way, David, no more complicating your life. I'm so sorry for everything. It's all been very unfair to you."

She started to release him. She felt somehow relieved, unburdened. She had practiced her final words. They needed to be just right. She knew no matter what had gone before, the video, the affair, that David had viewed her as a murderer. That he could never accept her after that. But now, maybe he would see it differently. "If you ever feel like it, you should come spend a little vacation time on the Rio Dulce. I think you'd like it. I love you, David. You've been the best friend anyone could ever have hoped for through all this. I really mean that." She gave his arm a squeeze.

David didn't respond.

55

The double garage door rose at his touch of the opener. He drove in. The garage looked naked without the tomato red Saab convertible. How excited she had been when he surprised her with it. Most women wouldn't drive around Denver with the top down. But she had, at least when it was sunny. The car might be gone, but the piles representing neglected projects were not. They remained right there for him to complete.

David sat down in the den. He was still numb. Could he ever believe what she said in that room today? Did he want to believe her? He reran the story endlessly, fighting not to, but not succeeding in the fight. He was mired in what-ifs.

Where had he gone wrong? What if he hadn't challenged Ramsey? David might not have liked himself very well, but he would have survived. Ultimately, Ramsey would have exited the picture. He couldn't go along screwing clients and partners and get away with it forever. And Hill & Devon would have prospered. Even great firms sometimes choose the wrong leaders and live through it.

David would not have found himself forming a team with Gates McGarey to avenge what Ramsey had done. Not that they could take credit for all that befell Ramsey or Hill & Devon, but they had been catalysts.

Things would have been different with Ellen. Without the pressure of the law firm fight, their relationship would have been so much smoother. Without the videotape horror, there would have been a magnitude of difference in the tension in their lives. She might not have ever fallen into Asher's hands.

With Asher, again David had been pressured to take the easy way out, to understand, to forgive, to forget. These things happen, unfortunately, even in the world of psychiatry. No matter that Ellen had ended up in a psychiatric ward. If David had been willing to go along, Asher wouldn't have died, and Ellen wouldn't have had to play the role of murderer.

Go along. Go along. Dance the dance. Forget what's right.

Rerunning it all was useless. He didn't have the opportunity to relive it. He'd done the best he could. He remembered Stephen Hill's remark at lunch that the biggest mistakes he'd made in life were in the things he didn't do, not in the things he had done. But when you do something, you know the result. When you don't do it, you can only speculate as to what the result might have been. Speculation is worthless. The fact is that he didn't know, and never would, what might have happened if he'd taken different actions.

His head fell back on the couch. Tears dropped to his cheeks, to his shirt, to his loosened tie. He slumped sideways on the couch. He pounded his fists into the pillows and then buried his face.

⚖

Much later, in early morning, he awoke. He had fallen asleep on the couch. His tie was on the floor and his coat across the room where apparently he'd thrown them. It was cool, but the air was close. He walked to the French doors and opened them. He looked out at the terrace and the lawn and trees beyond. He sat down in one of the metal chairs at the terrace table and gazed at the garden. How he had loved that garden. It had, in times past, given him a feeling of tranquility to be there. It was probably what he liked the most about the whole place. The house itself had been an icon for him. It represented something he'd never had and that he'd earned. But he wasn't inspired by the sight this morning. No longer an icon, he felt loneliness there, not warmth. The spirit was gone.

Leaves were swirling around the terrace with the help of a slight wind. The chair and table legs became resting places for small piles of them to gather. He looked down at one of the legs of his chair and pushed the leaves away with his shoe. He stood and walked to the den and then upstairs. He went into the bedroom. He looked around. Purple letters flickered on the wall, the shattered door hung from its hinges. He blinked repeatedly. Shook his head. They disappeared. He'd go for a run. It would clear his mind and release the tension that was gripping him.

He changed into light sweats and running shoes. He went down the stairs and out the front door to the giant American elm next to the brick path leading to the sidewalk. This tree, his usual stretching spot, was one of the few survivors of the blight that had devastated its type in the city. He used it to stretch, thankful as he always was that it still stood there to grace the entrance to the house. He turned and started down Race Street. If only he could never enter that room again.

ACKNOWLEDGMENTS

While this story is set in Denver and is generally faithful to that locale, liberties have been taken concerning certain details of the environment of that city, the most significant of which is that there is no Denver City Ballet Company.

I am indebted to my wife, Linda Vaughn, for her editorial assistance, her patience, and her constant encouragement; to Beth Slattery and Hensley Peterson for their editorial comments; and to Lorenzo Semple Jr., who caused me to believe that there was a story worth telling.

A number of people with the law firm from which I have retired, Paul, Hastings, Janofsky & Walker, have contributed in a variety of ways, including sharing their experiences and war stories and offering legal and technical advice. Principal among them, in no order other than alphabetical, are Larry Barcella, John Brinsley, Vicki Cundiff, Ethan Lipsig, Paul Perito, George Stephens, Geoff Thomas, and John Trinnaman. The consistently high ethical standards and steadfast integrity demonstrated by the lawyers of Paul Hastings throughout my fifty-year association with the firm prove this work to be truly one of fiction.

Many others have also provided information and advice. My thanks go to Al Dietsch, Germaine Dietsch, Mike Hamilburg, Steve Kenninger,

Steve Knous, Esteban Londono, Dr. Robert Mack, Dr. James Maloney, Robert Rich, Susan Sheridan, Judge Stephen Trott, Ron Watkins, and to my brother, Bill Vaughn.

Finally, I want to thank the Aspen Writers Foundation for the opportunities for learning offered through its programs.